Moon On An
Iron Meadow

Books by Peter Tate

MOON ON AN IRON MEADOW
COUNTRY LOVE AND POISON RAIN
GARDENS ONE TO FIVE
THE THINKING SEAT

Moon On An Iron Meadow

PETER TATE

DOUBLEDAY & COMPANY, INC.

GARDEN CITY, NEW YORK

1974

To LESLEY PATRICIA TATE,

sweet love of my life

ISBN: 0-385-02422-3
Library of Congress Catalog Card Number 73–10977
Copyright © 1974 by Peter Tate
All Rights Reserved
Printed in the United States of America
First Edition

ACKNOWLEDGMENTS

The Green Town of this piece is an amalgam—part Waukegan, Illinois, part Kent, Ohio, part the sidewalks of my mind.

Waukegan would not have been possible without the friendly and abundant postal assistance of Mayor Robert Sabonjian, his council and the Waukegan League of Women Voters, whose guide to their fair city gave more insight than a three-month visit.

Kent, Ohio, was but a skeleton in the campus cupboard when I read *Kent State: What Happened and Why*, by James A. Michener. He and his research team furnished the flesh and a portion of the urgency for *Moon On An Iron Meadow* and it is because of them and because of people like Senator Richard D. McCarthy, whose Operation CHASE anti-campaign provided another portion, that I was better able to qualify my attempt.

The sidewalks of the mind need no thanks; a writer should have them, is all. But he has need to be grateful to many pedestrians on those sidewalks and in my case never more so than to that fabled pedestrian Ray Bradbury. When he was making his first sales to *Weird Tales*, I was making my first purchases of the magazine over the paperback counter of Woolworth's, British tradition owned by that American lady Barbara Hutton (so thank you, Barbara Hutton, also). And there was something about those *Weird Tales* that lingered a lot longer than *Texas Rangers, Detective Stories* and *G-8 and His Battle Aces*. . . . I knew the chills before I knew the bylines and when, at ten or eleven, I got around to *The Silver Locusts*, I was amazed to find the myths were familiar (old-friend familiar, not no-not-again familiar, that is). From then on, it was my story, Brian Aldiss's story, 95 per cent of all S-F men's story, deeper and deeper into the genre, pubescent first writings, kindly first rejections, dreaming of the day we might share a contents list with our heroes.

And finally—well, here comes novel number four. As part payment of a debt to RAY BRADBURY, who taught me the avoirdupois of words and now must bear a small, warm consequence.

Peter Tate, Cardiff, 1973

Threshold

Koza stayed out of the city. He had made his choice, electing primitivism for progress in the wake of the steel typhoon. He had scurried from cover to cover during those blazing three months between April and July of 1945, neither Japanese nor American, while the antagonists played "Please, Jack" across the stepping-stone Ryukyuan Islands.

And the Americans had won. That fact alone didn't bother him. It was that there had been a winner—and that Okinawa was no longer his possession.

Naha, the capital, was an architectural apologia, all glass and Harvard ideas. It housed some 350,000 people, and that was too many for Koza to take.

When Koza cut loose, he made for the jagged spine of the island and built his home by wedging tough cherry wood into natural enclaves of rock. Two typhoons a year were the local average, with winds up to 190 miles an hour just testing their muscles as they headed for the Asian mainland. He wasn't willing to keep replacing his home, so he drove it at the outset deep into the vertebral stratum.

And while he built high against hurricanes, the military built low. One installation, ten . . . fifty . . . one hundred and twenty . . .

Koza had heard that in some of these places they stored the mushroom that had poisoned Hiroshima. This was the way he heard it and accepted it, as a Babylonian learned to put his fearful trust in Ti'amat, the dragon with the power of life and death. As a legend.

Remote by choice, but still needing to move, he threaded his way hither and thither across the island, charting the bases in his mind and giving them a wide and superstitious berth.

Years passed with Koza dodging the gum-chewing, happy-go-lucky servants of the mushroom. Not that they directed terror upon the populace. The two life-streams flowed side by side, unturbulent but unmixable.

Nevertheless, Koza knew them by their outfits. He associated them. He went his way busily ignoring them, secure in the knowledge that his attitude was not unique. That soon, when they were ignored sufficiently, they would disappear.

And sure enough . . .

It took twenty-five years for the first indication. In 1972, there seemed less of the servants. He even got brave enough to tour the one-fourth part of the seventy-by-several-mile island, counting the occupied installations. Eighty-eight were still inhabited. But thirty-two were empty.

In the subsequent years, he made it his regular pilgrimage. Dry season, walking—and year by year, the number went down and down.

Koza, today, had happened upon what he counted to be the last of these places. He had learned that the servants all wore the same dress with small differences of elaboration. Here were few such uniformities but the cluster of buildings was surrounded by two layers of high fence which might take you and throw you some distance if you laid a hand on it. A gate with a couple of men guarding it, seemingly. And a pastoral setting among woodlands at the north of the island.

He had gone as close to the fence as he dared. The place was not bustling but it was not empty. His small curiosity appeased, he retreated into the woods, looking for a meal.

The rabbit, unfamiliar with the geography, unschooled in the fear of men, did not take flight at his coming and wriggled hardly at all when clockwise and anticlockwise hands caught it up and snapped its neck.

An old man doesn't know how hungry he is until in the presence of food. Koza's saliva glands were active as he gathered branches, then hollowed out a base for the fire and built it. He had to wipe his mouth frequently as he skinned and gutted the animal. But in a little while, watching the meat as it turned in the flames, Koza felt his appetite diminishing.

Instead, suddenly and without warning nausea, he vomited. An abrupt fall in temperature followed the retching. When he tried to stand, to offer some kind of battle, his legs would not hold him and he went face down in the undergrowth, still retching dryly, for the scant contents of his stomach had gone.

He was shivering, he was sweating, his teeth were chattering, his chest was on fire.

And it was as though the fire had burned its way through his bronchi, because very shortly he could not breathe and soon after that stage he was comatose and within seconds he was dead.

The servant with the stripes of a master sergeant who had crouched in the bushes while Koza enthused over the meal he would never eat moved now to the edge of the clearing.

He had been seeking the rabbit for three hours, knowing what he must do, and his sojourn in the bushes had been made uncomfortable by the equipment needed to that end. The short-handled spade had dug into his kidneys and the large flask of gasoline had rubbed the skin off the outside of his left thigh.

He stood now bracing his back with gloved hands. According to his instructions, he lit a rather special menthol cigarette before he began digging a trench six feet long by six feet deep by three feet wide. Koza was a small and withered man but orders were orders.

He lit a second cigarette off the first, a third off the second as he toiled. He was sweating less now than he had been with nothing to do but watch Koza cook up his death. The abundant clay of the island soil made his task relatively easy and in a way was an aid to his next move.

Whatever he had to do could be contained and controlled in this trough. The ground was therapeutic.

Drawing on his fourth cigarette, he took Koza by the bare heels, dragged him to the edge of the pit and toppled him in without ceremony. Then he went for the can of gasoline he had unhooked from his belt and sprinkled the contents liberally into the trench. He followed it up with the now-cooked meat and the remains.

He worked his gloves off over his fingers inch by inch, careful that no outer surface made contact with the skin of his hands. He dropped the gloves into the trench.

Then he went back to Koza's fire, selected two brands and tossed them upon the corpse.

He picked his way well back into the woodland while trench and contents were devoured. He gave the operation a designed half-hour, switching to a more orthodox brand of cigarette to pass the time.

The subsequent inspection of the pit showed him destruction had been to a degree well within prescribed limits. What was left would do nobody any harm.

He started shovelling the clay back into place. The operation had assumed one complication which had been absorbed. Who was going to miss old Crazy Koza, anyway?

Hands of Love and Hate

Simeon and Tomorrow Julie dropped out of the Illinois landscape and into Green Town like figures from a Dalí unstill life. They were a flamboyant pair and built to last. Not colourful in the way that a student's first away-from-home habits are colourful, but carefully considered and resplendent.

Simeon, mid-thirties now and feeling the weight of them, had traded his hoverhop within a very few miles of the California Pacific coast and breezed along for three years on what providence, good intent and occasional poetry furnished.

Julie's misty beauty had become more clearly defined and she had assurance. They both had assurance, discovered together, sharpened upon each other, a currency that worked between them.

Green Town, which cannot live with its landscape quietude forever, nor even for a single sentence beyond this one, was going about its business in the simple Illinois way with hardly noticed traffic passing there and by along the turnpike. A '74 Chrysler stopped, put out its two easy riders and . . .

Simeon and Tomorrow Julie in Green Town. Splat!

They had come north via North Chicago and their chauffeur had dropped them midway down Dugdale Road, which ran on diagonally across town to the lakefront. He would have taken them further into the centre but Simeon had a landmark. Twelfth Street intersection with Dugdale. It was but a short step from that point to their destination. His destination, really, and Julie's because she was his wife. For better or worse.

And when they had made those vows in a small adobe church in the hills above the ocean, with a hurricane racing towards them across the water, she had wondered how much "worse" that meant. In fact, very little. Simeon was a dreamer but now practical with it and he no longer needed comfort toys like cliff-top swings. Julie came to Green Town to make Simeon happy even though the desire had been unstated; merely one more direction for itinerant feet.

Twelfth Street intersection. Going inland now, Rosewood Street, Willow, Evergreen, Maple.

Oak Street and the numbers went from right to left. A voice in his mind said "97."

They walked and found 97 with its lawn sloping to the pavement where the lightning-rod salesman had stood in some distant October and seduced Jim Nightshade and Will Halloway with a metal device, half crescent, half cross, its surface pitted with an acne of strange languages and incomprehensible formulae.

The house was as it should be, with gaunt cupola windows set high to give boys good views and a clapboard verandah where a swing might hang.

A swing?

Simeon was glad not to see a swing.

They climbed the steps and touched the bell. A woman came, bringing a delicate refinement to go with the tended sward before the door.

"Mrs. Halloway?" asked Simeon, partly because it made an easy introduction and partly because, by some miracle, she might well be.

"No, I'm not Mrs. Halloway. Perhaps if you tried in the next block . . ."

"Well, forgive me. I may have got the name wrong but I'm sure about the number. It was ninety-seven."

"This *is* ninety-seven."

"And I understand you may have a room to let."

"Wrong again, I'm afraid. I have a spare room but no intention of taking in lodgers." The woman had become wary.

"I—we—we're just here for a few days while I look around," said Simeon. "I had a friend who told me a great deal about Green Town and I felt I just had to come and see for myself. It wouldn't be like lodgers."

"I don't know. I hadn't intended . . ."

Julie let her breath out in a long sigh. "We wouldn't be a nuisance at all," she said. "Believe me, we understand your reluctance. It's so difficult to be sure of people these days. If I had a house, I'm sure I wouldn't rent out rooms to anybody. We travel a lot. My husband is a writer. He takes in atmosphere like a plant synthesises sunshine—do you know what I mean? So we seldom stay anywhere long. But we have found it increasingly hard to convince people that we will do them no harm. They seem to want to look at our arms for the marks of the syringe and express surprise when we reveal that we actually are married and happy with it. It's no easy task to be orthodox unless you are exactly like the person next door. And of course, if you were the person next door, you wouldn't be looking for a room for a couple of days . . ."

"I couldn't provide meals," said the woman.

"It's all right, Mrs. . . ." said Simeon. "I'm sorry we bothered you." He started to turn away.

"But I dare say you would find the room to your taste. And it's Mrs. Dilger. I do enjoy a good book. Do you write good books, Mr. . . . ?"

"Simeon. I try."

"Under your own name?"

Strange how many people made that the second question of their interrogation. Never heard of you and rather hoping your alias would turn out to be a household name—or rather surprised that you would add your actual identity to anything as shameful as a novel. "No. A lot of non-fiction and some science-fiction. I'm a journalist more than a storyteller. I guess I'm funny about lights and bushels."

"Well I'm sure I must have read something by you. I must check in the library."

"The library?" Simeon was at once attentive. "Do you know, that is always the second place I go, wherever I am. Libraries are treasure houses to me. Is it far?"

"On the corner of Clayton and County. Not far if you are used to big cities. Quite a way if you have lived in a village where everything is within one hundred yards."

"I know both."

"I'm not sure you can see it from the room. Would you like to come up and see?"

Mrs. Dilger led them up two flights of stairs and into one of the dormer rooms. Beyond the window, making a mirage upon itself, the lake succeeded the roof-tops.

"I thought not," said Mrs. Dilger. "But it's over that way." She swept her left arm through an arc of forty-five degrees from front to side. "I haven't spent much time in this room for some years. But it is aired and the sheets are clean. That gives me an interest."

"Oh." Julie sounded concerned. "Is there no . . . Mr. Dilger?"

"Not for ten years. He died."

"Death isn't the end, Mrs. Dilger. If it were, life would be more pleasant."

"Do you believe that, too, Mrs. Simeon?"

"Implicitly. We must talk."

"I'd like that. Now I'll see if I can find you something to eat."

Mrs. Dilger made short work of the stairs. Simeon came away from the window to embrace his wife. "You have so much love."

"And so much guile," said Julie.

"You mean that was . . ."

"Of course not. No, I meant that. I like her and I think we'll get on. By guile I mean that, left to you, we'd never have got through the door."

"I'm grateful."

"Are you going to tell me why?"

A lot later, fortified with tea, the women sat on the verandah and watched the sun sink into the distant Chicago haze.

Simeon was kneeling on the lawn. He held up a yellow flower. "That's why," he told Julie. "Sweet lord, even dandelions."

"They keep coming back," volunteered Mrs. Dilger.

"You're so right." Simeon's heart was full.

"Do you know what he means?" Mrs. Dilger was bewildered.

"Only most of the time," confided Julie.

"And the rest of the time? When he talks in riddles?"

"By the pricking of my thumbs," said Julie.

If you want to see a rickettsia thrive, feed it a healthy cell. The weaker you are, the stronger you are with the same kind of up-turned logic which gives the patients the edge on the nursing staff when there is an outbreak of viral hepatitis in a kidney dialysis unit.

That is the Australia antigen.

A cancer virus works the same way, finding rubicund cells far more to its taste than wasted, ageing organs.

That is the oncogene hypothesis.

At Station Deva, behind two electric fences on Okinawa, they had been developing an effect that hailed from Detrick and combined the talents of yellow fever, the transmissibility of psittacosis and the strain variables of Q-fever with the dogged determination to succeed of a little-known local condition called Yeze fever.

They had toyed with infectivity, arguing for the optimum effect from injection or ingestion. They were up to dosages, with delivery systems earmarked for the next fiscal year of research, and all had been going well.

Until one of their California white vectors decided to act like a rabbit and disappeared from its piece of potted pastureland. They had ended the electric fencing at surface level, which provided no problem at all for the digger.

The Medical Corps personnel with their mandatory Japanese laboratory aides—part of last year's Okinawa Extension Treaty—had poked and petted their animals with infra-red spectography and electronic microscope. They had isolated host organs and tested the virulence and dissemination of rickettsiae so stored in a whole suite of cloud chambers.

But they had not cleaned the guts out of a rabbit with a peasant's hands and then used those hands to wipe saliva from the lips. That was the best and fastest delivery system.

It had been unknown to them and now they were not going to be able to improve on it.

The sergeant who shall be nameless as so many good military men are nameless was making his report to the commanding officer who shall be nameless for the benefit of his remaining reputation in the field of aerobiology.

The sergeant was reaching the crux of his report.

"Not quite all, sir. It happened that a civilian got himself involved."

"A civilian? In what way, Sergeant? Did he see what you were doing?"

"No, sir."

"Then in what way . . . ?"

"He died, sir."

"You mean you killed him."

"Not I. The—the animal, sir. He killed the rabbit before I could get to it and then it killed him. At least—"

"This should have been high up in your report, Sergeant."

"I was going chronologically, sir. What happened was that he caught it, cooked it and then appeared to become ill."

"Could it have been anything else that sickened him?"

"Too much of a coincidence, I considered."

"Good thinking. Did you manage to get his body back here without anybody seeing you?"

"No, sir."

"You mean somebody saw you."

"No. I mean I didn't bring his body back."

"What!? You didn't just leave it lying—"

"Of course *not*, sir. I dispensed with it using the same method as had been recommended for the vagrant animal. I burned it and buried it. . . . It was only an old man, sir. Nobody would miss him—"

And when the commanding officer unpicked himself from the ceiling:

"I guess it didn't occur to you that we might want to carry out an autopsy."

The sergeant's patience was fraying. He considered he had handled the complication in exemplary style. "You can't do that, sir. You can't just pick up a body and take it away for an experiment—"

"We'd be wanting to find out how the man died. That's all."

"You know how he died. From the rabbit."

"Yes, but how, Sergeant? You see, I mean—how? What organs were affected? What course did his illness take? Was the killer thrust to the brain or heart or lungs or nerves?"

"Look, sir, I am a security officer and that is the job I do. I am not expected to exercise scientific curiosity as well."

"Well, Sergeant, that's"—chewing on a word—"I guess that's fair. So this old man is a total write-off now. Little chance of gaining any kind of pathological information."

"I could . . . er . . . dig him up. My motivation was that I considered he might have become infective. That was why I acted in the way I did. I hope you follow my reasoning, sir."

"I think so, Sergeant."

"Well let me see if I follow yours. You were expecting me to bring this man back here not because he was dead but so that you could see how your germ agent had worked on a human."

"Are you being supercilious, Sergeant?"

"No, sir, just getting things concrete in my mind. I want to have a proper awareness of what my duties are, so that if anything like this happens again, I will know what you want me to do."

"I can't get rid of the idea, Sergeant, that your attitude is somewhat deprecatory."

"No, sir. I'm just trying to be a good soldier—"

"And one further thing. There won't be another occasion. You should be clear on that because it is a security matter."

"Right, sir."

But that wasn't the close of the matter. A soldier trained into disdain for certain well-defined sections of the living compensates for that professional hatred with a strange compassion for the dead.

In a corpse there's a dignity to be protected. A soldier can get quite emotional about it. And the cold, objective application of scientific method to a piece of meat that couldn't care less anyway touches that sentiment come lately and wrings expression from the fighting man.

Like to the guards on the gate at Station Deva.

After all, nobody had told him to keep quiet about it. In any event, he had an entitlement to state his opinion.

"These medical guys are ghouls," he said, and the gatemen shared his horror at the prospect of taking a cadaver and wounding it still further.

"Poor old stiff," said one of them. "Just looking for a break. Matter of fact, I saw him round here this morning. Looked a little— tetched, you know? Looked a bit like a cottontail himself, skipping out of our way and into the bushes."

The other guard was philosophical. "Too bad," he said. "That's the kind of guy who always gets the poisoned meat."

They chatted about it, angling it this way, that way. The sergeant put himself in the dock. Did they think he had done the right thing? Well naturally, Sarge. You were in danger yourself if there was a risk of infection. We all were. Well done, Sarge. It was a pleasant academic exercise as the evening came down and the rice-flies started fracturing themselves on the compound lamps.

Not ghoulish, either. Not the way *we* talk about it, hey, fellas?

And, of course, somebody heard them.

Spangle by spangle, drib by drab, Green Town sloped off into night. Simeon, perched above the swell like a schooner figurehead, counted out the lights with an action of exhalation.

In days of dandelions, one Douglas Spaulding had done the opposite from a cupola bedroom so close to this one that there might not even have been a wall between. He had felt the tall power it gave him, riding high in the June wind, the grandest tower in town. Everyone yawn, everyone up, he had said to the yellow squares being cut in the dim morning earth.

"Everyone yawn, everyone down," said Simeon to the streetlights flickering in distance like candles upon a black cake.

"How about you down?" whispered Julie from sheets as white as Kilimanjaro.

"I have to keep hold of it. Lose sight of it now and tomorrow I'll look out on slums and smoke and steelworks."

"Rubbish," from the cotton glacier.

"You know what I mean, Julie. It is the start and—well—something wonderful can happen here."

Alone in her soft ice-house of Parma violet fragrance, Julie committed an unnoticed tear to the pillow. She knew now what her husband would discover only out of pain and too late: things are not the way you want them to be, not anywhere, not ever.

The tear was an acknowledgement which Simeon must not see. Presently, there was little to separate him from the youth who had ridden a swing, kicking out at the Pacific three years before. A little of the enthusiasm had gone over to reality in the practice of providing. A great deal of the fantasy had gone over to fact in the discipline of co-habitation. But here, now, swaying above a town that starred in another man's dreams, Simeon's stature was in doubt.

Swing or cupola bedroom, what difference? At Playa 9, Simeon had at least been Simeon but here he was a boy called Spaulding, another named Halloway (or was it Nightshade?), a writer entitled Ray Bradbury.

"I know what your fear is, Julie."

Wonderful. An assurance. An identification. Only Simeon can know what Julie's fear is.

"I guess you think I'm going to give you the same kind of calliope ride you had at Point Conception. I may love the words that go to making this place in somebody's fond memory; I may feel I want to find a little of that enchantment and in so doing find a little more of that somebody.

"But I told you, Julie, this is just a holiday curiosity. We've worked hard at getting to know each other and what we do, we do together. And me sitting on this window-sill blowing out the lights of Green Town, that's just harmless fun, recognised as such. Don't worry about me. Not me or you or us."

Julie stirred upon the freezing slopes. "I—I only worry that you're going to catch cold. On a pollen night like this, you get miserable with catarrh."

"Not this pollen. Not this sunflower dust. The bees keep it all on their fuzz in Green Town. Sneezing is on rota and by arrangement, new men at the bottom of the list."

"Everybody yawn," said Tomorrow Julie. "Everybody down."

And Judge Charles Woodman turned in his four-poster, dislodged a legislative tome, woke himself, doused the light, away across the town.

Lucia Lorensen let her tired right arm fall as darkness took away the task of masking her and Frank came quietly so as not to wake her from his propaganda room, hung up his elegance and laid a kiss upon her hidden brow.

The nut-brown eyes of Mrs. Fenella Buchman, in her penthouse above the library, reneged on Thomas Hardy and Wessex and drifted into the obscurity of Jude.

Charlie Frei, disguised as a shadow, went abroad with a paintbrush, adjusting the billboard scripts for the following day—twitching out of sight at one hoarding as Patrolmen McAree and Frolich flashed the sidewalk.

Jim Ruffner slept and the day animals on the prairie and William Filo plus Allison Miller and the stranger within the city gates. Movement was on the edge of the world, where daylight persisted as did the machinations of men, at the place Charlie had meant when he started "OK—" and had to sketch "—INAWA" on the apple-blossom air, making for home.

The message said "YANKS GET OUT OF OK—." No compulsive grafitti man would leave it like that, the law resolved and shut off the cruiser's power to wait. By which time Charlie had gone like a cat across a dozen limelit lawns and up the steps to his bed.

Each was unaware of the others but a subtle tilt of life and landscape would end all that in a very few days.

The only Green Town wakefuls now, Simeon and Tomorrow Julie. Simeon would not leave his platform. Julie came down off her mountain and found warmth as he wrapped her into his arms and let her blow out the two last lamps.

General Matthew Perry took the blip on the golf course north-west of Naha. Now that the U.S. military presence had diminished to a token handful, he was finding more time to unwind and only in-grained discipline had dictated that he bring the transceiver with him, clipped into his windcheater between a ballpoint and a briar pipe.

The sudden buzz startled him out of a crucial putt. But the mes-sage, carefully worded to mean nothing in itself, containing only the trigger that denoted a hasty return to his office, had him think-ing of more things than strokes over par.

"Washington wants a typhoon report today." "Today" meant "now." "Typhoon" had a kind of open-ended meaning. It signified any situation likely to cause concern; normally, there weren't too many crises to choose from and the word was adequate.

Perry sent his caddy lieutenant along to bring the car to the course periphery. He followed at a more thoughtful pace, the num-ber four iron bouncing on his right shoulder.

Try as he might, he could not identify today's "typhoon." And it wasn't a straightforward request for weather data—there was no dismissing it—because blip frequency was classified knowledge. Any of his meteorological officers could have dealt with a genuine inquiry of that nature.

Nevertheless, he would hold a rapid briefing before he connected with the Pentagon. He was uneasy and the reason was simple. Washington thought he knew what they wanted. And he didn't.

Back in his airy third-floor office in downtown Naha, where the wind hissed and hated around the glass corners and flying but-tresses, he could get at a blue-grass whisky and sharpen his mind ready for partial invention if no local answers were forthcoming.

But it was not to be. Waiting in his office with head on one side and eyes distant, as though he had some special understanding with the lyrical draughts, was Mitsui, who operated the Japanese interests in Okinawa under the umbrella of a flourishing import/ export concern.

Mitsui gave the lie to the oriental's legendary inscrutability. He was an enthusiastic person, expressive with his hands and animated with his features. When he was excited, the need for protocol could do little to calm him.

He was excited now. Which made two riddles.

"I'm sorry, Mr. Mitsui." Perry's philosophy was simple; take one matter at a time and if a queue forms make sure the one at the head is the one that can do the most damage. Maybe another of the departing military had left a local girl with more than a memory. Maybe the liquor bill was outstanding—or not as big as it used to be. "I have to deal immediately with a matter of some urgency. If you like, I could come round to your office later. . . ."

"No need. I fancy both our purposes might be served with a short conversation now."

"But you don't know what my purpose is," said Perry patiently. "Give me an hour, Mr. Mitsui, and I'll telephone—"

"No, sir. It is you who are uncertain of your purpose. I know you have been contacted by Washington with a specific and mystifying inquiry. I also know what they are talking about, even if you don't."

Perry slung his windcheater across a hardback chair, invited Mitsui to move closer to his desk and turned up two glasses. He was seasoned and not given to hypertension. His hand on the decanter hardly twitched when Mitsui said, "It is germ warfare."

Perry tried a laugh for size but it fitted him badly. "Ours or yours?"

"Most definitely yours."

"Where?" Perry sat down because he felt safer that way.

"Here on Okinawa."

"Not that VX container again. Hell, that was nine years ago. . . ."

"Please, General . . . Even I know the difference between chemical weapons and biological weapons. Germs I said and germs I meant—and not nine years ago."

"Then I'm afraid you have me at a disadvantage." And that was a sorry admission to have to make, he thought. The one U.S. installation left on Okinawa apart from the offices in the capital was a biological research station, arguably involved with germs but for purely medical reasons—at least that was the military–industrial dogma which made its presence on Japanese territory permissible.

Perry knew little of its functions and would have known even less, given the chance. The kind of war fought with dirty water and pox-ridden blankets was not for him. Notwithstanding, this unit seemed the only possible source for what Mitsui was suggesting.

15

Mitsui, with a physique that was more South Pacific than Nipponese, was perspiring heavily into his ample shirtfront. Perry's only comfort was that his caller felt less than qualified to relate the details of the violation.

"A man is dead," said Mitsui.

"Where?"

"In the woodlands to the north of the island. Near your installation."

"Dead how?"

"Disease is likely."

"Only likely?"

"There are circumstances, General. I would say very likely."

"Perhaps you had better tell me the circumstances, then."

"The man is an islander, of no particular consequence. There is no one to whom compensation will need to be paid." Mitsui smiled, slightly heartened by his small insolence. "He was preparing something to eat and died of it."

"Could be straightforward food poisoning."

"No, sir."

"You have a medical report?"

"No, sir."

"Then we cannot be sure."

"Yes, sir."

"How can we be sure?"

"Steps were taken to dispatch this unfortunate with minimum delay. A trench was dug, the remains of man and meal burned with kerosene and the residue interred. It was, shall we say, a prompt and comprehensive operation."

"I don't know anything about this." And Perry didn't.

"I believe you. But I would add that it is now important you should find out as much about it as you can."

"I don't need you to—you don't need to tell me that." The general was holding to the niceties with difficulty. "You are saying that our people are responsible for the death of your citizen?"

"I am saying that a rabbit was responsible for the death of our citizen and that your people were responsible for the condition of the rabbit."

"Look, man, we can't take the rap for every rabbit on the island—"

"I appreciate your anxiety but I would repeat that it was a member of your agency who stepped in so quickly to remove the offending articles and that it would be naïve to believe that this indicated anything but complicity. I have already said that I accept that you know nothing and I am sure my principals will not hold you personally to blame. But to be fair to you, I must tell you that details such as we know them have been passed on to Washington—not with any thought of malice but because we considered we must properly raise the matter. No doubt your superiors are now seeking your side."

Argument in the absence of facts was futile and ridiculous. "I'll find out what I can and come back to you," said Perry. "I am sure we can come to some reasonable arrangement."

Mitsui stood up. "I am empowered to say that under the terms of our Okinawa Extension Treaty of last year, there is only one arrangement we would consider reasonable."

Mitsui headed for the door. Perry said nothing, knowing the Japanese entrepreneur was just waiting to be asked what that was. He could read the exchange better than Mitsui, but that was hardly a victory . . . hardly a draw.

On the threshold, Mitsui said what he had to say, question or no: "The arrangement is that you take your research station and go."

Perry was left wondering how he could put that in a weather report for Washington.

Sunday on campus. A phenomenon not recorded by the Green Town quill, observed trotting Simeon with reluctance, possibly because summer of '29 had landed softly on sun pastures and moon meadows where the Little Fort college complex now stood.

He had started off walking in the cut-grass smell of mid-morning. Dawn would have been opposite, to see the first jingling trolley run out of the lakeside terminus. Last darkness might have been better, with the surety that one was rising alongside the first of the Green Town citizens.

But for a man in Simeon's position, with a wife to consider and a fixation which, at best, might be described as an indulgence, the action had to follow a decent amount of sleep and a leisurely breakfast and coffee and niceties with the new landlady.

The streets were warm when he ventured forth, which meant the magic oxygen failed to spike his senses. People prevailed, with no way of telling which was the early-riser of the Bradbury psalms, which the charlatan who had come to Green Town only in the last forty years or so.

Too many people, too many machines. Green Town buzzed when he wanted it to hum. So he trotted, thinking an increase of pace would bring him the sooner to the town he had come to see. Instead, it was bringing him the sooner to the knowledge that the town he wanted was beyond the limit of any running, almost beyond the stretch of any imagination.

Now slowing to catch his breath, he came upon the Brasilia magnificence of Little Fort. Young folk rapped and rolled upon the sward, stood up, stretched, poked their middle fingers at the day or his faith or some such thing. Maybe me, thought desolate Simeon. Maybe I am the abomination.

Not for any better reason than that he had been thinking them the same. They were too old to know a lightning rod if they saw one, too sour to find joy in dandelion wine.

His informant's childhoods always stopped at twelve. Was that when the man's family headed west on Highway 66 looking for work and finding the Inspired Chicken Motel? Such distant and conclusive days. Go away on lightweight tennis shoes. Come back troubled.

Simeon knew it in his water. His dream, his indulgence had gone west from here. Therefore, metaphysics and kidney divination, anything that came east from west would be the reverse of what he wanted.

"Fellow." The freshman was so big that he loomed. "You STARE!" Simeon, out of focus, had been regarding the boy.

"What are you looking at?" Territorial aggression.

"Nothing much," said Simeon. He had meant that in the whimsy sense. Now it was out, it sounded like a reflection of the other's worth. If they had been putting less clay in the feet of football idols this year, he might have suffered by the entendre. As it was, the kid left him to stare, merely removing himself from the line of vision.

In any event, the contact had been traumatic enough for Simeon. Not only was Green Town somewhat less than he had wished it, but the natives were pretty hostile, too.

If a student is a native. Shipped in to learn and spurn—how much of a native is that? A campus is an island, wherever it stands. Little Fort wasn't Green Town, he philosophised hopefully.

But it will be. You watch. Thus spoke the realist in him. Why does realist rhyme so closely with nihilist?

Simeon trotted on with all the prospects of a migrant who had missed the fruit harvest.

Tomorrow Julie, meanwhile, talked to Mrs. Dilger over coffee which the good lady called "yet another," it being staple to her diet.

Julie had known she was asking for trouble or despair, at least, when she had offered comfort on Mrs. Dilger's ten-year-old bereavement. Instinct told her to get rid of the subject now, at the outset, while relations were good, and not later when the recollection of such ready intimacies might be an embarrassment to all. What it all came down to, she confessed to herself and nobody else ever, was that she could not trust Simeon to keep things steady and good for long. Make an alliance and you win an allowance and that was how you cushioned yourself for life with Simeon. She felt a stab of guilt at being so level-headed.

She had a belief over death that was more Christian than that of Christendom but she never phrased it in theological terms because people got uncomfortable. She kept it clean and kept it there. She knew her Hebrew Scriptures and "hell" in most cases was "*sheol*" and that just meant "grave." Gehenna, the other sobriquet for death, had been the plain outside Jerusalem where the bodies of criminals were burned. No actual hellfire. No sweat. Heaven? The Book talked of a calling forth from the memorial tombs. If elevation was instant, what was the need for that call?

Paul had said it to one of his more distant congregations—the dead were only sleeping. Somehow she had never doubted that there was a state beyond earthly life. It was faith or specialist knowledge or both, because the former feeds from the latter. Julie's creed had room for evil spirits—so many famous and Blishian intellects accepted that much, anyway, and she read them as proof positive of the balancing forces for good—but to place for Mysteries. Mysteries had been invented to keep the repressed ignorant.

And along these lines, she waited to say the words to Mrs. Dilger. Only to find they weren't needed.

In the lady's understanding, Mr. Dilger's absence was purely academic. His clothes, lovingly tended, hung in the wardrobe they had shared. His picture abounded. His opinions still fashioned the thoughts of his widow. Because she had known them and understood them and loved them.

He had insured her comfort financially—not affluent but in the manner to which they had been accustomed. He had gone away and would be back. He loved books and would have enjoyed talking to Julie's husband.

Come to that, where was Julie's husband?

When the problems were aired, the first out was Julie's.

"Researching," she said. "It's a grand word but all it means is that he is walking around trying to recapture atmosphere, to absorb this place into his bloodstream."

"I don't think I'd enjoy that," said Mrs. Dilger.

"You don't have to. With you, it's there . . ."

"No. I mean, I don't think I'd fancy being wife to a man like that. It would make you feel you had to keep a grip on him the whole time. Now with Leonard it was all the other way—I had to push him out to get some peace."

She laughed apologetically, lest some shade of Leonard Dilger should be listening.

"If we all liked the same kind of man . . ." began Julie.

"I know, I know. I'm sorry. That comment was less than genteel."

"Actually, it isn't so bad being married to Simeon. He takes these flights of fancy and they wound me. But oh, the pleasure when he keeps coming back. Do you understand me, Mrs. Dilger? With a man who has never known anything else but his home—nothing personal, Mrs. Dilger, just an illustration—a woman might get to thinking she was on safe ground."

"I was never in any doubt with Leonard, young lady—"

"No, of course not. But you had the talent, you see, to keep the life so attractive. Think of lesser women—perhaps you know a couple—who thought they could keep their men tethered with too little effort and then lost them."

"I do, I do know a couple and that's exactly right—"

"Now what gratifies me about Simeon, Mrs. Dilger, is that he samples all these other enchantments, all these substitutes for settling down—I don't mean other women; there are none of those and I would know—and discards each one in favour of me. That's what boosts my confidence."

"Whatever turns you on," dimpled Mrs. Dilger. "Isn't that what you young folk say?"

Julie smiled. "A long time ago."

"I don't quite—"

"The young people don't say it any more. You know phrases, they go out quicker than pop groups."

"Do they? I mean, do pop groups go out quickly, too? There—
and I thought I was so clever to use it."

"You had the sense of it precisely right," conciliated Julie.

They fell to drinking yet another while the generation gap
yawned.

Perry had set to pondering on his reply to the Pentagon and had
arrived at an answer without too much sweat. His responsibility was
for the U. S. Army personnel on the island, but that had never
been crystallised as extending to the scientists who worked at
Station Deva, an installation which seemed to give proper nominal
dignity to the oriental deities on the face of it, but provided a better guide to function when the words were juxtaposed.

They were civilians and U. S. Chemical Corps graduates who
weren't really army except in the most peripheral sense.

If they had lost one of their laboratory animals, that was their
look-out or the buck belonged in Detrick—the buck, huh; a small
smile for the pun—but in any case, not with General Matthew
Perry.

His cable to Washington said simply, "Glass dropping and wind
building up. Could do with some relief."

If the Pentagon knew the situation, they would know what to do
about it. He would sit back and wait for the man they dispatched.

And sure enough, the man came in haste. Another full-blown
general who—as it turned out—had supervised the devolution of the
stateside military germ and gas houses into legit public health
agencies and now found himself suddenly back in the old routine.

Kenyon Sebright was studious, slightly stooped, with eyes no
longer good enough for the artillery and heart too heavy for the
missile program. He didn't exactly bring all his hang-ups with him
but Perry could tell, just by watching the way he downed his
Bourbon (so similar a fashion to Perry's own), that this was a
basically unhappy man, a man who might now be contented with
small victories.

How much of that was long-term and how much due to this
current assignment was not immediately clear. Besides, Perry had
little enough time for psycho-analysis.

Kenyon Sebright had been up to Station Deva and had sought
only information on their product.

It was Yeze fever, he told Perry over lunch, talking fast because they were due to meet Mitsui and others early that afternoon. That was classed as a rickettsial disease, involving micro-organisms which shared the properties of both bacteria and viruses but were more versatile than either. Furthermore, this strain had succeeded in telescoping the ten- to twelve-day incubation period into a few minutes with healthy individuals and paradoxically longer for weakened individuals with faulty cell structures.

Perry was not interested in the organic niceties. He wanted to know where the human element had failed. Here, Sebright was less than informative.

"The matter was under control," he said, "until this local stepped in and grabbed the rabbit."

"Then it was never under control," said Perry. "If it was that easy for a local to step in and grab a rabbit, control is not the word to use."

"The animals were given a fairly free run," conceded Sebright. "They were so used to their domestic environment that they had provided no trouble hitherto. This one was some kind of throwback. It dug its way under the fences. Naturally, the body count soon revealed the deficiency and a patrolling guard found the hole. . . ."

"You're saying is that what sent the system awry was a rabbit that behaved like a rabbit."

"Their reaction was commendably prompt—"

"Doesn't matter how prompt they were after the event. The idea is to avert hazards by anticipating them. And what was the matter with this guard that he couldn't recover the bunny without killing the native?"

"The native was dead, anyway—the moment he came in contact with the rabbit's innards. The guard only did with the man what he was supposed to do with the rabbit. In the circumstances, my feeling is that he acted with considerable merit."

Perry spluttered into his soup. "With considerable merit, is it? Well, I guess life's cheap in the scientific service."

Just a hint of tightening around Sebright's mouth. "We still have to go quite a way before we devalue it to the level of Vietnam."

"You eggheads beat us to that a long time back with a wonderful peacemaker tried and tested in Hiroshima and Nagasaki. When you're talking to Mitsui and his friends this afternoon, you might remember that world is a lot nearer the surface than any Vietnam."

They ate out the meal in a silence that started off stony and ended up pensive as each worked out his approach to the interview.

Mitsui was on time and sweating predictably. He was accompanied by two suave and miniature gentlemen of clear Nipponese stock. He introduced them as Mr. Malecki and Mr. Keio, both of the Japanese Defence Ministry.

To Perry's surprise, Sebright took the lead, seeing them comfortably seated and supplied.

"I am here on behalf of my government," he said, "to offer you our sympathy in this matter and to assure you that disciplinary measures have been taken and that we are happy there will be no repetition."

Mr. Keio leaned forward. "We are happy, too, that there will be no repetition. We trust that a week will be sufficient for you to wind up your undertaking here and remove all trace. As for the matter of the tainted beasts, arrangements have been made."

Sebright was unperturbed. "We can understand your anguish, but really we would implore you to reconsider this notice to quit. It is common knowledge that your economy, on this island particularly, has been based almost entirely on the spending of our personnel and the aid we have supplied—"

"Common it may be," said Mr. Malecki, echoing Sebright's disarming smile, "accurate, it is not. We do not need your money. Japan is a rich nation."

Thanks to America, Perry thought, but he left it unsaid. The interview was not going well but at least it was going. A comment like that, designed to degenerate the exchange into an open argument, would have been foolish.

"Thanks to America," said Sebright. Perry swore under his breath and waited for the worst.

Mitsui threw him a troubled look. At least he could see the resident general's difficulty.

"That may have been true at some stage," said Keio calmly. "But Japan has long been competent to create her own wealth. The money we took from America was a matter of grace so that she could assuage her own conscience. We feel she has paid her debt."

"But we are not about to let her incur a new one," said Malecki, who was rather less collected than his companion.

"I think it's about time I said something," put in Perry desperately. "What General Sebright says about our investigations of this event is true." It wasn't but the truth was not accessible to his visitors. "What he says, too, about our measures to alleviate similar accidents is also true. The fact is that we like it here. We are reluctant to leave for a number of reasons and strategy is not one of them. This was an isolated incident which we regret but I would appeal to you not to take it out of perspective."

"I will tell you what we consider is perspective," said Malecki. "On this island, we discover, we have the wherewithal to destroy the whole population by plague and I don't know how many more beside. If the measures we now employ would seem to be extreme, it is because we consider the situation extreme. You will not persuade us otherwise."

Then Sebright compounded his stupidity. "How did you find out?"

"For crying out loud . . ." responded Perry.

Keio asked quietly, "Was it your intention that we should not find out?"

"No . . . I . . ."

"I think what General Sebright meant was that it was unfortunate from our point of view that you should have been informed of this from a source other than ourselves," said Perry. "We would have looked better if we had told you."

"But you did not know," said Malecki. Perry flashed a glance at Mitsui. "You were in the dark yourself until Mr. Mitsui told you."

"I was on the point of taking the matter up with Station Deva when I talked with Mr. Mitsui," countered Perry. "The deficiency is in timing only."

"Your Pentagon knew before you did," persisted Malecki.

"I am aware of that. What's your point? I mean, apart from answering my companion's question."

"We found out because we were told," put in Mitsui. "By someone who considered the incident was not covered by the provisions of your stay here. You will appreciate that we don't intend to name that person."

"Am I to understand that our establishment was infiltrated?" asked Perry. It was foolhardy but he had to try and retain a little of the draining decorum. "If so, how does that fit in with the provisions of our stay?"

Keio's smile had not altered by one degree. "There is nothing clandestine here, General. We did not need an agent at Station Deva to acquaint us with a situation he considered 'bestial and inhuman,' to use his somewhat repetitive words. The abomination produced the informer, it was as simple as that."

"Then there must be some other reason." Sebright had taken Perry's suggestion as a lead and was prepared now to proceed forcibly in that direction. "It has been suggested to you that you could benefit from making full use of this incident."

Malecki laughed. "By whom?"

"The Chinese."

"They're your friends," prompted Keio.

"The Russians, then. You've been pretty much cheek to cheek with them lately. Maybe they've told you they'll help you if you can get rid of us."

"But we don't need their help any more than we need yours," protested Keio.

"Then maybe they've told you that what you suggest will cause us a great deal of trouble and that's what you want. . . ."

Perry could not be sure that the Japanese tolerance was going to stand much more of Sebright's empty-headed passion. He suffered no lack of patriotism but the Pentagon man's continuing outburst was sounding more and more like the ravings of a petulant child caught out in a misdeed and less and less like an adult appraisal of the problem. "What *are* you suggesting?" he put in forcibly. "Let's get this discussion on a realistic level." By that he hoped to communicate that he did not sanction, could not control, Sebright's display.

"You are going home and the rabbits are going with you," said Malecki.

"We could destroy them here without hazard."

"We don't find that satisfactory."

"Well, all right. We'll get them ready to ship out."

"No."

"But you just said—"

"*We* will get them ready for you to ship out. You, meanwhile, will get all the rest of your personnel and equipment ready to travel."

"That's not necessary," persisted Sebright. "Our staff is quite capable of preparing the rabbits to move—"

"We are not satisfied," repeated Malecki. "We prefer our own men to do the job. I am sure it is obvious why. We will listen to what you say. We will take the risk. But we will put the rabbits on your ship."

"All right." Perry was hurrying to be practical. "We'll convey the rabbits to America and destroy them by incineration."

"We have no objection to incineration."

"Good. We make headway—"

"Only we must nominate the man who will carry out the destruction. That way we can be sure the job is done and the carcasses are not returned to us in our meat supply."

"We wouldn't do that—"

"We are not going to give you the opportunity. Our man is an associate of Mitsui's. He has meat warehouses in New York."

"Then we can take them the whole way by sea. Through the Caribbean, past the West Indies, via the Panama Canal and up the Atlantic coast—"

"We're sorry," said Keio.

"But what's the matter with that?"

"The Panama Canal is closed."

"How do you know that?" queried Sebright.

"We're businessmen, General. The canal has been closed to the shipping of livestock by the Panamanian authorities. They are fighting an outbreak of Venezuelan equine encephalomyelitis and this ban is one of the statutory measures. You can check with your representatives there if you have any doubts. And we are not even going to suggest flying. There would be difficulties enough with porterage were it not for the delicate state of the rabbits' ears, anyway. It is our opinion they have been caused discomfort enough."

"So that leaves only one route—here to a port on the U. S. Pacific coast and across the width of America by rail."

"That's out of the—" began Sebright.

"That would seem to provide the answer," said Malecki.

"Maybe we could kill the animals on the boat and put them in cold storage. . . ."

"No." This time the objection was from Sebright. "These organisms are pretty unstable. There is no information yet how they react at temperature extremes. They could thrive on cold storage. We have to keep the animals alive. But we—we couldn't let people know what we were doing. . . ."

"The condition is outrageous." Perry was sure the manoeuvre was a set-up but could not fault it. "I'm beginning to think myself that what you're insisting upon is a penance and I'm afraid we don't see our position that way at all. . . ."

Keio stood up. Malecki joined him. Mitsui hovered. "Do you

mean," asked Keio, "that you would have trouble shipping these rabbits across your country? We could always banish the need for secrecy by explaining exactly what you were doing and why—"

"No." Perry cursed himself for sounding so desperate. "We had enough trouble railroading nerve gas eight years ago. No . . . we can't do this."

"It's blackmail," said Sebright, who seemed to have a talent for exasperation.

"It is the Principle of Strong Position," said Keio, "and really, you Americans should not complain on the infrequent occasions when the principle works against you."

They turned for the door. Malecki delivered the parting shot. "We shall take lack of action as reluctance. Then I'm afraid we shall just have to start putting the word about."

Sebright settled back in his seat when they had gone, content for some reason. "Well, I think we handled it pretty well. We gave them something to think about and our honour is still intact."

"We're still moving out," prompted Perry, mystified, "so what honour is that?"

"We didn't admit our guilt."

Perry plunged headfirst into the drinks cabinet. Concession thinking of such a high calibre he could not contest.

The library, then, at three-fifteen of a Monday afternoon, steeped in great drifts of silence with books scattered boulder and tree-trunk style on the tundra of eternity, shelves so tall the snow of time fell all year round.

That wasn't exactly how the master had put it, but no amount of good intention could make Monday afternoon Sunday night and June October. Simeon had come to look last night and found the place locked and deserted.

He had expected to ascend Jim Nightshade's twelve steps but had found instead a floor-level entrance to a building hardly high enough to take the dew, let alone the snow of time. And Clayton and County when it should have been . . . Well, he didn't know where it should have been because the dreamwelder hadn't said; just spoken of Will Halloway rising at two in the morning at his home in Oak Street to go to the bathroom and seeing a single light in a high library window.

Standing at the corner of Oak and Thirteenth, he would have to get a good deal closer to the lakefront and about forty-five degrees off to the north-east to reach Clayton and County. As far as that went, it was "across town" but he could not be sure the wordspinner had meant just so; was doubtful, too, that any vestige of library roof could be pinpointed from upstairs Oak Street, not to mention a high window.

But this was the only library in Green Town and if it looked too new, what could he do about that? He could be prickly.

The girl at the intake was ridiculously young. When she smiled, Simeon said, "I was looking for Miss Watriss."

"Miss Watkins?"

"Miss Watriss."

"I'm afraid we don't have anybody of that name here."

"Are you sure?"

"Pretty sure. I mean, we have a staff of thirty-six and it's possible she has joined recently and I don't know her. . . ."

"No. She would be one of the veterans." Staff of thirty-six? Up front was the desk where the nice old lady, Miss Watriss, purple-stamped your books. . . . There went Miss Wills, the other librarian, through Outer Mongolia, calmly toting fragments of Peiping and Yokohama and the Celebes. Way down the third book corridor, an oldish man whispered his broom along in the dark, mounding the fallen spices. . . . Staff of thirty-six?

"When was this?" the girl was asking.

"This was 1928." 1928? "What about Miss Wills?" Simeon said quickly. Nearly fifty years ago. Could it be possible?

"No Miss Wills either, I'm afraid."

"Mr. Halloway? Mr. Charles William Halloway?" An old man then and resenting it. How could he be alive now without Mr. Cooger's wonderful calliope? And that was broken up by Nightshade and Halloway Incorporated in—1928?

An elegant form moved behind the counter-girl. "I am the chief librarian," said Mrs. Fenella Buchman. "Can I help you?"

"The gentleman was asking for a Miss Watriss or a Miss Wills," explained the girl. "Or a man called Charles Halloway."

"I'm sorry," said the fair Mrs. Buchman. "There is nobody of that name and I would know. How long is it since you were in contact with them?"

"They were here in 1928."

"19—28?" Mrs. Buchman regarded the man before her. He was not above thirty-five—could not have come within a decade of

1928, hence—and his dress, though not unkempt, was without attention to what she called detail. She looked at his collar and it was clean. Eccentric he might be, but somebody was looking after him. The face? He had a pleasant face. Something of the mystic about it, maybe. A face to watch. But that didn't always apply. Once, she had flirted with the verse of Dylan Thomas and pictured just such a face. Only to be confronted with the actuality.

Bramley apple cheeks and small features which might have been attractive on their own but never in that particular order. And an awkward man in drink, as he had been at the literary gathering she was attending.

But this man . . . Something of the darkness in his eyes and hair. Celtic extraction and thereby having access to the tongues of myth and magic.

She was losing the drift.

"That was the time," he said. "I can't help the time." He made it sound like a challenge and that more of arrogance than an academic defiance.

"Then you—never met them personally. Perhaps your parents . . ."

"No. I met these people myself. Not in the orthodox way, perhaps. Through the printed word." Simeon did not know why he was being deliberately abstruse, except that one way to deal with his frustration was to pass it around a little. "They occupied a library in this book. Or I might mean they occupied a book in this library. No . . . I mean the first. . . ."

"Which book?"

"*Something Wicked This Way Comes.*"

"By whom?"

"What?"

"The author?"

"You mean you honestly don't know? Living in Green Town and you don't know?"

"We have four thousand volumes here—"

"Bradbury. Ray Bradbury."

"Oh, science-fantasy."

"Grief, what a well-laid-out mind you have. You even dismiss science-fiction. Fantasy . . . And yet how close we all are to his fantasy, how many chords he strikes in us. If you dismiss him, you've never read. . . . Let me tell you, proud analytical lady. . . . He made this place immortal and a lot of people in it. . . ."

"Well, I'm afraid he didn't make Miss Watriss or Miss Wills or Mr. Halloway quite immortal enough, Mr. . . . because they're not here now and I doubt if they ever were, except between covers."

"I'd say you read the classics," said Simeon. "I'd say you tried a couple of the other kind and found them less than dignified and dropped them very smartly. And the name is Simeon."

Mrs. Buchman drew herself up (which served to make her even more statuesque, as it happened) and said, "You are in error, Mr. Simeon. I provide a weekly column of reviews for the *News-Sun* and am an occasional contributor to the *U. S. Library Journal*. If my style is classical, it is a preference and not a pair of blinkers."

Immediately she regretted the outburst. She had been drawn into an attitude and had shown rather more of herself than was professional. "You may find something about your friend in our local lore section. If you haven't a ticket, I could allow you to consult any book you like at one of our study booths—"

"I've read all the books. I want the people. And the creatures—the thunder lizards, Pterodactyl, Kite of Destruction, G. M. Dark and his populated skin, *fantoccini* and the pandemonium theatre company and brother Tom Spaulding who counted every lick of every ice-cream and ticked off the petals in the dandelion wine—"

"I can't help you."

"You WILL help me."

And Simeon was sweeping off among the shelves, trailing his hands like antennae along the spines of the books.

Mrs. Buchman reached under the counter and pressed a button which rang a small, insistent bell in the police station just around the corner in Madison Street. She motioned the counter-girl and floating assistants towards the door. Then she went after the trespasser.

"Don't you see, we can't help you," she called.

Simeon countered over his shoulder. "It's a matter of having to. A matter of being the last and only place."

Meandering left hand dislodged a volume. Simeon spun and caught it a foot above the floor. He gentled its pages, inspected its binding and replaced it. Mrs. Buchman was disturbed by the caress. Is a madman that sympathetic? Can a person who cares so much about books be all bad?

Her mind fled back to the button and she wished it unpressed. But that could not be so.

Even now, Officers Frolich and McAree came through the door with side-arms drawn and scanned the network of text and leather.

Mrs. Buchman withdrew from Simeon's trail and hurried to meet them. "There'll be no need for—those." She nodded at the guns. "It's a small disturbance. I can handle it myself."

"We were called, lady," said Officer Frolich. "That's our authority."

"It was a misunderstanding."

"Do you have a difficulty here?" Officer McAree.

"I thought I did. Now . . ."

"Now you're not sure?"

"The summons may have been a little hasty."

"The faster the better with summonses, Mrs. Buchman," said Frolich. "We'll clear up your misunderstanding. No blood on your books, though. Okay?"

"Then I go with you. The man is just a little—bewildered."

"Did you press the bell?"

"I was bewildered, too."

"Maybe you'd like us to leave altogether."

"Would you?"

"We're guardians of the peace and the community, Mrs. Buchman. We can't turn our backs on a call. There could be injury—even to property. It's our responsibility."

Fenella Buchman felt like a tennis-ball volleyed between racquets. "Come with me," she said. "Behind me. I can only show you what I mean."

She led them into the labyrinth. Anthropology, biography, cuisine . . . no sign; meteorology, nuclear physics, orchestration, nothing; radio, submarines, tautology . . . nowhere to be seen.

"What was it exactly?" asked Frolich.

Mrs. Buchman, wondering why she felt relieved in the midst of her mystification, perceived a line of escape. "I was sure I saw somebody dodging among the shelves. Perhaps I was mistaken. So many plots here . . . My imagination . . ."

"Like one character in search of an author," said Frolich.

Mrs. Buchman laughed. Frolich did not.

"You wouldn't be trying to fob us off, Mrs. Buchman?" said McAree quietly.

"There doesn't seem to be anybody here now," the librarian volunteered weakly. "You can see that as plainly as I can."

"But there was somebody."

"I thought so."

"You must have been certain to press that bell."

"No matter how certain I was then, Officer, the gangways appear now to be deserted."

"And you'd like us to stop looking."

"Officer Frolich, I'm not sure your condescending attitude wouldn't interest the members of my committee. I'm not in the habit of making a fool of myself or of making rash movements towards that alarm. It was a genuine mistake, I'm sure."

"I'm sure," echoed Frolich.

"Pigs," said a voice from the air. "Pigs and tyannosaurs. Who said you armour-plated specimens died out? You just got a change of uniform."

Simeon was lying atop a ten-tier shelf. He could have stayed there, said nothing, remained safe, but it looked as though Mrs. Buchman was going to end up embarrassed. The fun, then, was over. The madness was gone except for a few tatters that might make for easy fright but no more.

"What in Sam Hill are you doing up there?" McAree wanted to know.

"Waiting for a mumbo-jumbo jet," said Simeon.

"Wise guy, huh?"

"You said it, baby. Let me tell you, Officer, if you want to trade B-movie clichés I can keep it going until the cows come home."

"Keep it going all down the side of that book-case," said Frolich, waving his piece. "And you dislodge one volume and I'll give you a lump of lead for your knee-cap."

"That's civilised."

"Nixon said it for me. Students aren't civilised. Students are bums."

"And look what happened to Nixon," Simeon came back. "Besides I'm no student. Don't give the academics credit for all the lawlessness."

"Then you admit you're being lawless."

"As sure as I'm on this shelf."

McAree's neck was sore from looking up. "Come on down. We'll talk about reasons at the station."

"I'll tell you now—I'm looking for the pandemonium theatre company . . . the Dust Witch, Mr. Electrico, the Dangling Man, the Monster Montgolfier, Mademoiselle Tarot, Egyptian Mirror Maze—"

"Up *there?*" Frolich's upper vertebrae were aching, too. "Man, *you're* the only pandemonium up there and not for long."

His foot found a space on the bottom shelf. He kicked a gap on the second, started climbing, fingers gripping sixth and seventh.

Simeon, so lately mellow, could not take his eyes now from those upcoming fingers. He shrank back. Frolich kept going.

"G. M. Dark in person." Simeon's voice was high-pitched with awe and uncertain in timbre. *The Illustrated Man.* He heaved himself off the remote side of the book-case, let fortune guide his feet to the floor.

Then he ran and didn't stop until he was flat on the wood-tiles with McAree's arms wrapped around his thighs and spread-eagled Frolich shouting instructions from six tiers up.

The officers gave him perhaps half a second to say sorry to Mrs. Buchman and prodded him on towards the door. He was subdued, with the cumulus of consequence piling up and the first salt raindrops already there when he ran a grubby hand across his face.

Out in the Clayton Street sunlight, Frolich put his iron away and rubbed his hands down the sides of his trousers. The action reminded McAree of something.

"Your fingers," he said. "That's what spooked him."

"What about my fingers?" Frolich splayed out his oversized mitts palm-down.

The right hand said "LOVE." The left hand said "HATE."

The L'Enfant Plaza offices of the Department of Transportation were on the White House side of Washington and General Nathan Young, anxious to keep at least a semblance of interchange in his dealings with the DOT, volunteered that he should go to them.

He took the scenario and Captain Richard Grass with him. Carl Whittier, head of the Federal Railroad Administration, did not keep them waiting.

"Good afternoon, gentlemen." He put his cards on the table straightaway. "I hope you don't have another Operation Chase for us."

Captain Grass cultivated what he considered the proper facial degree of askance, but to the general it was a reference not easily laughed off.

Briefly, CHASE (short for "cut-holes-and-sink-'em") had visualised sending more that eight hundred railroad cars filled with poison and tear gas and possibly unstable explosives across the United States through Indianapolis, Indiana, Dayton, Ohio, and Elizabeth, New Jersey, to waiting liberty ships at Earle, New Jersey.

In all, some 27,000 tons of gas weapons and storage tanks were involved—12,000 tons of GB nerve gas, 9,000 tons of mustard gas in one-ton canisters, 2,600 tons of leaking GB rockets encased in concrete, 3,000 tons of contaminated containers and thirty tons of CS gas in concrete-encased fifty-five-gallon drums.

The munitions were to be marshalled on rail sidings at Rocky Mountain, Anniston, Alabama, Edgewood and Blue Grass, Kentucky arsenals, and loaded aboard more than a score of trains for shipment to the New Jersey coast. The four liberty ships were to be towed out some 250 miles and sunk. This turned out to be an error. It was closer to 125 miles.

This wasn't the first CHASE operation, but the largest. The disposal program already had a history of accidents. One ship, the S.S. *Village*, had blown up five minutes after sinking—luckily, not one of the three (out of eleven) which had been carrying poison gas, or the seaboard populace would not have been alive to see the 1969 project.

Another ship, the S.S. *Isaac Van Zandt*, had been bounced around so heartily while it was being towed out of Bremerton, Washington, that it broke free and two navy tugs spent an anxious six hours trying to recover the severed rope.

All this at a time when derailments were reaching an unprecedented level in American railroad history.

The subsequent expert testimonies delivered to a panel of the National Academy of Science—set up because of the hoohah which subtle revelation of the military plans had prompted—had motivated a unanimous recommendation that CHASE be scrapped, that the nerve-gas bombs be demilitarised, that the mustard gas be burned and that a special panel of munitions experts devise a disposal plan for some of the other gas weapons—by this time reaching a critical level of deterioration.

The successful harnessing of the Pentagon plans had been seen as a triumph for the conservationists—and one which had taken them off alert for a considerable time afterwards. All it meant to the military was that they did their dumping more regularly but on a smaller scale—and without giving the program the dignity of a title.

Now, Whittier had bridged the years and evoked the old taboo with his opening gambit and his little pile of memoranda from the Office of Hazardous Materials.

In fact, opinions were all he was equipped to offer at this point. The Defense Department was a law unto itself and could outweigh the DOT without trouble. The documentary sanction he was prepared to offer was not so much a blessing for the Army as an exoneration of his department.

Nevertheless, the general accorded him the courtesy of discussing the matter and outlining their plans.

"This time, nothing on that scale. A one-shot from A to B. A consignment of two hundred rabbits being taken from San Francisco to New York to be destroyed."

"Why?"

"With respect, Mr. Whittier, that exceeds what I am obliged to tell you. There is a need and a purpose, but all that concerns you is that the journey is being made."

"How are the animals to be ferried?"

"Compound fashion, one would suppose."

"Is that a little old-fashioned?"

"There's no more modern arrangement for providing plenty of room, plenty of food and plenty of comfort."

"These must be very special rabbits. What is their origin?"

"They have been used for government work in Japan."

"What kind of work?"

"Does it matter?"

"Of course it matters. It matters how you carry them, what safeguards are necessary."

"That factor has been considered and resolved."

"You have to allow us a little say in this, General."

"We don't, Mr. Whittier. But I'll tell you we have taken trouble to see that we are not in violation of the authorisations you are going to give us."

"How do I know that?"

"Because I tell you so. Sir, we try to avoid alienation with your department but we are bound to feel a certain amount of pique when we find you don't trust our intentions."

Captain Grass laughed quietly from a chair behind Young.

"Captain?"

"I'm sorry, sir. I thought you were making a joke."

"The DOT and ourselves have a good working relationship, Captain Grass."

"Perhaps the captain accepts the charade for what it is and is amused by it," said Whittier. "There is a certain wry entertainment to be drawn from the actions of two men trying to slow down the inevitable to less than indecent haste."

"I don't know anything about that," returned the general, "but because the outcome of our exchange is assured, I see no reason for that to preclude proper discussion. That is why I come and see you instead of just getting you to send round the forms."

"You might as well have them, anyway." Whittier pushed two documents across the desk. Young handed them to Grass to keep him quiet.

The unfortunate captain noted a memorandum, which explained the DOT's part in the arrangements and discharged it from responsibility in the areas outlined, and a special permit.

The memorandum stated:

In accordance with the regulations of this Department, shipments of explosives or other dangerous articles offered by or consigned to the Departments of the Army, Navy and Air Force of the United States Government must be packed or otherwise freighted, including limitations of weight, in accordance with such regulations or in containers of equal or greater strength and efficiency as required by their regulations.

Special Permit No. 9199 authorises the Department of Defense to ship livestock in trailer on flat car (TOFC) ensembles without the five-year electrokrypton retest. The permit was issued on June 20 and is valid for twelve months.

The containers are built to Department of Transportation specifications and are authorised for commercial shipments of livestock. The purpose of retest is to determine whether the containers have been weakened by abuse or other means. From a continuing quality control and test program, DOD has found such containers are adequate to their function. The specific trailers have not been in transportation since their last use by the military authorities and it was therefore appropriate to waive the retest requirements.

Our regulatory authority over hazardous materials relates only to safety in transportation. We do not tell DOD (or any other shipper) where materials may be shipped, nor do we have anything to say about the disposition of materials after they reach their destination.

We are satisfied that we have taken every practicable precaution to ensure safety in transportation of these animals. The proposed shipment meets our standards for transportation safety, so that Special Permit No. 9199 is sufficient authority in all respects for the shipping envisaged, so long as all terms of such permit be fulfilled.

Determinations as to scheduling, routing and destinating of the livestock which are the subject of this permit have been made by the Department of Defense. Therefore, inquiries and objections raised in these areas should be directed to that agency.

The other item said:

Special Permit No. 9199

Pursuant to 49 CFR 170.13 of the Department of Transportation (DOT) Hazardous Materials Regulations, as amended, and on the basis of the June 18 petition by the Department of Defense, Washington, D.C.:

Special Permit No. 9199, authorising the shipment of livestock, recognises that the arrangements made by DOD for this shipment fulfil DOT requirements and are therefore sufficient to allow unlimited access for the shipping train.

Retest requirements on the cars to be used have been waived since said cars have not been in operation since last used for military purposes, at which time regulatory inspection was made.

Any shipments of different nature to this present must be approved by recourse to us, the Office of Hazardous Materials or the Bureau of Explosives, when a new permit may be issued in respect of that proposed use.

When Grass looked up Whittier and Young were watching him.

"Do you find them in order?" asked the railroad man. Grass felt a stab of pity for the man at the mercy of the military machine.

"I'm not qualified to argue," he said. "They certainly look O.K."

"And they wouldn't be anything else," said Nathan Young.

"Tell me"—Carl Whittier was settled back in his chair, arching his fingers—"now that we've given these cars an apocryphal clean bill of health, maybe you'll say where you got them from."

It was General Young's turn to laugh. "This'll test your capacity for railroad history. Do you remember a case back in 1971 when the La Salle and Bureau County Railroad was alleged to have stolen two hundred and seventy-seven Penn Central freight cars and repainted them and changed their numbers?"

Whittier looked blank.

"Don't worry," comforted Young. "I only remember because I researched it and thought it sounded interesting—like rustling on wheels, huh? Well, the FBI was digging and La Salle insisted the cars had been bought legitimately by a company that was using its workshops for renovations. The case dragged on, the cars were suspended from use—just lying there in Illinois, idle. So we commandeered a handful and very useful they've been. Where did you think we got 'em, off Barnum's circus train?"

Whittier looked about to say something and then thought better of it.

"You think it sounds like stealing," Young prodded him. "I'll cite the Army Appropriation Act, 1916."

"Cite what you like," said Whittier. "I'm only concerned about keeping my railroads safe. For my part, I'll give you Lorenzo S. Coffin."

Young stood up—somewhat sharply, thought Grass. "If our business is over, we'll be going."

Whittier was looking happy for the first time as he shook their hands.

Going down in the elevator, General Nathan Young said, almost to himself, "Lorenzo S. Coffin. I don't believe it. It's a made-up name."

"No, sir," responded the indefatigable Captain Grass. "He was one of ours—with an Iowa infantry regiment in the Civil War and then a pioneer for railroad safety. He didn't like the way brakemen kept losing their fingers in link-and-pin coupler accidents and he spent most of his life lobbying for air brakes and automatic couplers. . . . Got them, too. Railroad Safety Appliance Act, signed by President Benjamin Harrison on March 2, 1893—"

"Captain Grass!" The aide had to skip to keep up with the general crossing the plaza.

"Sir?"

"You talk too much."

The one-way system made it a long journey around the block and McAree and Frolich were not disposed to brighten the ride with conversation. McAree drove the cruiser and Frolich stayed in back alongside Simeon.

When they trundled him upstairs, along a corridor lined with doors on either side and into a charge-room straight out of Ed McBain and proud of it, Simeon felt obliged to comment. Something simple like: "What's the charge?"

In actuality, the silence of the arrest had been in Simeon's best interests. He had used it as breathing space to regain his composure.

Frolich wasn't prepared to answer until he had a ballpoint in his hand and an incident report before him. "What's your name?"

"Simeon."

"Is that a forename or a surname?"

"It's my identification. Just . . . Simeon."

When Frolich looked like losing his cool again, McAree said, "If that's how people know him, it serves. Where do you live, Mr. Simeon?"

Simeon gave them the address in Oak Street. They would check it and he would be moving on, dispatched by Mrs. Dilger, but that was for tomorrow.

"Marital status?"

"Yes."

"Not sufficient. Are you married? If so, what is the name of your wife?"

"What has that got to do with it? She's not on a charge."

"Her name."

"Julie."

"Julie Simeon."

"No. Tomorrow Julie. It's a good name. Pity to change a name like that. We've got rings and papers. We really are married, you know—"

"Don't try to patronise me, Simeon. I don't care what your arrangement is—don't make it sound as though you're being old-fashioned for my benefit."

"My goodness," said Simeon, but he didn't add what was in his mind about the up-tight policemen.

Frolich waved his arm in the vague general direction of the corridor. "Put him back in a cell while I make the call."

"What call?" Simeon hoped his plight was not going to be introduced to Mrs. Dilger first and Julie second over the telephone. Best they should hear it from him. Better than best if they could be spared it altogether—not for dishonesty but because his wife did not deserve to share his consequence and was troubled enough just by his being in Green Town.

"Campus police," assured McAree. Something of Simeon's anxiety must have filtered into his carefully genial expression. "For corroboration."

"But I told you in the library, I'm not a student."

"Right," said Frolich, but he went on dialling. McAree took Simeon's arm and turned him towards the corridor.

"They won't be able to help you," persisted Simeon.

Frolich pointed at the corridor. McAree said, "This way, Simeon." Six paces nearer the cell, he said, "Just let us do what we usually do and it will save trouble."

"But I'm trying to save you trouble—"

"We're not used to that. Let us hear it from elsewhere. We need that." He said "we" but he meant Frolich, Simeon was sure of that.

"Frolich isn't going to like it when the campus police come down and blast him."

"You don't have to worry. You told him. And don't think anybody is going to blast Frolich. . . . Say, Simeon—that's a kind of biblical name. Are you Jewish?"

"Out of the Land of Shinar. Aren't we all?"

McAree didn't know whether that was an admission or not. He was still trying to decipher it when the lawmen from Little Fort State arrived and he had to retrieve Simeon from the cell.

With the last classes of the day still in progress, campus patrolmen Clark and Montague were not sure what kind of a case they were going to find at Madison Street and the city police had been less than informative. That was the situation from way back. Too many broken store windows and the mistaken belief that campus was sanctuary and college police were pro-student had ensured no happy working relationship could be achieved between the two sets of guardians.

But when Frolich and McAree produced Simeon, the riddle was over.

"He's not one of ours," said Ramsey Clark.

"How can you be so sure?" asked Frolich quickly. "You've got ten thousand students up there and you can't see most of their faces for hair anyway."

Harvey Montague ran his eyes over Simeon's patched but tidy frame. "Too old," he ventured.

For some reason, that brought a sting like pepper to Simeon's eyes. He might have been accused of harbouring a disease. "I'm not so old. . . ."

"No, he's not so old that it's out of the question," said Clark. "But—"

"What about the G.I. Bill of Rights?" suggested Frolich, but resolved quickly that the defendant didn't look like any kind of a fighter. "What about—these regional traveller people. They're, like, mature. Maybe he's a political activist just passing through."

"I've told you I've nothing to do with the college," said Simeon, who was still short on patience after the reference to his advancing years. "How many different ways do you have to hear it? You're trying to tie me in with these things and it doesn't make sense—"

"Doesn't make sense sitting on top of a library book-case talking about mirror mazes and dust witches," countered Frolich. "More what you might call an intellectual pursuit. And you were molesting that librarian."

"I—"

"You were making trouble. We don't like that in Green Town."

Harvey Montague coughed. "If you don't require us any further—"

"The matter's not settled." Frolich was unrepentant. "Is he a member of your college? If not a student, a member of the faculty?"

"Nothing to do with us," said Montague. "Why don't you listen to the man?"

"You could be mistaken."

"So could you, Frolich. And look here—"

Clark stopped Montague with a hand on his arm. "We are not accepting responsibility for him," he said firmly. "That's all you want to know and I'm giving it to you. He's yours to do with what you will. Now we're leaving."

And they left, with Clark muttering to Montague as they

went: "Why do you take him up on it, Harvey? You know how the guy loves to prognosticate."

Another strained silence followed their departure. McAree broke it finally with a piece of procedure that had somehow been left to afterthought. "Do you want to call a lawyer?"

"I don't know one."

"We could recommend somebody."

"It would be a waste of time until I know how I'm going to be arraigned. . . . Even then, I . . . No, I don't want a lawyer."

"Breach of peace, violation of citizens' rights, trespass . . . we'll leave the exact terms to the city prosecutor," obliged Frolich. "There's the question of bail."

"Do you have any bondsmen here?"

"That may be difficult in view of your lack of residential and work qualifications. Any regular income of your own?"

"Occasional free-lance writing. And"—Simeon smiled wryly—"the government sometimes pays me to stay out of trouble."

"I'll believe anything you tell me, naturally. But it occurs to me they'll stop the payments now—"

"Once they know," conceded Simeon.

"So that just leaves you Tomorrow Julie."

"That's all I need. That's all I ever need."

"Noble but it doesn't solve our problem."

"He won't skip," McAree said quietly. "Will you?" He waited for Simeon to confirm.

"I can say no. I can even mean it. But everything hinges on whether you accept that as currency. . . ."

"I'll accept it," said Frolich surprisingly. "I guess when I find you telling the truth and still don't believe you, I owe you an apology and maybe a favour. I'll guarantee you turn up to see the C.P. and at any subsequent hearing, and if you let me down, don't try hiding in the library or anywhere else in this neck of the universe. Now get out of here. . . ."

McAree conducted Simeon onto a darkening Madison Street. When he got back to the charge-room, Frolich had his hands splayed out on either side of the incident report and was looking almost quizzically at the right. The one that said "LOVE."

He caught McAree's eye. He stabbed at the right hand with his left as though the digits at issue were not part of his body. "What do you think about that?"

"Beautiful," said McAree. "You know you must have had the thing written there for some reason or other. . . ."

The quayside at Naha, remote from the hurricane side of the island and overlooking the Sea of Japan with the Korean coast a couple of hundred miles away, was accustomed to the rumble and drag of army traffic, but the stuff moving out today was ancillary and almost unmilitary—glassware and anonymous containers, all handled with so much caution that the exercise could not help but look subversive.

Miyake Mitsui had kept an eye on the operation from one window of his import–export business overlooking the bay. At regular intervals he had noted the presence of General Matthew Perry, becoming progressively more disturbed as his strength on the island diminished with each shipboard lading.

Mitsui was well enough able to keep tally from his window and knew the general would not thank him for counting on the quayside. The denouement left no room for deception, in any event.

Perry and his executive personnel were being given a few days of grace to complete paper work, but everything which constituted a manifestation of the U.S. menace was being removed.

Scientific, medical and security staff had moved out of Station Deva even as the nominated Japanese destruction crew had moved in. They had been allowed to take records, germ cultures, instruments. But their two hundred common white cottontail rabbits were left where the Japanese could make a confidential check on them, uncluttered and uncensored and unseen by U.S. manpower.

It was an insult by any standards but one the Americans had to bear. A man had died as a result of contact with the tainted beasts. He was a civilian and, more important, a Japanese national.

Perry, once he had obtained confirmation of the death, had been unwilling to press further. It was better that the prognosis should be death by disease than that he should find the man had been removed in some other way because he had discovered a secret.

That might be an unnecessary worry—Perry believed the American conduct on the island had been honourable. On the other hand, Perry had believed that quarantine measures at Station Deva were sufficient and had been proved wrong.

The behaviour of the many was no guarantee against the dubious practices of the individual. He had seen the soldier who had burned and buried Koza and had been impressed by the man's professionalism—an impression not shared by Sebright from his earlier and harassed visit to the scene but all the more astute for that. However, a classic soldier could be just as easily a classic liar.

He did not so suggest. He merely asked no more questions. In any event, the Japanese seemed ready to accept that Koza's death had come from the fever. And the result was the same—the Americans were out. But in a slightly better light than if there had been a rape or a murder.

So the Japanese were taking the last steps at Station Deva and it was their responsibility to bring the laboratory animals to the quayside in whatever conveyance their administration recommended.

Perry, still pacing the wharf while the small waves washed up against the ancient Amami stone, was waiting for them now.

Mitsui glanced at his office clock and then at the schedule he had been provided.

According to plan, the rabbits were five minutes away. Time enough now to take a stroll down and exchange last pleasantries with Perry. Sure, the man would be here a little longer but when he went, Mitsui felt, it would be with the minimum of fuss and farewell—and Mitsui didn't qualify for any special intimacy.

Mitsui descended to the open air and directed his steps to intercept one of the general's tacks. "Good evening," he said.

Perry grunted.

"I hope you don't think badly of me for what happened," said Mitsui. "I am only an agent here and very much in the hands of my government."

"Very much," echoed Perry.

"Almost as much, I would say," purred Mitsui, "as yourself."

That kept the points even and it made Mitsui feel better though it did little for Perry.

"I don't think badly of you," lied Perry. Not you particularly, just everybody in general. "We brought it on ourselves," he added with an effort. Command meant collective responsibility. All right, he was ready to stop playing footsie with the Japanese but he wasn't ready to stop being a general.

"An unfortunate accident," comforted Mitsui. "To tell you the truth, I'll be sorry to see you go. As a trader, I have to confess that it will very soon cost us more than the little profit we have at present of saving the status quo. Gestures are all very well when you can afford them and in Tokyo they can. Here in Okinawa, we don't get much of the glow from the Asian phoenix."

It cost him precisely nothing to say that. In his business guise, anyway, it was no more than the truth. In his second self as a diplomat, it didn't cut all that deep. One of the assurances the phoenix had given was that it would make good any deficit the island suffered as a result of the U.S. expulsion. But of this, Perry was not aware.

Perry, in fact, was warming almost against his will to the Polynesian-style plenipotentiary who had made his stay on Okinawa all the more pleasant for providing good liquor with his messages from the Japanese legislature.

"I'll be sorry to leave," he said. "The islanders have made us very welcome and if they are going to suffer on our account, it saddens me. I don't suppose your principals would hear of the idea of financial aid."

"I don't suppose *your* principals would hear the suggestion," countered Mitsui. "Not when there was no visible return."

"Maybe not—though we have been known to do things out of the kindness of our hearts."

"Not for the Japanese," Mitsui reminded him. "For us, you paid to right a historic wrong."

"It wasn't entirely unprovoked . . ." Perry flushed and bit his lip. This was Pearl Harbour land, fighting a war thirty-odd years over. No percentage in—but if Mitsui chose to—

"Anyway," said Mitsui. "One way or another, we feel you have recompensed us now far more than was deserved. . . . Look at it that way, General. There must be a thousand places where you can carry out your medical research with many more facilities than you had at Station Deva. Let's say we're saving you the rent."

And before Perry could respond to that, the rabbits were there from Station Deva—a couple of Kimshu wagons bouncing along the quayside with the maximum noise and what looked like the minimum protection.

A Japanese in a white coat jumped down from the passenger seat of the leading wagon and came over to Perry and Mitsui. He ordered the wagons opened and the contents brought forth.

In a short while, the job was done and Perry was staring, speechless, at twenty wicker baskets with unprotected air openings and the comings and goings of the occupants discernible.

Finally, he turned to the man in the white coat. "Am I to understand this is how your authorities have elected these animals should travel?"

"Certainly, General."

"Well, even in my faulty judgment on security, these baskets are somewhat marginal in their safeguards."

"They may look fairly ordinary, General, but the fact is that the creatures can't get out on their own and careful handling will ensure that none of your personnel will be able to get in."

"Are you being sarcastic?" Perry was back on the defensive.

"I don't think so," put in Mitsui. "What this gentleman means—"

"I'm perfectly able to say what I mean," hastened the health official. "These baskets are quite adequate. They give you a firm advantage."

"Over whom?"

"Over Koza," said Mitsui. It was what he had come down from his office to say.

Perry could see his loaders moving restlessly near the gangplank of the cargo vessel with the merchant coding. Weighing up the possibilities of a bite, maybe. He didn't want any more trouble, least of all from his own side. He gathered the remnants of his poise about him and said, "Then you won't mind having your boys carry them aboard and stash them in some suitable place."

He called the loaders to him, dismissed them to the Iansho bar and went to buy the first drinks. He didn't invite Mitsui or the man in the white coat.

Shigajiro Malecki chose carefully as one must when one uses the media. First, he had to figure what kind of impact he wanted to make. A bland statement outlining the American demise and released to the Western press was too obvious a violation of the loose assurance he had given to Sebright and Perry; not that the fact would have deterred him if there had not been other and better reasons.

Break it down into essentials. First, it was vital that the news was leaked to America somehow or other. Second, the sources should not be readily traceable. Third, the details should be rather less than accurate, allowing speculation of several sorts.

Even in the midst of his urgent sobriety, he had to smile. The American Government would know immediately that his office was responsible for the revelations, might go so far as admiring the panache with which he was carrying it off, but could do little to prevent the outflow of embarrassing information because too conspicuous an outcry on their part would alert the great force whose ignorance was absolutely vital—the American public.

They must deal with the disclosures as they were made.

Fourth, there must be several versions of the truth, each incomplete but embodying a trigger for curiosity. Each version could be released consecutively. No—the object would be better served if they were concurrent, converging upon the United States with a sinistration that would place heavy pressure on their agencies of guile.

Start in Okinawa. His office located Mitsui and by that time version number one was ready. When he was satisfied Mitsui was able to handle the release, he said, "A man called Koza is missing from his home. Relatives are concerned because they are aware he has been in the habit of touring U.S. installations on the island. Draw attention to the fact that these are now almost totally out of use.

"Suggest that he may have come to some harm on one of these abandoned sites and state also that inquiries are being made at the one remaining installation.

"Give the *Naha Star* three hours with that and then get back on and tell them the badly charred and unidentifiable bodies of a human and an animal the size of a cat, a rabbit or a small dog have been found in a shallow woodland grave near the Station Deva biological research unit of the U. S. Army, but foul play is not suspected—"

"*Not* suspected!"

"That's what I said, Mitsui. It always looks that much more convincing when we appear to be hushing something up. Now . . . follow my instructions to the letter."

Malecki broke the connection. He was happy enough with the start and considered it nothing short of ingenious. Once the *Naha Star* knew questions were being asked at Station Deva, they'd get through with a few of their own—and find the place empty and Perry's staff so touchy they would be sure to let something slip. Even if they didn't, they would probably issue a denial so curt it would merely heighten suspicion.

That took care of versions one and two. Next call was to Fujita, an ingratiating soul of limited usefulness in the Ministry Press Office.

"If anybody asks about a report that the Americans are pulling their last installation out of Okinawa, no comment," he instructed. "Do I make myself clear?"

Fujita fumbled momentarily. "Not altogether, sir. I have heard no such report."

"Then you know it to be nonsense, otherwise you would have heard."

"Yes, sir, but—"

"What?"

"Is it nonsense?"

"I have told you what to say."

"Yes, sir."

Malecki replaced his hand-piece, again well pleased. Fujita would be dialling away right now, seeking out one of his press favourites with the tit-bit.

"I can't tell you any more than that," he would be saying, "and for Jimmu's sake, don't quote me. Insist on speaking to Malecki and say if he can't or won't comment on the report, you'll just have to publish it as it is, citing 'informed sources.'"

Malecki left his office, still smiling. He wasn't ready to be available just yet. He would keep out of the way until the report had been filed and columned. Then, when the wire services had picked it up, he would be ready with version number four.

He bought himself a generous meal and then went to a bathhouse to get the excess weight sweated and slapped from him. The clock moved on four hours while he enjoyed himself.

His secretary was putting her stenog away when he got back.

"Minister, the telephone has not stopped buzzing," she said. "The press—"

"What is the matter that our press office cannot deal with it?" he said mock-irritably.

"They insisted that they should talk to you."

"Did they say what they wanted?"

"A report of a U.S. pull-out from Okinawa. Even the Okinawa papers have been calling."

Good. By now the discovery of the charred body would have been "made." The details were beginning to stack up in a certain way.

"There is no need for you to stay, Chibiko," said Malecki in a softer tone. "Your work is done for today."

"Thank you, Minister. Is—is there anything in these reports?"

Chibiko was halfway out through the door. Her boy-friend was already restless in the foyer.

"I'll tell you," said Malecki carefully, "when I hear them."

Then the telephone grated. Malecki waved to the closing door. Into the mouth-piece he said, "Malecki."

"Ah, Minister," said an English voice. "It is an honour." Peregrine of the *British Guardian.* He made it sound as warm and runny as any Fujita but Malecki was not so repelled. Peregrine was a sharp character, a tough and intelligent newsman who was nice when he wanted something but could be ruthless in pursuit—and part of his success lay in the fact that he didn't try to hide his conflicting selves. With Peregrine, you knew what you were up against. Malecki could not have asked for a better opener.

"John," he said. "Good to hear your voice. Have you tried before? I've been—unavailable."

He baited the hook and Peregrine rose to it, not out of fish ignorance but with a determination to pull the angler into the water. His "Oh, yes" begged a massive question.

"I don't know that I like telephones," said Malecki. "How long would it take you to get to my office?"

Peregrine laughed. "About thirty seconds. I'm in the foyer. I don't like telephones, either."

Perfect. "Well, you know the way up," said Malecki. He had two tall scotches poured by the time Peregrine came through the door with a kind of flourish that was knock and entry combined.

The newspaperman slung himself over an easy chair, having somehow grabbed up one of the glasses during his descent. "Shigajiro," he said. "You are picking up rather a nasty Western habit. You are becoming elusive."

Malecki let it go with a smile. "Talks," he said.

"Of a confidential nature?"

"How do I answer that? If I say 'no' it's no news; if I say 'yes' you can't have it anyway."

Peregrine sucked at his scotch. "Then why ask me up?"

"Not ostensibly to talk about where I've been. I understood that various members of your corps had been trying to locate me. Maybe I can take this phone off the cradle"—which he did—"and you can act as a kind of spokesman. I'd like to go home tonight in the certain knowledge that I'll get some peace."

Peregrine had unhooked his leg from the arm of the chair and was perched more conservatively now, like a man about to do business. "Then you know why we were calling."

"A rumour that the Americans are leaving Okinawa."

"And is it a rumour?"

"All right, a report."

"A report, Shigajiro—is it a *true* report?"

"Yes."

"Why are they leaving?"

"That you must ask them. It is a matter of protocol."

"Then it is their decision."

"I didn't say that."

"Well, is it or isn't it? If it isn't theirs, it must be yours."

"That's speculation."

"You bet your sweet life it is, but what else am I to do when you're going round and round the mulberry bush—"

"My humble apologies—the mulberry bush?"

"Fencing with me, Shigajiro—the conspirator one minute, the innocent the next. What is it you want to say officially about this pull-out?"

Malecki played his trump-card. "There are good diplomatic reasons for it."

"Then they've done something—"

"John, you know I can't—"

"Violated something. The Okinawa Extension Treaty—one of the terms. Which one, Minister?"

Malecki cultivated a mien of helplessness. "John, you have gone beyond the point where I can help you."

"We had a snap on a couple of charred cadavers, one human, one animal, near Station Deva just as I left the office. Is it to do with that? Do you know what they've been doing at Deva?"

"I cannot confirm anything that you say to me."

"And you will not deny it."

"I cannot deny it. Surely you can see you're putting me in an extremely difficult position—"

"Come on, Shigajiro. You know damn well you've led me this far. You might as well tell me why."

"No, John. You brought yourself to this point by your own perspicacity. Now you can be content with what you have or you can wait until the whole matter is revealed through official channels in the fullness of time. I have a feeling your patience won't last that long."

Peregrine unwound himself from the chair, slightly flushed with a newsman's excitement. "All right, you old buzzard. And thanks."

He made for the door. Malecki called him before he could turn the handle. "There's one thing you're forgetting."

"What's that?"

"I asked you to be a spokesman."

A shadow of disappointment passed across Peregrine's face. "You mean you expect me to tell all the rest of the mob about our exchange?"

"No."

"What, then?"

"Only what I said."

Peregrine was out through the door with the same tenacity. Malecki heard him whistling down the hall and was rubicund with satisfaction. Four separate news items which would presently link to make some kind of sense were all circulating.

Phase One of the project was well under way. Malecki was setting up no interviews yet on Phase Two, if he ever did. Phase Two was the knock-out.

They walked for four hours a day and were tired. Circuits of the community centre attached to the rebuilt church of Matobacho, which was immediately behind Hiroshima railway station.

Two hundred. Some had been hairless from the Beginning (or shortly after the Beginning, to put a fine point on it). Some had been born years after the Pikadon and their genes were treacherous and their knowledge of the pika-for-lightning and don-for-thunder was a kind of scarred hearsay.

Like so:

The sky falls and falls.
I take its fragments
Upon the skin where once hair flourished like leaves.
Now is always autumn and the rain fills the furrows of my brow
Until it falls full spate into my pitted mouth.

Streams on my fissured back.
Floods in my ruined lungs.
Sky fall and why
Do I live to suffer it?*

* Author's note: These lines are mine but in the spirit of much post-Bomb poetry.

That was the question Dr. Ichiro Domei had to answer. Explanation, even now, was impossible. It involved an evil too vast and terrible and profound for the two hundred minds to encompass and this was just one rehabilitation clinic in a hundred in the city and he was just one doctor in a thousand. If explanation were beyond belief, then something must be found to fill that spiritual vacuum, that curiosity of being.

Domei's approach was practical. He trained his *hibakusha,* his survivors, to live. He built them up with diets rich in protein, vitamin, salt and calcium and watched their corpuscle counts when they weren't looking.

Two hundred. A month ago, they had tired of their exercise in two and a half hours. A year ago, they would not have begun the exercise. The progress made him wonder whether perhaps the Roentgen rays of time were beginning at last to dispense with the blood-debris.

He gave them a promise. Using the figures available to him now, showing them their forward step that they could not deny, he gradually brought them round to thinking of a future when the sun would throw the mushroom shadow behind them.

He used the therapy gently as one might rouse a child. This was late June by an occidental calendar. Tomorrow, next week, next month, he would teach them a new word and shed the label of "survivor." He must work on it, a compound that bore no inference of ashes or even rebirth, that denoted purity but not peculiarity. It was a complex equation in semantics and he put it aside. Again.

Even as he so resolved, the swing doors of the clinic yielded to give access to a stranger. The man was not the least bemused. Though Domei had never met him, he came straight to the doctor, extending his hand.

"Good afternoon, Dr. Domei. Where else would I find you but here?"

"Forgive me," said Domei, "but—have we met?"

"I know you through your records and results. My name is Keio. My occupation is with the Defence Ministry. It is a great pleasure for me to meet you and congratulate you."

"For what?" Domei had little love for the administration, for a man who took so much for granted and for a position so close to the stigma he was trying to dispel.

"For your work. Your success has earned special attention."

"From whom?"

"You don't have to be modest, Dr. Domei. There is no shortage of people aware of your qualifications."

Domei saw his survivors were slowing up, not so much with fatigue but because the visitor was providing a distraction. "We'll go into my office," he said. "Then you can stop beating about the bush."

He did not know what it was about the man that had alienated him. The approach was not so very fatuous among natives of a land where long-winded courtesy was legendary. Perhaps the fault was in himself because he was used to breaking down conversations into solid bricks of words, easy to understand and short to remember.

Before Keio could say more, he produced two glasses and a bottle of sake and said, "I'm sorry. I'm not used to formality."

Keio accepted the climb-down graciously. "I should have known better. Informality is as much out of habit to me as its opposite is to you."

"Then perhaps we could . . ."

Keio smiled. "Get to the point? But of course. I started off congratulating you. That was twofold—for past successes and for the tribute that has come your way now because of those successes. We want you and your people to help us."

"My people? My staff?"

"No, your—patients."

It was some time since Domei had heard his charges described thus. He did not like it but could not fault it. "I prefer to get them away from the idea that they are being treated," he said. "We are sharing an experience."

"Forgive me." Keio sounded genuine. "Indeed, 'experience' is a far better work than my own. It is an experience that we are intending to provide and we would very much like you to share it. We want you all to take a journey."

"What kind of a journey?"

"A straightforward movement from A to B."

"Where is B?"

"America."

"I forbid it. Are you mad?"

"Why mad? It is not enemy territory."

"That's your view."

"Are you still fighting the war?"

"How can I do anything else? The A-Bomb is my employer."

"No."

"Believe me, without the Pikadon—"

"No. I was going to say the Japanese Government is your employer."

"I don't see the point you are making."

"Merely this—that greater administrative minds than yours or mine have selected your charges for this honour."

"In Meiji's name, what honour?"

"Of showing the Americans that we have no hard feelings, even among those still tainted by their mischief."

"No hard feelings . . . mischief . . . ?"

"Dr. Domei. The war is over—"

"I know the war is over—you keep trying to tell me that without letting me tell you how I consider it. I want it forgotten. I have cleansed their minds of it and you're trying to . . . to . . ." The concept was so immense that it defied easy definition.

"To what?" Keio forced him to say something.

"To—turn my people into some kind of trophy. To undo all I have endeavoured to do and tie them to the Bomb as surely as if this were August 6, 1945."

"Dr. Domei. I can understand your anxiety to protect these people from events and recollections that have caused them so much pain. But don't you see that you are creating another unreality if you send them back into the world without their pasts? Memories are terms of reference. They need those guidelines or they will have to keep coming back to you for even the smallest decision. Should they be honest or dishonest? If they are taught that the world owes them a living, perhaps they will not understand the principle of payment. Or maybe that's what you want—always to loom large in their lives . . ."

"And why not?" Domei admitted without thinking. "Haven't I done enough for even a small corner in their hearts? If they listen to me, they will do little wrong . . ." A stomach cramp gripped him. He knew he had spoken foolishly, knew he had revealed an obsession no true healer should have had, given a glimpse of the Frankenstein feeling. The fool words ground to a halt.

Keio said nothing and left the eloquence to the heavy silence that now lay between them.

"There's an unreality in determining to get what you want at all costs," ventured Domei. "If that hadn't been the object up to 1945, perhaps I wouldn't still be repairing bodies and minds."

"Who will repair them from your damage?" said Keio quietly, toying with his glass. "All right, you can forget it."

"You mean"—the tortured doctor grabbed at the straw—"you mean you are going to spare me your tribute?"

"Yes."

"Thank you, thank you."

"But not your patients."

Domei hung like a rag on his chair. He was not strong enough to win but could not allow himself to lose.

"I—I have made my feelings known to you. In rather more emotional detail than is sophisticated, I am afraid. As you must surely see, my life is my people. I beg that you don't separate me from them. Perhaps I can at least ensure that they come through this holocaust."

"Thank you, Doctor."

"You knew I wouldn't be parted from them."

"Yes."

"You don't think I'm—bad—for them?"

"You may well be bad for them but the rest of us would be worse. They could certainly not take such a trip without you. I trust you will come to see that it is beneficial. For this reason, my government is insisting."

And there it was, a fine statesmanlike finish to an exchange that had taken more out of Domei than he yet realised.

Keio's smile stayed with him, Cheshire-cat style, long after the Ministry man had left the church of Matobacho, gone next door and boarded a fast train to Tokyo. Long after Domei had dried his eyes, blown his nose and gone to walk with his children.

Sentimental Searcher Misses
Library
Lizards

The Lake County courthouse was set back from Washington Street with an access road off West Dunlap.

It had what Simeon had begun to call the "Green Town Look" about it; designed by local architects Hausen and Hausen, who had fashioned the monopoly of the town's public buildings and schools (including the library, which had so provoked the defendant) and built perhaps a dozen years ago. Beyond that, he was unacquainted. The edifice, grouped around a square, comprised a tower block at the north and sections two to four storeys high on the other three sides.

As courthouses went, it seemed to have a light airiness which might find some reflection in the kind of justice dispensed. He hoped so.

St. Therese Hospital was visible across Washington Street. There had been some huddle among the arresting officers about a psychiatric ward. Simeon was already around to the opinion that psychiatric wards were among the few remaining refuges for sane people, but at the same time he wasn't sufficiently dogmatic to let his beliefs take him out of circulation—even if his convictions did, he concluded ruefully.

Better to play safe than sane, and upright folk don't go shouting for thunder lizards in libraries and running from Mr. Cooger and Mr. Dark.

The city prosecutor, Theodore Elmwood, had not been empathic. The ordinance he quoted was part riot act, part Athens statute. In Green Town, there were things citizens did not do. How much less, than, casual (he made the sound like "undesirable") visitors. This was not so much a prosecution as a retention of the status quo. He was apologetic about precedents, determined about enactment.

And Simeon, whose anxiety of consequences had crystallised into a fear of the reaction from Tomorrow Julie, had kept it all from her until he had a conclusion.

Simeon, pinned by the folly of his conduct, the torture-stake of his folly, the persistence of his torture-stake, could not summon his legendary eloquence as advocate. It worked in only so many ways and never when Simeon felt his accusers might have some justification.

He was outspoken when he knew he was right; otherwise, he would offer little to deter punishment. He even welcomed the penalty with a relish he suspected was masochism masquerading as a lively conscience. In fact, it was the other way about.

Simeon had grown so accustomed to paying for his indiscretions as to make it almost a science. He put it all down to experience and the wallet in that pocket was getting to be weighty. Come the day, he would be able to pay out with interest. Thus he turned the eloquence inward to explain away a lack of confidence.

Elmwood statutorily had drawn his attention to his rights, had recommended several legal men. But Simeon had had it with lawyers. He could not expect any counsellor to work with the kind of mitigation he had to offer. If he was unable to outline the riddle to himself, he could not enlist another agency.

They would give him a chance to volunteer a plea but he still did not know how to plead. It was a simple enough matter to deny charges of public order violation or sub-sectional vagrancy. The hard part was phrasing a lesser admission—and he might as well accept the axe at the outset if he could not put his extenuation into words.

Admitting guilt might save a lot of trouble and for all he knew that was a consideration with the judge. Nevertheless, disappointment was not a violation. He could not plead disappointment. But he could fight for a chance to describe it.

Then if the ruling was St. Therese, at least he hadn't copped out. The punishment was as much living with his performance as shouldering the ruling of the court.

He pleaded not guilty. Loud and clear. The judge was expressionless. Elmwood was irritated. The pressmen were relieved, Green Town *News-Sun*, Lakeside *Examiner* and Station WKRS having been warned that the case had a chance of turning bizarre.

Elmwood rose to begin his indictment. The judge waved him down. He nodded at Simeon. "Are you represented?"

"No, sir."

"Do you want to be?"

"No, sir. I think I know what I want to say."

A shadow of a smile from the judge. "You're not overawed by the surroundings? A lot of our clients, weaned on Perry Mason and Portia, feel they want to defend themselves, only to find their tongues have cleaved to the roofs of their mouths."

Scattered laughter. Simeon waited. "What I am asking," said the judge, "is whether you feel competent."

Simeon stirred himself. "Perfectly. I am innocent of the intentions so necessary for the success of these charges. It is up to Mr. Elmwood to prove whether there is sufficient reason to doubt my word and lay these charges."

Now Elmwood's mouth flickered. "Your Honour. I can assure you I would not try your patience, let alone this defendant, if I were less than certain of success."

His Honour made an indistinct gesture and addressed himself again to Simeon. "Mr. Simeon, my name is Charles Woodman. My assurance is that I am as willing to be persuaded by you as by Mr. Elmwood and that my only criterion is truth."

"Thank you, sir."

"Now—Mr. Elmwood will outline his case and perhaps you will make notes of points of contention and put them to the prosecutor at the end of his arraignment."

Judge Woodman waved Simeon on to his seat, settled back and signalled to Elmwood. Who stated:

"Your Honour . . . at three twenty-two on the afternoon of June 20—yesterday—Police Officers Frolich and McAree were called to the public library building at Clayton and County by the senior librarian, Mrs. Fenella Buchman. She complained that the defendant had approached her in an eccentric state—she will elucidate shortly—and had then proceeded to make his way among the bookcases in a manner likely to damage contents and disturb patrons.

"At the approach of the officers, you will hear, defendant became even more agitated and was eventually taken while lying face-down and full-length on a topmost shelf.

"There was some conversation which would seem to corroborate Mrs. Buchman's statement that the defendant was in an eccentric frame of mind—"

"Mr. Elmwood," rapped Woodman. He had noticed Simeon moving restlessly. "I do not care to see this defendant branded as a madman from the outset. A woman's impression of 'eccentric' is not sufficient reason for the irresponsible use of the word in your opening. What may appear to be eccentric in ignorance or isolation soon ceases to be so when the action in honoured with a context. Present your case in a less partisan manner—and defendant does have a name."

"I am sorry, Your Honour." Elmwood was not one jot dismayed. "What you are saying, in effect, is that I should let the evidence speak for itself. That is my immediate intention."

"What I am saying, in effect, is nothing so fundamental, Mr. Elmwood, and you know it. Nevertheless, since you seem about to reach your point, I shall not delay you with a lecture on semantics. Call your first witness."

Mrs. Fenella Buchman brought a rare elegance to the halls of justice. She was neither aggressively intellectual nor waspish in her style of dress—and she was not haphazard in her use of adjectives. She had described Simeon's course as eccentric. Perhaps, said Mr. Elmwood, she would tell the court why she had chosen the word.

She seemed in no hurry to oblige.

"This gentleman"—she indicated Simeon, trying not to catch his eye—"entered the library at about three-fifteen yesterday and asked at the desk for Miss Watriss or Miss Wills.

"My desk-staff was not familiar with the names but before they gave a definite denial, they called me, thinking the ladies might have worked here some years ago.

"I knew of no such people. Mr.—Mr. Simeon then said, 'If they are not here, this cannot be the place.' It was the kind of comment that warranted some response and I asked him whether he could give me any more information about them.

" 'Summer of 1928,' he said. "Well, my feeling was that—"

"No feelings, Mrs. Buchman," interrupted the judge. "Just details."

But the librarian was undeterred. "It is a detail, Your Honour, that 1928 is close on fifty years ago and if I were to feel it unlikely that Miss Wills or Miss Watriss should still be connected with the library or that such a young man could hardly have first-hand knowledge of them, that would not be too personal an opinion to be valid."

Some kind of deeper interest was kindling behind the judge's brow. For the moment, his lips moved as though a smile was caught and held. "In the event, I will allow the observation, ma'am."

"I asked whether they might not now be married or even dead. The suggestion seemed to trouble Mr. Simeon.

"'And Charles Halloway,' he said. 'Surely he . . .' and then he paused. 'He was an old man then. I guess he . . .'

"I apologised for not being able to help him. I told him the present library had been erected only by bond issue in 1965. At that, he became even more bothered. He said, 'But surely there must be something . . .'

"He seemed at a loss. I asked if he would like to look around the shelves to see if he could find something to help him—we have a very comprehensive local history section.

"No, he said, he had memorised the words that had led him to us. Something like:

"'Up front was the desk where the nice old lady, Miss Watriss, purple-stamped your books. . . . There went Miss Wills, the other librarian, through Outer Mongolia, calmly toting fragments of Peiping and Yokohama and the Celebes. Way down the third book corridor, an oldish man whispered his broom along in the dark. . . .'"

"Mounding the fallen spices," finished the judge, but proffered no explanation. He was watching Simeon with a definite interest, careful to switch his scrutiny elsewhere if the accused man should raise his lowered and attentive head.

Theodore Elmwood read the diversion as a threat. "I think, Mrs. Buchman," he said, "that the judge would like to hear why you described the defendant's conduct as eccentric."

Mrs. Buchman picked her gloves up from her lap and laid them down again. "On reflection, I'm not sure 'eccentric' was the best word to use."

"Nevertheless," Elmwood reminded her gently, "it was the word you used."

"Then I'd like to change it."

"I'm sorry. It's not possible to alter your deposition at this stage. You read it and signed it yesterday. Then would have been the time to have any second thoughts."

"Mr. Prosecutor—yesterday, I was still having first thoughts. Contact with your police officers is not exactly . . . comforting."

Elmwood stiffened. "Are you suggesting they were less than humane, Mrs. Buchman? Because if so, it becomes a very serious matter indeed."

"I'm not suggesting that. I am merely pointing out that most women—most *people*—would find making a statement to the police somewhat disturbing. I am sure I am not unique in feeling that I might perhaps have made a fairer job of the statement if I had been allowed to think on it—"

"Or perhaps might not have made it at all, Mrs. Buchman."

"What do you mean by that?"

"Yes, what *do* you mean by that, Mr. Elmwood?" echoed the judge.

"There is a point to be made, Your Honour. Mrs. Fenella Buchman is a lady of rare self-assurance, a lady not easily flustered and not readily pressed into saying something she doesn't mean. What she is saying now is that she was flustered—"

"But why might she not have made a statement?"

"I understand there was a certain reluctance when the police arrived."

"Are we to hear evidence of this?"

"Not from my part."

"Then I would advise you it has no place in the prosecution."

"Your Honour, this is a very capable lady, a trained nurse working part-time in the casualty section of our town hospital—"

"I fail to see what that has to do with anything," said Mrs. Buchman.

"Nor I, Mrs. Buchman," said Woodman. "Mr. Elmwood, it seems to me you are going to quite hazardous lengths to secure the repetition of this word 'eccentric.' If your case is that sure, you are wasting your time sweating on one word."

"Your Honour, the reference to Mrs. Buchman's nursing activities, for which I feel no apology is necessary, was to exemplify her high capabilities as a person. The word I pursue happens to be important because it illustrates exactly the state of the defendant."

"But the point this witness is making is that the word does not identify the state of Simeon—is that not right, Mrs. Buchman?"

The fair librarian nodded and smiled graciously.

"What would be a better word, in your now well-considered judgment as an arbiter of good taste and a nursing sister?"

"Your Honour, I thought we agreed—"

"Mr. Elmwood seems to think the qualification adds authority to your answer."

"I meant—before—" said Elmwood limply.

"Come now, Mr. Prosecutor," said Woodman. "This is still the same Fenella Buchman. Your word, Mrs. Buchman."

"A word I used before, to the arresting officers, Your Honour. 'Bewildered.'"

Elmwood relaxed visibly. "The prosecution will accept the substitution of 'bewildered' for 'eccentric' in this witness's testimony."

"You are sure, Mr. Elmwood?"

"Certainly, Your Honour. It is a very small point, I concede."

"Forgive me, I thought the whole case turned on it. Pray proceed with your examination in chief."

Elmwood let the jibe go and was promptly back on key. "What was the defendant's reaction to your suggestion that he should consult your shelves for some way out of his—bewilderment?"

"He went among them."

"He accepted your suggestion."

"Not exactly."

"Then what? I'm sorry, Mrs. Buchman, but we seem to depart from your deposition again. I'm reluctant to lay my own interpretation upon this—"

"He did not appear to be consulting any particular book. He did not wait to have me show him where to look."

"How would you describe his progress among the bookshelves?"

"Somewhat disorderly."

"Eccentric, Mrs. Buchman?"

"Only in the geometric sense."

"I meant it in the behavioural sense."

"Then bewildered, Mr. Elmwood."

Simeon was laughing despite himself, forgetting momentarily that he was the person on trial, watching the starchy librarian of yesterday wrapping up the stiff lawyer of today. He caught Judge Woodman's eye, found the amusement shared, but had to restrain himself when the judge laid a finger alongside his beak.

He had gained a great deal of confidence, principally because he suspected he had an ally on the rostrum and he fancied the case was falling down, quietly. And in that realisation, he had to stop short because he was not being honest. He had, after all, made mayhem in the library and Elmwood's inability to present the misdemeanour convincingly should not prevent justice from being done.

Judge Woodman watched the pulse flickerings of Simeon's emotions, knew them for what they were and stored them for later.

But Elmwood, made a fool one second, was a wise man the next. "Was it at this point that you pressed the alarm which summoned the police?"

Mrs. Buchman acquired a great deal of colour and could offer only a faint, "Yes."

Simeon, on the point of volunteering a guilty plea, bit down hard on the words.

"Why?"

He watched Fenella Buchman struggle and cursed himself for bringing her to this.

"The procedure is laid down," she said. "Whenever we get a patron we are not able to handle, we summon help."

"Then you admit you were not able to handle the defendant."

"That was my judgment at the time. I regretted it almost immediately."

"But not before you had pressed the button."

"Obviously not. My later thought was that I had misread Mr. Simeon and the situation and I could deal with it. But by that time, it was too late."

"Thank you, Mrs. Buchman." Elmwood was quitting while he was winning.

Simeon, for all his soul-searching, knew this present initiative was unfair. He had to take steps to get the fundamentals reiterated—more for Mrs. Buchman's case than his own.

When the judge asked, "Does the defendant wish to question the witness?" he responded quickly.

"Mrs. Buchman"—he tried to comfort her with a smile but it was the wrong time or the wrong man smiling—"did I actually harm or interfere with anyone in the library?"

"No."

"Did I damage property?"

"It is not possible to say."

"How so?"

"You—you were found on top of a shelf. Later, I noticed marks on the woodwork at that point."

Elmwood came out of his chair quickly. "Your Hon—"

"You're out of turn, Mr. Elmwood," said the judge.

Simeon continued, "Then what is your difficulty?"

"Well, one of the arresting officers also scaled the book-case. It is possible he could have caused at least part of the damage."

"Would you accept, Mrs. Buchman, that I habitually wear sandals and tread softly?"

"It isn't up to me, Mr. Simeon, to accept—"

"Stand out, Mr. Simeon," said Judge Woodman. "Let us see you treading softly."

Simeon obeyed and returned to his bench. Questions at an end, he sat down.

"Mr. Elmwood? I recall you wanted to speak when there was mention of damage. I will just say I incline to the belief that sandals do little damage to woodwork."

"No questions," said Elmwood.

Next up was Officer Neil Frolich, and Elmwood took him right through his evidence without intervention from judge or defendant. Simeon, in his time in the cell, remembering a favour wrought by the policeman, had reduced Frolich to size and got rid of the C. M. Dark whim, almost.

To return to Fenella Buchman the sympathy she deserved, he had to recall something of the exchange he had heard as they hunted him; for his own sake, he had to let the court see why he had suddenly been seized with such panic. He paid special attention to the end of the officer's testimony. Then he took him back to the beginning.

"Is it true that when you arrived Mrs. Buchman described the summons as a misunderstanding?"

"It's true." If Frolich had been expecting an easy time from Simeon in return for his impulse of last night, he did not show it. This was the arena, where favours were forgotten. Simeon picked up the vibration, blunt and without eloquence, and felt better for it. "And your response was?"

"I was reassuring, as I recall."

"Can you remember your exact words?"

"No. I didn't note that portion of the exchange."

"Was it something like 'We'll clear up your misunderstanding'?"

"Could well have been."

" 'No blood on your books, though, okay?' "

"I don't remember that part."

"Mrs. Buchman said she would go with you because I was just a little bewildered?"

"I'm sorry. If I had thought I would be questioned on the sequence, I would have taken special steps—"

"Officer," said the judge quietly, "at what point would you say in general that an incident commences from the police point of view?"

"From the time we are called from the station, Your Honour."

"Then you should be prepared to be questioned upon any matter subsequent to that time."

"Quite so, sir. I—just human, I guess. The dominant points are the ones first to mind. I also recall now that I said something to Mrs. Buchman like 'We're guardians of the peace and the community. We can't turn our backs on a call!' "

"Had anybody suggested that you should turn your back on this particular call?" Still Woodman's interrogation.

"Not in so many words, sir. But Mrs. Buchman, when we arrived, seemed somewhat reluctant to co-operate."

"She said she might have been mistaken."

"Yes, sir."

"Did it at any time cross your mind that there might be a misunderstanding worthy of your cool consideration?"

"No, sir."

"Not even as a courtesy to a lady?"

"Your Honour, we had had a bona-fide distress call. Now, ladies in distress often do irrational things like defending the lion that just bit them. . . . In fact, events immediately following proved there had been no mistake and that there was indeed a disturbed person —the defendant—on the premises."

Judge Woodman sat back and motioned Simeon to continue his examination.

"What would you say your attitude towards Mrs. Buchman was?"

"Well . . . helpful, I guess." Frolich tried to laugh it off.

"You and your companion, Officer McAree?"

"Sure, both of us."

"But at one point, when Mrs. Buchman believed I had disappeared, did you not make some comment about 'Like a character in search of his author'?"

"I did."

"Was not the suggestion there that the—intruder—was a figment of Mrs. Buchman's imagination?"

"Certainly not. I was just trying to be—literary. I am familiar with Pirandello."

"And just after that, did not Mrs. Buchman have cause to say, 'Officer McAree, I'm not sure your condescending attitude wouldn't interest the members of my committee'?"

"You must take that up with Officer McAree."

"Fair enough. Did you not later say to me, 'I'll give you a lump of lead for your knee-cap'?"

"That was a deterrent statement made when you appeared to be considering resisting arrest."

"Then, believing me to be a student, did you not say, 'Nixon said it for me. Students are bums'?"

But Frolich was not to be shaken. "I admit to that comment immediately prior to your admission to me that you were behaving in a lawless way. You then proceeded to justify your actions with talk of a—a pandemonium theatre company, a dangling man, a monster Montgolfier. When you refused to descend, I was forced to climb after you, whereupon you leapt to the floor shouting something about an illustrated man and were arrested."

"All that is true," yielded Simeon—and was surprised to find an expression approaching disappointment on the judge's face. It jolted him. Just in time, he remembered to say, "Would you show the court your fingers, please?"

Frolich obliged. The court-room could see the blue-pin hieroglyphics but did not know their message. "Would you tell the court?"

"One hand says 'LOVE,'" explained Frolich. "The other says 'HATE.'"

"And how close does that come to being a personal philosophy?"

"Your Honour." Elmwood was on his feet. "I consider I have granted this defendant considerable latitude with his questioning but this really is too much."

Judge Woodman ran a weary hand across his eyes. "I'm inclined to agree with you. Unless, Mr. Simeon, you can justify this line of questioning I am going to have to stop you."

Simeon's lips were dry and his stomach crawled with the near-nausea of having offended a friend. "In my defence, sir, I was trying to say that I was in a whimsical state of mind and that these tattoos gave depth to that whimsy."

"And is that *all* you want to say?"

"Your Honour," put in Elmwood, "I do have another witness."

"Officer McAree?"

"Yes, sir."

"For corroboration?"

"Yes, sir."

"But nothing is being contested."

"There is the matter of McAree's alleged attitude towards Mrs. Buchman, Your Honour."

The judge looked hard at Simeon, who flinched. "Not valid, Mr. Elmwood."

"I accept your wisdom, Your Honour," said the prosecution.

"And I will finalise by repeating my invitation to the defendant. Now, Mr. Simeon, would be the time to make your statement."

Simeon was standing with his head bowed, not wanting to see the pain in the eyes of the legislator. He had come to fight his case for no better reason than to have it said. He had affected innocence for so long that he had gained the favour of the judge—only to blow the whole thing by failing to distinguish between degrees of guilt.

There was no exoneration but there might have been extenuation. Instead, all he had done was to waste Woodman's time and sympathy.

"I admit the fairness of the evidence against me," he said. "If I am thereby guilty of the offences as charged, my plea is one of guilty."

Only then could he look up.

The strain was gone from Woodman's face. Simeon knew the judge could not dismiss him now, but there was some salvaged nobility, surely, in acknowledging his sins and saving the man the task of apportioning blame.

Woodman said it with relief and it was just. "I find you guilty of violating the ordinance governing proper conduct in our public buildings and the subsidiary or alternative charges are withdrawn.

"Your sentence will be a day in custody. In addition, you will be bound over in the knowledge that repetition of this offence or any other violation will bring you a much more substantial penalty."

The judge withdrew his timepiece from a vest pocket and checked it against the clock on the court wall. The hands stood a little off four.

"Since the defendant has spent this day in the court precinct awaiting and participating in the hearing of his case, my ruling is that the term of custody has been served. That being so, I propose to release him immediately."

Then Woodman was gone into his chamber without another glance at Simeon and the news media were filtering towards the exits. The trial had been an amusement but not as much good copy as they had hoped. It would make a ten- to twelve-paragraph funny on most of the wire services and for that, in his reduced state, Simeon was thankful. There was Julie to be told it all now. And a place to stay if Mrs. Dilger cut up. How many people would see it?

Just enough. And very soon he was going to have to face his real sentence. . . .

The marching orders came for Dr. Ichiro Domei at the church behind Hiroshima station one day after Keio arrived, and outlined in such detail that his visit could not even have been a formality, merely a scene-setter.

Domei and his party were to board a Tokaido Line stopper which would get them the 450 miles across Honshu Island to Tokyo in around eight hours. From there they would be shipped northeastward across the Pacific to San Francisco. At San Francisco they would be met and the arrangements for the rest of their journey explained.

So it was to be. For Domei, the problem was simple to see if not to resolve. His years of dedication were at stake. All the work that had gone into humanising the *hibakusha* could be lost if he did not dignify the situation with a string of right decisions.

He locked the instructions away in his desk as an old sensation moved along the corridors of his body. It was not welcome. He had felt it first as he picked among the rubble of the Hiroshima hypocentre in late August of 1945, little more than a student, with emotions that turned on superstition almost more readily than they did on fact.

The Japanese had a word for it—they had had to find words for so many new aberrations. It was *sabishisa,* the sentiment of being unutterably lost. Within a very short time of that induction, he had been feeling its opposite, *kangeki,* an elation, when he came upon small acts of decency, attempts to behave properly. The emergence of the two poles might have been a paradox in Western civilisation but in Japan it was a restoration of metaphysical balance. The horror had produced the anti-horror. The oriental spirit had shown it could survive. That was the Beginning.

He had felt the *kangeki* many times since as he watched his children improving on their performances. While man tried to make it up to himself for the terror, the ultimate effrontery, there was little call for the other.

Now, here was the *sabishisa*—and back to stay until he knew that he could handle these demands upon his personality and these drains upon his charges.

He could postpone the approach no longer.

He went to his children, touching an arm here, lodging a smile there, imparting a whisper, stressing his affection.

"We are going on a journey," he told them. "It will mean a ride on a train, then some days on a ship and then perhaps some more days on a train. But at the end of it, we will have seen a large portion of the world."

They watched him, uncertain how to react. He had tried to sound enthusiastic, to make it enchanting, but obviously he had not tried hard enough. The excursion still seemed like an ordeal.

"It is because you have done so well," he said. "There are people above me—people who look after us all—and they are very pleased with our little class. They are so pleased that they want to give us a reward. They want to take us to America."

The silence was chilling. He had taken a gamble in naming their destination, thinking it was better that they knew at the outset instead of discovering suddenly during their journey.

He gazed upon the two hundred. The older ones were forming the word with their lips. America . . . They were remembering they had little for which to thank America.

"My children . . . In our little family here, we are happy—is that right? That is so because we have been helped. A great deal of that help has come from America. A long time ago, America made a mistake, as all establishments run by imperfect people make mistakes—as we could just as easily have made a mistake. It is true we have been suffering many years for that error.

"But she has, too, in different ways. We can do something, perhaps, to prepare ourselves for living in a new way. America can do nothing to wipe out that mistake. She may try with money and facilities and even with gestures of love, but always there is the knowledge that none of these things would have been necessary except for that error—and that there are those here in Japan who remember only the suffering and will not accept any attempt, however honest or sincere, to make amends.

"Our family is founded on love and we do not have this bitterness. Because our love is so strong among ourselves, we should be proud to show it off to others not just in our own island but all over the world. Our love is our richness, but love is no good unless you share it. You cannot be greedy with love and still say that you love. When you deprive others of love—whoever they are—you devalue your own wealth. We go to show these people we can be and are happy. Thus we can help a little with their pain. Our own people were not blameless in the time when our suffering was inflicted. Each of us provoked the other—that is the tragedy of war—until we lost sight of reason and were able only to trade blow for blow.

"The Pikadon ended that senseless time and ushered in an era which has allowed us to develop this community. The history books said that the Americans had won with their Pikadon but there are no winners in war. If you don't pay during war, you pay afterwards. For more than thirty years, America has been pouring out her goodwill in an attempt to say 'sorry.'

"Now we go to show these people that they can stop feeling sorry because we have recovered. That was why that man came yesterday"—they had all seen the man and Domei had offered no explanation; this was timely—"to explain what our government wants us to do. He told me it was an honour and we must feel it so. We have been chosen as very important ambassadors. I have spoken to you before about finding our place in the world—and that place has been shown to us.

"In all conscience, we cannot refuse this opportunity to show off our strength. For that reason, I have accepted on your behalf.

"If any of you are apprehensive—if any of you feels he or she will have difficulty making the journey—let me know now. Remember first of all that we shall be together and this will be a constant comfort. And remember, too, that I would not have agreed if I thought it would be any tax on you.

"Today, I received further details of our journey and we will leave in a very few days. I am looking forward to it and you will, too. America is a fine country full of beautiful sights and gentle people. We will find warmth and friendship there.

"Now . . . There are arrangements to be made and I must go and make them. Come to me if you have questions."

Talk started up among the *hibakusha*, but no statement was addressed to Domei. He took his time passing through the midst of his children, trying to gain an impression of their feeling. The one he got brought him little comfort.

They seemed excited.

Which meant they accepted what he had told them. When he felt he had been dishonest in emphasis and spirit, his success was an extra persecution.

He reached his office, closed the door and slipped the catch. If anybody wanted to come in, he could claim an accident. At that moment, he needed a small privacy.

He had expected to feel close to vomiting, even close to tears. Instead, there was just a burning indignation that already his relationship with his charges had been compromised.

He dialled the Defence Ministry and asked for the extension number on the card Keio had left. Shortly, he was talking to the smooth civil servant.

"I have primed my people for our journey," he said. "You will be pleased to hear that they are even excited about it."

"That is excellent, Doctor. I congratulate you."

"Spare me that. I didn't manage to excite myself."

"You would not be a responsible healer if you did not have the interest of your patients at heart at all times. Rest assured we will provide you with everything you will need."

"Provide me with one thing first."

"Of course. What is it?"

"The real reason why you need my people for this jaunt."

The massive sprawl of the Bay City sea-link complex defies the capabilities of cartographers, and foreign novelists and traffic controllers cannot be bought.

But Herb Latimer had a way through the jungle. He went from Bay Area Rapid Transit outlet to Coast Guard, from Coast Guard to Customs and Excise and from Customs and Excise to Pier 93, in low gear all the way, keeping off longshoremen's toes.

All the while, Hayes Whitney, his immediate chief at the Port Health Authority, argued that the U. S. Department of Agriculture ought to be along on this trip.

"Maybe we'll find them there," consoled Latimer.

Whitney waved the copy in his hand. It bore the distinctive USDA motif. "Not a chance. They've made it clear. They need our rubber stamp, but this consignment has already been cleared, to all intents and purposes."

The vessel at Pier 93 was a nondescript all-purpose cargo boat with a Portland coding. The objects of their inspection had been introduced on deck, activities confined by some unstable fencing.

The rabbits looked healthy enough, as far as Latimer could tell. Their movements weren't sluggish and eyes and fur seemed without blemish.

Latimer was no veterinarian. He had walked into the Port Health Authority office in Frisco in the early winter three years ago. His movements before that were anybody's guess because he kept them to himself. But a Romantic would have noted a semblance of flame somewhere behind his eyes and said that whatever had happened prior to his arrival at this point had been good and was lasting.

Whitney knew nothing of Latimer's lost years and accepted the easy dismissal of other members of the PHA. Latimer was something of an eccentric but then you had to be to work here, anyway.

Besides, it came with the generation, weaned on LSD, learned to walk in student demos, learned to talk in ghetto raps and when that was no longer enough—well—this vagueness, this lack of purpose.

And in truth, his observation from the remote side of fifty wasn't such a bad one. "Lack of purpose" said it all.

In summer and autumn of 1975, Herb Latimer had witnessed the events of Playa 9, had been an essential and breathless part of them. When Simeon was tied to the swing, Latimer had tried to dislodge him. When Simeon was free of the Thinking Seat, Latimer had found a friend.

He had not understood the finer points of the giant desalination plant at Point Conception and its effect upon the sea, which had been the focus of Simeon's concern. Then, Latimer was too involved in the student affairs of Ballantyne, trying to be a leader but mostly being a front-runner. There were no real leaders then. There were those who said, "Let's do this, let's do that" but never, "You will do as I say because it is best."

They introduced ideas, promoted them to the point of action and then disappeared round the back of the militant crowd. But Simeon . . .

Well, Simeon sat on his ridiculous perch knowing it was ridiculous and using that awareness as strength, almost, to show he was not bothered by ridicule.

He introduced ideas, too. But his ideas were more like seeds likely to flower in time, not fuses that had to burn towards the powder-keg.

And he had proved himself more radical than the volatile because he had shown that a passive approach could work—even that a condition of the heart sometimes got a lot of inexplicable help when a condition of the mind eventually failed to explain itself.

Three years ago, nearly. Simeon had gone his way with Tomorrow Julie and an exhortation that his friends could always find him if they cared to look in the newspaper.

It was a strange and somewhat grandiose claim and Herb Latimer would have forgotten the man long since, because a thousand daily papers had yielded no such proof. Except for one thing. Latimer had been an asthmatic, part allergic, part nervous. His contact with the Simeon catalyst had brought about a strange chemical adjustment.

Every time now he climbed steps and breathed easily at the top; every time he lay among bedclothes without wheezing at the coccinidae who fed on microflakes of his dead skin, he remembered Simeon.

The man was with him now because he would not have been able to get close to a fur three years ago.

Even conceding that, though, he had to allow that he was losing impetus. Simeon was too long gone. The seeds had flowered and proved not to be perennial. The inhaler he had found at Playa 9 needed recharging.

That was his sadness, his present vagueness. But it was not uppermost now as he went about his PHA business.

This consignment of live rabbits for shipping inland needed the sanction of his department. Ten years ago, they would have been stuck in a dockside pound for six months to satisfy quarantine regulations. Today, they were vaccinated against any mobile infection and the coming and going was easier. Rubber-stamping was about the strength of the PHA.

Nevertheless . . .

Latimer picked up one of the rabbits, persuaded its mouth open and examined its teeth. Whitney was stirring restlessly.

"You don't mind if I look at one, do you?" said Latimer. "We do have to go through the motions."

"Why?" Whitney was in an uncompromising mood. "Really, I'd sooner we just got the things on the train and left them to it. USDA has done all the necessary."

The rabbit flinched.

Latimer, moving his hands gently among the fur, found a small raised area and knew as the animal struggled, its legs pushing against his jacket, that this was the cause of the discomfort. At least . . .

His searching fingers found more of the lumps, very, very small, no bigger than the raising a needle might leave on the arm.

He held the rabbit still and approached Whitney. "Feel these."

"Vaccination marks," said Whitney, without obliging. "They all have them. It's a little delicate for a couple of days."

"So many?"

"I don't exactly know how many," said Whitney. "Look, USDA knows what they're doing."

"And this is USDA?"

"Who else?"

"Hell, they must have been working with their needles all night. I'd like to see somebody now and ask—"

"There's no need." Whitney's voice had an edge. "What do you think, the rabbits are junkies?"

"What I think is, the rabbits don't have any control over what they are. . . ." Latimer was inside the pound now, picking up animals at random. Each one winced before his touch; every one bore the marks.

"They're laboratory animals," he said suddenly.

"That's not our business." Whitney's temper was rising.

"Where have they come from?"

"Japan. That's all we've been told."

"And you're content."

"Of course I am."

"What if they are carrying an infection?"

"They've been inoculated. They wouldn't be here in the open if there was any contagion risk."

"I don't like it."

"Latimer, you don't have any medical training."

"I do have some experience of the administration, though."

"I don't know what that's supposed to mean—"

"And I'm not about to tell you. . . ."

A couple of idling deckhands had stepped closer now, attracted by the conflict. But then, even noting that, Latimer was struck with a certain way they moved, not exactly the roll of the seaman's gait (ship stabilisers may have killed habits but not genes), more the surreptitious agility of—security men?

Rubbish. He was trying to read some enchantment into the situation. Security men on an old tramp like this and for what? Maybe they were in the pay of the vivisectionists—here he went again.

One leaned on the pound close to Hayes Whitney. "Trouble?" he inquired sweetly. "Boy, those rabbits. We'll be glad to have them from here. The stench and the cleaning up—"

"No trouble," said Whitney. "My assistant was a little concerned that they were feeling their vaccinations—"

"Wouldn't you?" The second hand was fixing Latimer with his gaze.

"I never had a myxiamatosis jab," said Latimer. "I guess it's unpleasant." If his imagination wouldn't let him rest, at least he could keep out of bother until he had time to examine instincts, charisma, whatever. He looked at Whitney. "Are we through?"

"Hours ago," said Whitney.

"Then let's be away."

As he gunned the PHA Oldsmobile to life, the men were at the ship's rail. They waved for no good reason. As though the order was "Look casual." Latimer went into second gear too fast and got a small consolation from Whitney's inertia. But the rest of the day, he was thinking.

On his way home, apprehensive still but strangely buoyant, he made sure of a newspaper.

Tucked away below the fold on an inside page was a ridiculous item about a man who had gone hunting Tyrannosaurus rex in Green Town public library.

Ed Rinehart and Joseph Gaskell were men of peculiar talents and more costume changes than a three-ring circus. And the reference was apt, at least in Rinehart's case, for he had toured the world with a big-top outfit as an acrobat catcher until cramp of the extremities took him off the trapeze and gave him a job with the animals or nothing.

He tried the menagerie but soon elected nothing. The cramp didn't affect the way he handled a gun.

Gaskell in the meantime was the radio expert. With Nasa, his speciality had been S-Band, picking up Apollo vocal contact as well as the usual telemetry. He had blown that by complicity in an astronaut moon-postmark plot. Though it was all prank and not misdemeanour, he had been invited to look elsewhere and his present employers recommended not to blackball him entirely. He was a short-wave operator now, with his index finger as used to transistors as it was to triggers.

Rinehart was looking after animals and Gaskell was making vocal contact. Both were in the employ of the military-orientated National Security Agency on an assignment which sounded funnier each time you told it. Between them, they had coined the codename "Bugs Bunny," but it was too dependent on instant charm to last long with a mission which was already dragging. Besides, the epithet was so close to an actual revelation that they would have been jobless again if official circles grokked it.

Bugs Bunny had dressed them in seamen's clothes for the voyage from the Orient and would press them into the superior suiting of bullion guards for the subsequent rail journey.

Now while Latimer nursed his doubts and cradled his thoughts before hurtling east to see a man who still chased dinosaurs, they were in the midst of changing guises.

Twenty wicker baskets, ten animals in each. Aboard ship, Rinehart had been able to lay them all one beside the other. But these piggyback containers hadn't been made with that kind of floorspace, so that meant piling. Which brought a worry about air supplies—not that it made much difference whether the animals were alive or dead on arrival, so far as he could see. But the orders said alive and that put an end to any arguments—and left him with this problem.

Rabbits had to have a run. They had to have somewhere to exercise, somewhere to relieve themselves. Now, was he to make a small enclosure in the midst of the piled baskets and let them out a few at a time?

That meant portering and more portering and he didn't fancy toting all across the United States. No, the enclosure would have to be a full-time thing big enough for them all and the baskets just vehicles within vehicles.

And the rabbits were still with rickettsiae? How did a rabbit like that look? Because these seemed normal enough.

Rinehart put the question to Gaskell and got some kind of an answer. "Well, they're carriers, aren't they—not fur-covered bombs."

"How do they pass it on?"

"This man was in contact with the entrails. We don't intend to do that."

"What if they bite?"

"Could be in their saliva, I don't know. Just make sure they don't bite you. Keep them locked up, Ed."

"They can't stay in those baskets all across America. They'd suffocate even if they didn't choke from inhaling their own . . . residues."

"That's a nice way of putting it, Ed. Almost affectionate."

"Don't get funny, Joe. I just think maybe we've given these particular creatures a pretty rough time and they deserve a little consideration now. A place to run is a very small thing. What I'm thinking is an enclosure where they can spend most of their time—"

"It's not in the orders," put in Gaskell quickly and a shade nervously.

"Nothing to preclude it, either. We just have to get them where they're going alive. I happen to consider this is an essential part of keeping them alive."

"But—"

"Cool off, Joe. Look, the Japs dictated the terms—right? They did it to safeguard themselves—right? The way we go, the method of travel, the type of conveyance. If they see fit to put these things in wicker baskets, then there's not much danger."

"I wish I could be so sure."

"You don't have to worry about anything. Just lock yourself in with your radio for the journey and leave the mucking out and the feeding and the doctoring to me."

"I can't stay in that cabin—"

"But these can stay in baskets, huh?"

Gaskell cursed. Then he laughed. If they were going to get on, they would have to be a little less electric with each other. "Point taken, Ed—you know what you're doing, so do it. And I may come in and feed them some lettuce leaves now and again."

That was how it was resolved—a roll of loose-knit plastic fencing commandeered from a dock complex do-it-yourself and then fashioned into a rough square inside the piggyback container with the empty baskets piled in three adjacent corners. If the rabbits tried burrowing out, they would make little headway against the steel framework.

Rinehart emerged from the kennel and found Gaskell smoking a cheroot as the sun dropped like a dull red stone into the Pacific.

"Children in bed?" asked Gaskell.

Rinehart didn't honour him with a direct reply. Instead, he said, "Have you contacted our men in Michigan?"

"Of course."

"Are you going to let me know what you said?"

"Well, nothing. I just told them the freight was loaded and we were ready to move."

"Mention anything about the boy?"

"What boy?"

"The Port Health Authority nose. Obviously you didn't."

"You mean Latimer. They've been told."

"How did you know his name?"

"I called Whitney."

"On what pretext?"

"Who needs a pretext? Whitney's in this thing as well, isn't he? Michigan knew about Latimer."

"But—"

"Listen, Ed—you just look after your rabbits."

The comment cost Gaskell another cheroot. Presently there were two glow-worms sitting on what used to be called a caboose, waiting for the adventure to begin.

In fact, Dr. Ichiro Domei had no further chance to tackle Secretary Chuta Keio until they were aboard the converted cruise-ship *Himawari-jo* (Sunflower Castle) and well out across the ocean.

The liner had become a hospital ship of a subtle and sophisticated kind, with all the appearances of a pleasure vessel but some special installations below deck. Domei's room was well appointed and the *hibakusha* had been provided with strings of bedrooms, cubicled off to convey privacy but at the same time open enough to enhance community living.

Keio was elsewhere in the ship with a cluster of minor officials whose function was not clear and Domei had not been acquainted with them or their location.

He examined the medical suite and found it lacking in nothing, generously supplied and imaginatively arranged. There could be no complaints on that score.

But Domei had not expected to find contentions here. This was not the basis of his misgivings. That lay back in Tokyo or ahead in San Francisco or wherever they were supposed to go from there—he didn't know.

The only person likely to give answers was Keio and he was mercurian and ubiquitous. Domei could start looking only when his people had been bedded down, their heads full of new visions but their eyes heavy with the viewing thereof. Keio and his staff were not around—the reasons declared would be that they were busy with paper work. But Domei would have been naïve in the extreme if it had not crossed his mind that they might be finding the presence and appearance of the *hibakusha* disturbing.

If that was how it worked for fellow-Japanese, how much more so for foreigners? This question above all begged solution. This factor predominantly made it impossible for Domei to believe he had been told the complete truth.

He ran Keio to ground eventually on the middle deck, emerging from a saloon which seemed to be equipped for games of chance.

"You've discovered my vice," said Keio. He tried to laugh it off.

"I don't know that I have," responded the doctor.

The civil servant was lighting a cigarette. "Meaning—that you think I have others?"

"I'm quite sure you do, like most of us. Those we admit to are seldom those that worry us most."

"And thus you defy me to lie."

Domei leaned on the rail and cast his eyes over the night sea. No smear of land anywhere on the dappled surface. *Sabishisa* hovered again, the aloneness of a place in the senses, a position of the mind that yielded no trace of familiarity. "I defy you to tell me the truth," he said.

Keio joined him at the rail, inhaling smoke.

Domei was anxious to fill the silence with something; more concerned, perhaps, that in the silence Keio might have time to work on his fabrication. "I'm surprised you can do that."

"What?"

"Breathe in smoke."

"I grew up on the fourth floor of a block of flats overlooking one of Tokyo's main thoroughfares. There you die or develop lungs of leather. Believe me, tobacco smoke—particularly this type with the benzpyrenes filtered out—is not the worst scourge."

"I'm prepared to accept that, too."

Keio took a last long draw on the cigarette and cast it into the ship's glinting wake.

He said, "You seem determined to provoke me. I don't know why. I accept you have your own views on what our government has asked you to do, but I'm only an agent. We're going to be spending a great deal of time together and it is as well if we get our respective positions clear. When I came to you in Hiroshima, I was acting as a messenger. Here, my chief concern is your comfort. Why that should lay me open to your bad feeling, I don't know."

Domei knew himself to be totally inadequate. For so long, he had dealt with people to whom simplicity was important and guile non-existent. Now, all of a sudden, he had to try and reason rings around a seasoned administrator. He did not feel equal to the task, but could not be satisfied until the ploy was made—and successfully.

"I cannot accept that your roles are so easily interchangeable," he said. "I give you credit for versatility. What I suggest is that your rationale of dropping one role and taking on another is a facile dismissal."

Keio was unmoved. "In other words, I'm being devious."

"If you like."

"I don't like, but you seem very fond of the idea."

"Then deny it."

"I deny it. Does that satisfy you?"

"No."

"Of course it doesn't. It is as easy for me to say one thing as it is to say another. You cannot force me to confide in you if it does not suit me to—even allowing that there was something to confide."

"My feeling is that you have not been totally frank with me. There are several matters which are—inconclusive."

"Because of my omissions."

"That is my feeling."

Keio was fumbling in his pocket. Shortly he withdrew a silver case. "You are making me smoke much more than I should."

"Why is that?"

"Because, for all my innocence, there seems to be nothing I can say that will reassure you."

"Except the truth."

"You have the truth. Tell me, why are you so sure you are being deceived? Are you no longer able to deal with normal people?"

"My people are perfectly—"

"I'm sorry. That was badly put. What I meant was—well, one gets into a certain way of thinking when one is acting as nurse and comforter. It is an artificial situation, inasmuch as it is far removed from the majority of worldly situations. With the result that when the world recalls you for one reason or another, you are at a loss to cope. Is this your difficulty?"

Domei could feel himself waning before the cool, professional rhetoric. "Whatever you are doing, truth is truth and a lie is a lie. Settings or habits don't alter that. I am saying I have not been told the whole truth."

"And I am asking what it is you want to know. You started this before on the telephone. I told you then this was a goodwill gesture on our part. Are you still not . . . ?"

"I don't like telephones."

"Why not?"

"You can't see faces. You can't see the other man bat an eyelid when he tells you a lie."

"There are many people who can tell lies without batting an eyelid."

"Are you one of them?"

Keio chuckled. "You persist, Doctor. As a matter of fact, I am. Does that advance you at all?"

"On the contrary," admitted Domei. "It's a setback."

"Then why don't you just put your problem to me? Failing that, why don't you believe what I tell you? What is it you want me to say? There you are—three good leads to follow."

"Why have my people been chosen for this—honour?"

"Because they are the best example of what we require—the successfully rehabilitated A-bomb victim. Should we send America less than the best?"

"It might serve better to show them what they did."

"They *know* what they did—and *you* know that is not our intention. We want to make up, not break up."

"I am not convinced."

Keio became serious. "Perhaps you have heard otherwise. Perhaps you have heard that we kicked them out of Okinawa."

"Did . . . ?" Domei's reaction was clumsy. "Yes."

"And you think we are trying to add insult to injury—or injury to insult might be a better way of putting it."

Domei was silent.

Keio went on: "The fact is that the Americans in Okinawa violated the terms of their occupation there. We had no alternative if we were to keep face. But we have no desire to make this a lasting breach. That explains the necessity of a goodwill visit."

"Wouldn't a trade delegation or diplomatic overtures have done just as well?"

"I can see you are an infant in the game of international relations, Doctor. It is important to keep all these moves in their right context. The American occupation of Okinawa was a direct effect of our failure at their hands during World War II. Our expulsion of them now is a direct effect of their failure at *our* hands. How, then, can we restore the balance? By proffering some gesture that will serve as a reminder to both of us that what happened in 1945 must never happen again."

"But why *hibakusha?*"

"You mean why *your hibakusha.*"

"That's hair-splitting."

"Doctor, I'm sorry, but your insistence leads me to two alternatives—either that you have so little faith in your treament that you feel your children cannot stand the situation or that you are ashamed for the people to see them."

Keio could not have dealt a more effective blow with a low-placed kick. Domei was winded and nauseated. The suggestion—either suggestion—was nonsense but it took time to cut his way through the forest of self-recriminations that sprang up all too promptly about him. He was drained of his last energy resources.

"I—I am only concerned that my people should not be commercialised," he mumbled. "They are not ready for that and never will be."

He went back to the medical suite. There, at least, he could keep score.

He did not see Secretary Chuta Keio reach for another cigarette with a hand that was almost as unsteady as his own.

Here came the judge. Simeon, loosely involved while his odyssey foundered and Tomorrow Julie shopped, had found his way to Uneeda Park and sat now on the promenade looking out across the lake with government pier 3,212 dominating his right aspect.

Judge Woodman neared at a sprightly pace, using his stick more for panache than support. Simeon saw nothing of him until the man lowered his bulk on to the bench alongside.

"A sad day," said the judge.

Simeon considered the warmth of the sun upon the backs of his hands and the gay sailboats offshore and marvelled at the man's reasoning.

"I'll get over it."

"Perhaps it isn't that easy."

"For a moment, I thought you were talking to help me."

Charles Woodman laughed. "You're right. I guess I just don't like things left in the air . . . The library you want was the one built on land willed to us by Oliver S. Lincoln specifically for that purpose. Andrew Carnegie paid for it, Patton and Miller designed it—"

"Ray Bradbury rendered it immortal. Where is it?"

"Not immortal. And it wouldn't make any difference if I showed you."

"Why?"

"No more bookshelves. Drill hall for the USO, recreation facilities—that rare and scented air of erudition is as long gone as your Tyrannosaurus rex. You would only be disappointed all over again. Perhaps more so."

Simeon shrugged. "Is that possible? Just like he never was. Douglas Spaulding doesn't live here any more."

"I'm sorry."

"And is the rest of his childhood just as passé?"

"How do you mean?"

"Mr. Jonas, the ingenious junkman, Mr. Tridden, who drove the trolley to the picnic ground—this picnic ground? Then there were Miss Fern and Miss Roberta in their wonderful Green Machine, Colonel Freeleigh and his Indian Wars, witch Clara Goodwater, Miss Helen Loomis, encyclopaedic lady of ninety lime-vanilla icecream summers, all . . ."

"Figments? Could be, Mr. Simeon. Coloured rosy by retrospect. We must surely have had junkmen. I know we had trolleys, courtesy of the Bluff City Electric Company. Indian fighters, witches and battery automobiles—probably. What small American town hasn't?"

"But what about the Lonely One?"

"The who?"

"The Lonely One—and the Ravine. There must have been some basis in fact."

"Certainly we have ravines. But who or what was the Lonely One?"

"A—well, he killed young ladies."

"Molested them?"

"No, just—killed them."

"I have dealt with several of the variety but the epithet isn't familiar."

"Maybe 1928 was before your time."

"Undoubtedly. But I have records, Mr. Simeon. I fear your friend's memories were—shall we say—fantasised by affection. Rendered readable. No harm done. Except to you, perhaps . . ."

"No harm to me." Simeon was readily protective, still. "Only magic to me—and my own fault for what I find if I try to look inside the conjurer's cloak. He made a lot of people content. I am here because I am greedy . . . though where the sense is when I *know*

the enchantment was in Green Town when it very-big-*was*, I can't
explain. Picture me, the dark side of thirty, hunting around for Douglas Spaulding's Royal Crown Sponge Para Litefoot tennis shoes, run
and messaged for, June 1928, dead inside like leaves by October of
that year. . . . Elmira Brown, I must be crazy. . . ."

For long minutes, a peace lay between them as though they considered the fragments of a spent dream together.

"My own favourite view is backwards," said the judge. "I'd push
you out of your place in the time-travel queue."

"But you're a—"

"A legal man? A practical, realistic fellow? Of course I am. It's
my guess you are, too, if you can just shake off the effects of all that
dandelion wine. I'll say something practical and realistic to you—if
any power could turn all our eyes to the past, that power could get
away with just about anything. What a weapon, nostalgia. Find the
right whimsy and genocide is in your grasp."

He climbed to his feet flexing the stick as though it had become
cramped and not him. "Think on that."

He walked a pace, thought, turned. "I'll even present my creden-
tials. . . . *Dandelion Wine*, page two—'Ready, John Huff, Charlie
Woodman,' whispered Douglas to the Street of Children.' . . . Page
twelve—' "Hey, hey." John Huff and Charlie Woodman running
through the mystery of the ravine and town and time. "Hey." . . .'"

Then he was gone along the path, feeling Simeon's wondering
gaze warm upon his back.

On another shore of Lake Michigan, backed by Battle Creek, two
intelligent military men who shall be nameless out of modesty were
casting a line of their own. One had found the other with a newspaper clasped in his hand. *Lakeside Examiner*. Headline: "Senti-
mental Searcher Misses Library Lizards."

"Our boy," said A.

"After all this time?" queried B.

"I knew if we waited long enough . . ."

Their wisdom in the Thinking Seat business had been unrecog-
nised and unmentioned. They had given the words to President
Keegan, who had passed them on to Point Conception Project Di-
rector Nicholas Freeley or Latimer, the Boy Spy.

Who passed them on to Simeon. The success of their brainwork had been—fitful. The representation of their ideas had been loyal. Simeon's reaction had been as predicted. In short, they had advised that he would do nothing and he had done nothing. Unfortunately, the effect of that nothing, coupled with the wild-card response of nature, had served to reveal Simeon as a victor. Of sorts. As much a victor as anybody got to be these days.

Keegan had been unable to pin them with any blame and Keegan had gone, casualty of the returning pendulum. A and B kept stars, status and posting. They also kept Simeon at the back of their minds. As a good idea.

And here he was, just across the water.

A plus B had familiarised themselves with his present anguish, were in conference now at a wharf-side bar adjacent to the ferry terminal. Not that they were actually going anywhere. Just that it would prime their tinderbox minds to know that they could.

"Douglas Spaulding," said B. "Who's he?"

"Literary alias of Ray Bradbury," supplied A. "Don't you never read nothing?"

"And Green Town?"

"Dive off this wharf, head westward and you're there. Pedantic maps call it Waukegan, Illinois. Site of an old Indian camp. Setting for his autobiographical works . . . *Dandelion Wine, Something Wicked This Way Comes* . . . *Summer of 1928.* Scent of sarsaparilla and any friend of Nicholas Nickleby's is a friend of mine. . . ."

"You lost me—"

"Keep listening. The genesis of every paradise discovered and hallucinated upon Mars, the joy in the 'Machineries,' the song of the Body Electric—Bradbury loved Green Town."

"And moved away?"

"Don't we all?"

"I think not. If I loved a place well enough, I'd stay."

"Not when your eyes were beginning to cataract with maturity. When the windmills start tilting at *you,* boy, that's the time to move. . . ."

"Hold it, A. Your acquaintance with Bradbury sounds more like an unsuccessful attempt at cannibalism. You keep spitting out bits of him and it doesn't get us anywhere."

A drowned the Muse with Kentucky rainwater.

B tried to reduce the exchange to a logistic equation. "What you mean is that Bradbury or more probably his work has struck a resonant chord in Simeon and there may be ways to utilise that chord and resolve our present dilemma."

"In a nutshell. If Simeon wants Green Town, we must endeavour to provide it. Make him happy and we are halfway there."

"What's the other half?"

"Make him talk. You know how we drew people to that swing in Playa 9—where he defeated us (and I wouldn't admit this to anyone else but you, friend) was because we couldn't control what he was saying and he was saying it before the blinkered experts had the truth of it, anyway. Here we provide him with a script and a gimmick and he's in our hands—"

"He's off swings."

"We wouldn't be fool enough to offer him swings again. Swings aren't Bradbury, they're Peter Tate. Black ferris wheels, maybe, Dust Witches, jeeps to Kilimanjaro . . ."

"Then what?" B impatient over an empty glass.

"Our problem is railroad transport."

"I know that."

"And we don't want to get too surrealistic."

"I'll take your word."

"So we think on railroads. Ray Bradbury and railroads."

"And our big-mouthed Nipponese friends and our baskets from Okinawa."

A chortled. B looked perplexed. A went away with the glasses, brought them back full, still laughing, not wanting to let go of it till he had extracted capacity.

B grumbled over his Bourbon. "Don't keep it to yourself."

"Okinawa baskets," said A. "Something wicker this way comes."

B raised the merest eyebrow. "Is that clever?"

"Not at all," countered A. "Finding it funny, that's the clever bit."

And the sun took the glint of his glass and bounced it all across the lake to Green Town, Illinois.

The six bars which stood cheek-by-jowl on North Water Street had no place in any romanticised recollection of a midwestern small town.

Orville's had the closest approach to respectability but only because it served bean soup and earnest conversation with its Buffalo beer. Big Daddy offered pizzas, J.B.'s and the Ron-De-Vou had the music, hot or heavy; the Kove held the proper sanity for the fraternity men of Little Fort S.C. and the Pirate's Alley was there for anybody with Spanish gold enough to afford it.

Individually, they broke down nicely into the kind of hungers possessed of college students. Taken as a conglomerate, as a squalid Great Off-White Way, they produced much of the ferment which activated the campus and even served as a jump-off for the motorcycle gangs and the runaway girls from Chicago and farther afield. To find the types mixing with no conflict as such would confound the sociologist. A possible explanation was that the university was putting out a tougher kind of freak these days who could give as good as he got when it came to broken bottles and Indian knives.

It was successful strategic arms limitation in microcosm. Surprisingly enough, the Greeks and the Chosen Few, the runaways and the academics, the athletes and the acid-heads had arrived at the belief that they had to live together if they were going to live at all. Their common ground was youth; their common enemy was age, as personified by administration.

Into this mish-mash came Tomorrow Julie, to whom the fever was no new phenomenon. She tried each door in turn, summed up the contents in a moment and elected Orville's as the spot where—though the gossip might not be the hottest—there was the best chance of hearing it.

The young folk had throbbed around her leaving a migraine where, three years ago, there might have been an empathy or an itch to join. She was thirty, the wrong age for a student. The right age for faculty status or revolutionary and that was the kind of attention she attracted.

The more wild-eyed youngsters grew silent at her approach, waiting for the word of a trashing, a blast, a Day of Terror. The instructors saw her but knew her not and took her for the ghost of Bernardine Dohrn, come to spread posthumous Weatherman propaganda.

But Julie offered no such thing. She asked the barman for cider and liquorice and found a seat near a girl whose hair obscured much of her face.

"I'm new here," said Julie. "I'm not sure where anything is."

"New as what?" said the girl. Her drink looked small and spirited.

"How do you mean?"

"Say what you are and I can tell you where to go."

Julie laughed. "I'm sorry. I didn't mean to be that stupid. I'm here with my husband. We are examining situations. His research is geared by observations of Green Town's past. I look to the present. That way, we can figure out the future."

"Is it a radical movement or a religion?"

"Neither. It's a life-style that happens to work for us."

"We have that."

"We?"

"I have a husband, too. He doesn't come here with me, either. He has More Important Things to do."

"Then you and I are well met. Ideology widows, I guess they'd call us. They think the thoughts, we carry the scars."

The girl's hand jerked suddenly and nervously to the hair, which fell luxuriantly across her cheek. "I'm—I'm Lucia."

"Julie," said Julie, intrigued by the small gesture. "Tomorrow Julie."

"I thought your focus was the present."

"When I got the name, today was tomorrow."

Julie chewed on the liquorice straw and watched her companion.

"You seem to be trying to be frank with me," ventured the girl, almost apologetic.

"Why not?" Julie found a poignancy in the utter baroqueness of the remark.

"I'm not always sure when people are doing that. I'm not always sure how to take it."

"Take it as a plea for honesty."

"I used to have clear ideas of what I wanted. . . ." Lucia's hand moving again, adjusting a lock that needed no adjusting. "I have a lovely house."

"That's nice."

"I haven't. Got a lovely house, I mean. I used to—like the clear ideas."

"A marriage can't stand too many clear ideas," said Julie. "The best kind have to be shared. Otherwise, spokes of a wheel reaching out from the hub, you know? And instead of being at the hub, you find yourself marooned on the perimeter."

"And the wheel moves," said Lucia. "It sure as hell moves. I have to cling."

Julie could not be sure how much of Lucia's condition was maudlin come from the bottom of the glass, how much a real sickness.

Whichever, it was a state that needed study and sympathy and she cursed because whenever she wanted help (help for what? some contemporary. Green Town spell to use on Sad Simeon, maybe) somebody showed up with a greater need.

"I'm sure there must be a way of stopping it." She wondered at her own off-handedness and pinpointed it in the next second as the protective reaction to a problem so recently her own. "Forgive me. That doesn't sound very positive. Is your husband a—dreamer?"

"No. Anything but. His bag is ultra-reality. He wants to change the world."

"And he's not a dreamer?"

"Oh, he'll do it. He'll think of a way. He's committed politically."

"To what?"

"To change. He changed me, all right."

"And your sadness is that change is not always a good thing."

"Obsession with change is not always a good thing."

"What about changing himself?"

Lucia said, "Huh! That's one thing the radicals never change. . . . At least you know where you are with them."

Her glass was empty. She stood up, looked down on Julie's half-filled glass. "Another one of those?"

"Thank you."

Lucia opened her bag, found a purse and took a high-value bill from a wad. She pushed the bag nearer Julie. "Look after that?"

"Of course."

The girl was gone through the melee, one hand clutching her glass, the other hovering near her face. It was a time for Julie to begin ordering her thoughts, deciding what questions might be put and how she could benefit best from the contact. The openings had been made. Little of mystery remained—except the major part; all that money and the girl's preoccupation with her face. So instead of setting up her gentle interrogation, Julie pondered over the unanswered.

Lucia came back with the cider and placed it in front of Julie. "Your own?"

"I'll be right there." And she was gone again, the right hand weaving a pattern like a southpaw's defence.

When Lucia was reseated, she said, "I guess you're wondering about all my money."

"No." The inevitable response from Julie. "Do you have a great deal of money?"

"My husband is very good to me in that way."

"It makes up for a lot."

"It doesn't make up for anything. It just provides the wherewithal for an alternative."

"You don't have to tell me—"

"I *want* to. You wanted to be frank. You listen to what I tell you."

"Just as you please."

"Frank has plenty. I don't ask where it comes from—Cuba, Red China, Moscow. I earn it. Every day I live in the Haunted House, that's haunted by the wreckage of what used to be my clear ideas —every time I walk around with my face like . . ."

Her right hand was moving again, offensive this time, hooking back the lustrous black hair to reveal the jagged scar which rambled like Jordan down her right cheek from eyebrow to chin. "Like this."

It took Julie's breath away. "I'm . . ." Could she say, "I'm sorry," when the girl wanted anything but pity? "I'm honoured that you took me into your confidence, Lucia. It makes me really feel that I've found a friend here in Green Town. . . ."

Had the husband done that? She wanted to know but could not press Lucia to tell her.

"You don't find me—ugly?"

"For crying out loud, Lucia . . ."

"In my disfigurement?"

"Believe me, that's nothing. It's not noticeable. You wear your hair exactly right for your face. Nobody would know."

"I know."

"Was it—an accident?"

"It wasn't intentional. Just how far you go towards making a thing likely by the way you act is a fine point. It wasn't expected or intended. I've talked about it enough now."

And Lucia was as cool and sober as a judge. As though the whole build-up to the revelation had been a charade. Julie wondered whether it was a nightly ritual, a kind of cabaret for one.

She was close to annoyance when she said, "Can I always find you here?"

"Here or at the house," said Lucia. "I don't go far, only sometimes

I go too far. I'm sorry our first meeting should have covered such a lot of ground, for instance. I thought maybe I could, with you."

"With me what?" And that must have sounded impatient.

"Being Tomorrow Julie."

"What's that got to do with anything?"

"You're something of an enigma yourself. I guess it just shows two enigmas don't make a right."

"You—*know* me?"

"As soon as you told me your name. Word gets around."

"What kind of word?"

"You and Simeon. Something of a folk myth. You can't expect a happening like Playa 9 to pass without notice or comment. But then, that's your business. My face is mine."

"I'm sure I didn't make it sound as cut and dried as that."

"My dear, when you expect that other people are always going to be rational, you do lay down certain guidelines."

"I'm sorry. . . . I mean it. For putting a price on my consideration. I hope we—"

"We did. We cleared the air. I feel better. You feel better. It happens—not always in the expected way, but always."

"So drink up," said Julie. Small mercies. At least and at last, Lucia's right hand was resting on the table.

There, on the world's rim, the lovely snail-gleam of railway tracks ran, flinging wild gesticulations of lemon- or cherry-coloured semaphore to the stars. So wrote Will Halloway's nom-de-plume.

There, on the precipice of earth, box-by-box with flexi-van flat to car floor to avoid air turbulence and cut fuel costs by as much as 10 per cent, there came the piggyback's offspring, the Amtrack container train, the basket-bearer, with a soft diesel sigh of apology.

It had branched north from Chicago, moving with the confidence of an unrealised clearance from the Elgin, Joliet and Eastern (outer belt). It was set for an extensive yard in Green Town, a sudden desirable haven by virtue of one inhabitant who might divert the heat and the attention from its lethal load; a handful of extra cars to add to the annual 28,000 incomers. Shortly, better conditions prevailing, it would join the average 7,000 outward bound.

Simeon, haunting the complex like he haunted the old rail spur in Rolfe's moon meadow hoping to find a Will Halloway tear on his cheek or a carnival train with death's head and cowcatcher, saw the thing threading its way like mercury between the container chaos of Chicago and North-Western, Illinois Central, Baltimore & Ohio, and was not suspicious.

The train Simeon sought had a Civil War chimney, dream-filled cars, an undersea funeral bell and a whistle with the wails of a lifetime gathered in it; the outgone shreds of breath, the protests of a billion people dead or dying. Now where would you find a train like that in a place like this?

Well, Bradbury did. Forget about Bradbury. Go home to your wife.

Simeon trod the high iron, barked his shins on switches and stumbled over continuous welded. For some reason, the mercury special drew him in its wake. He saw it stop, exhale, settle.

Then he couldn't believe. A vast, moss green balloon hovering above it, touching at the moon. Rubbish. Balloons make less noise, don't have blades and need wind, don't make it. A helicopter. Why?

Something wicked this way comes. Page thirty-seven. A tall man stepped down from the train caboose platform like a captain assaying the tidal weathers of this inland sea. All dark suit, shadow-faced, he . . .

Turned on Simeon with a weapon glint at his hip. "What do you want?"

"I'm . . ." Simeon floundered. "Looking for a ride."

"We're not going, we're coming. You got a ticket?" The man grinned, narrow mouth making a slash of matching mercury across his face. "But of course you haven't. Look, I wouldn't hang around here. You're likely to sever a limb."

"Thanks." Simeon didn't know what else to say but he needed to stay. He had been drawn. He looked up at the helicopter, tilted like a bowler hat and watching him. He turned his gaze back to the man with the weapon. "Bullion?"

"You name it."

"I'm not a train robber."

"You're not anything at the moment, friend, while I have a bead on you."

"Well, you can relax. I came out of curiosity."

"I thought you said begging a ride."

"So I did. Curiosity to know where you were going."

"We aren't."

"Then my curiosity is assuaged."

"Then what's keeping you?"

"I don't know. I . . ."

"Maybe he's enjoying the situation," said a voice behind him. Simeon half-turned. The man was milder of suit than his companion and bare-headed. "A little excitement."

Simeon followed the ploy. "Cherishing it. The itinerant life is dull."

"He doesn't sound like a vagrant," said the newcomer. "No four-letter words yet."

"Another of my campaigns. To bring a little quality back into the vernacular."

"But this isn't a vernacular railway," said blacksuit.

Greysuit laughed. "They're more Italian."

"And even more Swiss," put in Simeon to show he was getting the funicular message.

Greysuit passed between him and the cars, took his place beside blacksuit. "It's been nice talking to you—"

"But all good things must come to an end," added blacksuit. They had a kind of rapport but there were times when it was visibly strained. No Siamese twins but maybe servants of the same master.

"You want me to go," said Simeon.

"Unless you can think of any good reason for staying," said greysuit. "Don't get us wrong. We've enjoyed your company; we just don't see any useful purpose being served by continuing the conversation."

Simeon gathered his grace and dignity. "Thank you for your time."

He retreated slowly, stopped near a door flung back presumably when greysuit made his descent. The pair seemed tense. Greysuit gave him a wave too hesitant to be natural and just fast enough to be inspirational. Latimer would have recognised it. Simeon, just now, waved back and moved on a little wiser for the momentary pause.

Bullion should not smell of straw. . . .

All the way back across the complex, the helicopter trailed him. Like a Dust Witch. Will Halloway had routed the prototype with an arrow launched by hand to pierce the moss-green balloon. Simeon would have no such fortune with this sharp and oily counterpart.

At the gate, it came down close enough to send him grubbing on his stomach among the railroad gravel. Laughter came from the air and the piggyback lines as the chopper spun away.

He went home to his wife.

And an answer which, like the question, had come by train.

Three hours out of San Francisco, with the *Sunflower Castle* following the line of the coast now, planing north out of Monterey Bay and passing Santa Cruz, Keio called Domei to a meeting.

Domei had been restless for a day and a half, waiting for the instructions that had been promised on arrival at the Golden Gate. Since his uneasy dialogue with the secretary on the deck early in the voyage, Domei had kept to the quarters set aside for his party.

He had consoled himself with the reasoning that if Keio wanted him, he was readily available. In truth, horrified by his impotence before the civil servant's tangential argument, he was sticking to familiar ground.

Keio, for his part, had stayed with his staff, dealing quickly with the small amount of paper work, filing regular reports to Malecki and making frequent use of the saloon. He, too, satisfied his conscience by the device that if Domei wanted him he was in the obvious place.

He was not disturbed by Domei—not as he was by Domei's charges. Thirty-three years took him back into infancy and the mushroom meant nothing to him. By the time he was capable of feeling indignation, the offence was too old to raise such a response. He cursed more the sulphurous rains of Tokyo, the sky water poisoned by exhaust fumes which had rotted his father's lungs and made his mother an invalid before he was really educated.

The college years which might have versed him in the atrocities of war were busy while he found extra-curricular work to provide food at home and tried to achieve a sufficient depth of academe to enter government. He had had no time for the Zengakuren—the National Federation of Students' Self-governing Associations—and perhaps it was as well because the picture presented by the campus radicals was as steeped in propaganda as any they condemned.

The present assignment was as close as he had been to the horror of Hiroshima and for some reason the *hibakusha* filled him with a child-like awe and morbid fascination. Aware of protocol in so many ways, he was unsophisticated over this gap in his experience.

Like Domei, though in the active against the doctor's passive sense, he steered clear of situations he could not control.

That was why he called Domei to his suite—away from the mutants and as therapeutic to his needs as the medical suite was to the doctor's.

Domei came in his good time and while Keio might have fumed he resolved to say nothing on the score. Domei must be allowed his small indulgences—and besides, the session was going to be tough enough.

Domei, his corneas scarred on an illumination brighter than a thousand suns, had to blink at the subdued lighting of the cabin. Only gradually could he make out Keio and a man he didn't know who could have been one of the secretary's staff.

"Come in, Doctor." Keio was affable, comforting, professional. "Please find a soft chair."

It would have been hard not to, for the state-room was plentifully supplied with PVC form-fitters which moulded to support any shape thrust upon them.

"I thought it was about time we had another talk," said Keio. The approach was carefully chosen, indicating to Domei that this might well take up where the last exchange left off but to any casual observer would be merely another bland gesture of welcome.

The doctor was not prepared to trade niceties. "I knew we would have to speak sooner or later," he said. "There are instructions to be given."

"Instructions to be given," echoed Keio. "Such an unfriendly way of putting it. Couldn't we just say—arrangements to be made."

"Put it how you like," said Domei. "If the arrangements haven't been made already I'll be very surprised. And who is this?"

The man stood up and offered a hand. "Shinzo Yamaji," he said. "I've just come aboard with the pilot. I am to advise you on travel in the United States."

Domei took the hand. "My people need rather special facilities."

"We're aware of them, Doctor."

Keio was slitting an envelope with a miniature Samurai sword. "These are our instructions from Tokyo," he said, still picking his words carefully. In fact, he knew the enclosed directions intimately and the envelope was his own, sealed only minutes before he summoned Domei.

He drew forth a printed sheet and began to read. "It says we go inland," he said. "Strange."

Domei and Yamaji waited for him to elaborate.

"Our final destination is New York."

"But that's another"—Domei did a quick and not really accurate calculation—"another three thousand miles. Why land us in San Francisco if we have to go to New York?"

"New York eventually," said Keio. "Some stops in between."

"Where? I . . ." Domei was at a loss again. "I don't know what my people would like to see. Maybe . . . Hollywood . . . or . . . Disneyland."

Keio had a nightmare vision of these horror-picture inhabitants swarming over movie lots. "Not on our schedule," he said. "What about the Grand Canyon? Maybe even the Empire State Building?"

"I don't know . . ."

"I'm afraid we've had to be rather more organised than impulsive in setting out this programme," put in Yamaji. "I appreciate you want your party to see as much of America as you can while you are there, but the continent is so vast that we have to have a definite direction. In the circumstances, we thought all demands might be met by taking you across the country's waistline. There is an agreeable contrast of scenery from state to state, from desert to mountain to rich agricultural land to big city—"

"And of course . . ." Keio came in dead on cue.

"Yes?" Yamaji held his flow to let the secretary back into the conversation.

Keio was politely apologetic. "Whichever way I say this, it sounds like a censure. But this isn't purely a pleasure trip. We do have a serious purpose."

"I'm sorry," contributed Yamaji. "Forgive me. Is it other than—educational? From the itinerary I was sent, I got the impression that your prime purpose was to take away as much knowledge of the United States as you have in the time available. If I'm wrong . . ."

"You're not wrong," said Keio. "We'll be doing that, too. Just that we can't really extend ourselves as much as we would like."

Domei was tiring of the play. "Where do we go? How do we go?" he demanded.

"We go to New York," said Keio.

"And how?"

"Don't you . . . doesn't he . . . ?" Yamaji looked at Keio for instruction, took the slight flicker of the mouth. "You walk."

"We *what?*"

"Walk—well, march."

Domei turned his gaze on Keio. "Now I know you're insane. I don't even know how my people are going to be when I get them onto land again. Several of them have been badly sick. When they have to adjust again, it could make for all kinds of complications. You're not serious, surely. What did you really have in mind?"

Keio was thinking fast. The instructions made it clear—a procession of witness of some kind. But even he had to admit it was unreasonable in the extreme. He wished to hell Malecki had been at the Hiroshima centre to see exactly what the doctor meant when he reported his patients were walking four hours a day. Round and round a room was a lot different from striding across a continent.

"There must be some typing error," he said. "Obviously such a thing is ridiculous and out of the question. What was meant was that your people should walk about and mingle with the locals at the frequent stops we make."

"I'm not taking my people off this ship until I have an assurance that they have proper facilities for the rest of the journey. I can't think how such a mistake came to be made. If it was a mistake and not just somebody's idea of a—"

"Believe me," Keio hastened to comfort him, "this must have been an error in transmission. I am as distressed as you are and I am certainly going to take it up with Tokyo. Meanwhile, rail transport is no problem—right, Yamaji?"

"I'll see to it," Yamaji responded breathlessly.

"The train had better be there at the dockside for me to see," said Domei. "Otherwise, I don't move."

Keio smiled. "I accept that. Now—"

"Now I am going to put this to my people."

"Not . . ." Keio went with Domei to the door and put a restraining hand on his arm. "Not about us expecting them to march. That was a piece of clerical incompetence by somebody and they will pay. Believe me, your children will have a train. A beautiful train, tell them, with bubbles on the top where they can sit and watch the country on all sides."

Domei went quietly, examining Keio's words for catches.

Yamaji stood up. "That's a setback."

"A foreseeable one," snapped Keio. "And it should have been foreseen. I don't know what possessed . . ." He didn't finish the sentence because it didn't do to have a fairly minor agent like Yamaji being privy to his disenchantment. "As a matter of fact, if it has increased my credibility with Domei, it may do more good than harm. You'll have to see about a train. Can you handle that?"

"All the way to New York?"

"Unless you know something I don't know."

"The Americans have shunted the rabbits into Green Town, Illinois. They are trying to line up a character called Simeon."

"Then you do know more than I do. What is this—Simeon— supposed to do?"

"I don't think even they know that."

"Then the train's not a setback, it's absolutely essential."

"Why?"

"Because, Yamaji, there's no guarantee that they haven't found Simeon already. Or he them. So get to it."

When the agent was gone and Keio was free to express his ire, all he said was, "And you, my master Malecki, will just have to make everything happen that much faster."

Latimer had thought he would be bearded by now, but a man will not alter because you picture him so. It was sufficient that Simeon recognised him in his orthodox suiting and that small, warm moment served them as an introduction and gave Julie a chance to get among the coffee makings.

"Julie tells me you walk a lot," said Latimer.

"It's a shade less futile than swinging. When I walk, I see. That's why I do it."

"Always alone?"

"No, not always alone. Is that what she said?"

"No. My speculation. Forgive me. I have this idea of you searching, searching."

"That's authentic enough."

"Like looking for thunder lizards."

Simeon stiffened and then relaxed, one question posed, another answered. "I was wondering how you managed to find me."

"I read about it. You know what you said. 'When you want to find me, look in the newspapers.'"

"That was grandiose nonsense. Believe me, this latest item was a piece of folly, not a call to arms."

"Anyway, that's how I located you."

"In—where were you?"

"San Francisco. Not much mileage for three years."

"Sufficient if it gets you where you want to go."

"Well, you know I was never very positive in that direction."

"And you wanted to find me?"

"I do now. If you'll pardon me, Simeon, it wasn't until now that I—started looking."

"Don't apologise. Nobody else has ever bothered to follow me up. I—we were the wonder of the week." Simeon chuckled in his sadness.

Julie came with the Brazil blend and he took her hand and held it when she would sooner have been filling the cups. "We were really something."

"Speak for yourself," said Julie. "I still am."

He kissed her fingers before she could withdraw them. "Of course you are. And I am, too, I guess, when I get at it. If I get at it."

"*When* you get at it," affirmed Latimer. "That's why I'm here."

Julie flooded one of the saucers, though neither of the men noticed. They were too busy trying to read each other.

"That fall you left, I moved up the coast," began Latimer. "I took a job with the Frisco Port Health Authority—messenger stuff first of all but then moving on to real live issues like enforcing quarantine regulations, that kind of thing—"

"What about your asthma?" queried Simeon.

"The funniest thing—it just went."

"I guess you grew out of it."

"No. I—"

"Sure you did."

"Simeon," Julie said gently. "The boy wants to give you credit. Don't spoil it for him."

Simeon chewed his lip. "I'm sorry. Thanks. I'm glad. It was a traumatic time for all of us. A little exchange therapy and nobody benefitted more than I did, believe me."

"You were saying," prompted Julie, pushing Latimer's cup to him. "Port health."

"Yes . . . I've been pretty happy, you know? Enjoying my new trouble-free condition. But now, three years on, I find myself unfulfilled. Rather, I *found* myself in a vacuum. Now, perhaps, I have a way out. . . ."

He tried his coffee to cover an uncertainty. "Are you—fulfilled?"

Simeon caught Julie's eye and was reminded she had asked the same question silently for the whole of their marriage and more volubly before that. "We're well wed and remaining happy," he said. "You heard us say we are something special. We don't use the term loosely."

"But you walk and look," said Julie gallantly. "This summer, it's Ray Bradbury . . . something that has been with you since childhood. . . . I know it's innocent, love, and I don't mind it. But perhaps Herb has something a little more, well, tangible."

It was the kind of small sacrifice of self that meant more in terms of love than many physical expressions. "Stay mine," said Simeon. "You're my tangible."

All of which did little to reassure Latimer. He was close to resolving to take his problem elsewhere, though there was no elsewhere, when Julie said, "You've come nearly two thousand miles. Now, why?"

"I don't want to trouble you with it."

"We can stand it," said Simeon. "See how strong we are."

"Yes." And how—and what the hell, anyway. "This is what put me on the road to you. I was doing a routine health check. Everything was cut and dried. Clearance from the Department of Agriculture on some livestock shipped in from Japan. There was nothing for us to do. But I just happened to pick up one of these rabbits to look at it and it was covered with small swellings. Not disease but injections. Not vaccinations, too many of them—though that was the story they tried to give me.

"I took them to be laboratory animals. But when I started showing that much interest, a couple of pseud-looking seamen began to take a corresponding interest in me. I can't find out anything. I don't like government hush. And I don't like holes in rabbits for no good reason."

Two seamen looking unlike seamen. A black suit and a grey suit.

Rabbits! "Did you find out where they were going?" asked Simeon hurriedly, on the edge of excitement.

"Put in baskets, whisked onto a container train which left the Bay heading eastward. I don't know how far they were going."

Rabbits and the wrong smell for bullion.

"This far," said Simeon, joyfully, "and no farther."

In its time, the bed had been a glacier. Now it was a swan's back and the night drifted beneath them like untroubled water.

"Nice," said Julie.

"What?" There were too many nice things for Simeon and some not so nice. Which?

"That Herb Latimer remembered and looked and found us."

"And now he's here, how do we get rid of him?"

"Get rid of him! But Simeon—he only just got here . . . and he brought information that filled some gaps for you. You *told* him to come—three years ago."

"So the past catches up with me. It was a stupid invitation. Too much of the past is catching up." Simeon turned in the bed, scattered swan dreams and set off ripples.

"You can hardly be sure of that yet . . ." Julie thought she was seething at his ingratitude and then recognised it as another retrospective growth—feeling cheated . . . that then, the swing had been more than a swing; that now the bed was no more than a bed. "He's come all this way. He thinks he's brought you something you want. After reading about you and the thunder lizards—"

"What the devil have laboratory rabbits got to do with thunder lizards?"

"Maybe we just don't see it yet."

"Huh." Simeon twisted again in anguish, wished he could kick out, kick off . . . even felt the frightening old spasms in his legs.

Julie sat up, punching her pillows into a support for her back. "You don't have to act on what he told you."

"I was halfway there without any help. Why did he have to . . . ?"

"What?"

"Make himself useful. Now I owe it to him to do something."

"And maybe that bothers you more than the actual doing."

"It leaves me no choice. I would like a choice."

Julie raised him with cold feet deftly placed. "Settle one thing for me. Does it matter to you what he thinks about you?"

Yes, thought Simeon. It matters to me what anybody thinks of me. But if I admit to that, I reveal my readiness to have things as they were in Playa 9. And if that be so, how far have we come in three years? What is Julie worth to me? What price one thousand nights of togetherness when an old acquaintance can turn up out of nowhere with a story of ill-treated rabbits and grab me away?

"No," he said. "Of course not. People can think what they like."

"Then ignore him. Shut your eyes and he'll go away." Julie leaned over him and kissed him. Even as he gave her his lips, she thought, Liar.

But she was glad he had thought enough of her to lie.

Simeon shut his eyes and Herb Latimer was going away. Past the lines of Maple, Evergreen, Willow, picking up a late bus on Dugdale that would take him to the lakefront.

More switchback than swan's back for Herb Latimer, up one microsec and down the next, wondering whether he had done right, how he had done wrong, why he was wondering such things at all.

The Simeon of an hour back had been different from the man he had sought to sabotage at Point Conception and then come to—love? Maybe "love" was the wrong word but Simeon had made some glorious inroad into his soul and, in any event, had left him not needing his asthma spray.

This Oak Street man was older, slower-moving, less of an enigma, and didn't he have a right to be?

Latimer was sorry he had come and was almost around to deciding he would catch the next train back to San Francisco and his place with the Port Health Authority.

The eccentricity was still with Simeon but maybe the heroism was gone. True, he had been at the rail freight-yard tonight when the rabbit-carriers showed up, but not for *that* reason. He and Latimer could hardly be said to have found a common ground.

Latimer felt guilty. He had absorbed the warmth that existed here between Simeon and Julie and had seen the way first one and then the other guarded it.

He couldn't have stayed with them, of course, because they did not have the room. Had they a score of bedrooms, he would still have left.

No. Whatever was to be done about the rabbits, he would handle it alone, even if that meant ignoring it alone. No sweat. No come-backs. No blaming himself for ruining a rare relationship.

Lakefront. The driver whistled him out and bade him good night.

Back to San Francisco. South to Chicago, west to sanctuary.

Rail depot. First, find your rails. . . .

And there was the snail-gleam between him and the lake and looking right he saw the false orange of the sky and heard the sub-tle not-quite-quietness of distant locomotion and the occasional anvil-strike of trolley on track.

He could follow the road and reach the depot.

He could return with nothing done.

Now, to his left, before the glint of the Michigan, acres of hard-ware and rolling stock and somewhere in there the creatures whose condition had so offended him.

But where, for crying out loud?

Suddenly, like a lone vulture circling over a corpse, the helicopter, pinpointed in red at nose and tail. Why a helicopter unless to watch and protect? What else to watch but that pain-racked fur on its way to do more suffering for the government.

He found an access and plunged in among flat-car and stream-line, finding all too soon that his vision was impaired by the lowly level of his path, resolving before it was too late that he would keep swarming up ladders and bouncing on roofs until he got himself un-der the helicopter. And then?

Then would take care of then.

Fifteen minutes of such bouncing and climbing and each time wondering whether the helicopter would still be there when he breasted the cars and saw the sky.

Once, twice, three times he thought it had moved and panicked. And the fourth time it was back where it had been when he began his conscientious, carefully observed straight line. Obviously some kind of patrol route. He seemed to be making no progress and then, of an instant, he was sliding down a spiderway with his feet outside the rungs because he had come up so close under the chopper that its draught had flattened his hair.

Had anybody seen him? And now he was here, what?

Grab a rabbit. Get it to some independent source for tests and then feed the findings to a medium that could shake up the admin-istration. Plenty of time for strategy when he was on his way back to Frisco with the evidence next to his shirt.

Latimer scaled a set of couplings and stepped out upon a steel avenue, sniffing.

Follow your nose. Simeon had spoken about a scent of hay. He didn't know whether he could pinpoint that among the fragrances of oil, hot diesel and mobile gases.

Man in a black suit. Man in a grey suit. Helicopter. These were the hazards—these and the loose chippings which chattered and skipped from beneath his feet.

He kept to the shadows, bent almost double and all set to dodge out of sight if a guard should emerge at ground level or moving over roof-tops.

Something now. Just a trace, a nasal echo of fields under sun. He moved this way, it faded. He moved that, gone altogether. He stayed where he was and it persisted. This spot, then.

It was a piggyback container, a steel box of major dimensions aboard a flat-car and all sorts of clever things happening for the maintenance of stability.

He took a grip on the flat-car, swung himself up and flattened against one side of the door so that the fitful light of the setting would not be blotted out by the bulk of his body as he worked on the bolts.

Not by the bulk of his body. But by a shadow in the shape of a spider—and then the spider spat something that struck wide of his hand but not that wide and screeched off into the night.

He flung himself off the flat-car and made too-soon contact with the chippings. When he regained his feet he was grateful to find his joints were sound and he could move at pace.

But his knees were going hot beneath polymer tailoring and he knew the skin was off them. He found refuge under a car but knew that couldn't last. The forces on foot would be searching shortly.

Even as the adrenaline pumped, a plan was forming. He was excited and moist-eyed with his own ingenuity.

He backed out from cover and looked for the helicopter. It was going away from him but somebody was scanning because it began to turn.

He started to run in a vague southerly direction, reasoning that it would take him closer to where he wanted to go if he was going to get there and that the direction made no difference if he was not.

He tacked from shadow patch to shadow patch, hunched against more lead spittle from the spider. Wherever he went, he must go a long way in one line. That was contrary to the chopper's patrol route. It was taking the machine where it had not been before.

He zigzagged twenty yards, threading himself like a needle across the lighted spaces. Then he let the pilot see him going left, over couplings, down into the adjoining aisle. More zigzags. Then off to the right. Back to the original line.

He could see lights up ahead: big permanent lights, not torches. Faster, then. Cover fifty yards and then swap aisles, sixty yards and then swap back.

He was getting irresponsible, maybe, and the penalty for that was a bullet. But there had been no more firing. So perhaps the helicopter pilot was just seeing him off the premises. Then, Simeon had said something about the jockey making him crawl. That was arrogance.

Arrogance and pride. Pride goeth before a . . .

He knew he was near the end of his run by the humming which engaged his ears. His hope was that Johnny Upstairs was so full of his flying machine that he would notice no such change of pitch.

Buildings were shouldering up against the night. They meant power, telephones.

Cables.

Pride goeth before a fall.

He was wheezing badly now and if man's aerial facilities didn't intervene soon, he would be down on his belly like Simeon but with less chance of getting up.

Wrench.

Wrench and tear and zip and flicker.

Behind him.

Looking back, he saw the spider impaled on its webbing, the helicopter frying in high-voltage wires.

That one's for Simeon, he thought. And if the man ever finds out; if he only wonders why one of his foes has dropped out of sight, I've done something positive in any terms. On my own. Without troubling Simeon or Julie or jeopardising love. I have shed my guiltload. When I can put it into words, I'll pick up a newspaper, pinpoint him and explain or apologise or both. But no more face-to-face. I'll never be ready for what I see.

The emergency appliances hastening to the scene had little atten-

tion for the dishevelled youth who finished his track-walk at a leisurely pace, breathing with difficulty.

He waited an hour for his train and though the wheezing stopped,
he still knew he had done something exceptional with the chest
Simeon had restored to him, still marvelled at it when the locomotive
glanced right like a bullet and buried itself in the deep Midwest.

Simeon, raised from slumber and drawn to the window by the
lacerated sky over the freight-yard, hailed the sizzling skeleton as
the birth of Mr. Electro but not in any seriousness and thus missed
the death of his Dust Witch and the departure of a true friend.

Meanwhile, he reckoned, all the activity at the freight-yard was
going to have the men with the rabbits on pins. Serve them right.

Gaskell and Rinehart were ahead of him, rationalising like mad to
pass off the passing of their overhead guard.

"He was chasing something," said Rinehart. "Simeon?"

"Not again, I wouldn't think. Probably some hobo."

"A high price for a hobo," observed Rinehart.

"And even if it was Simeon . . ." pondered his colleague.

"Well?"

"Well nothing," said Gaskell. "If we nail him, we can't use him."

"So he could have got away with it."

"It wasn't him."

"How can you be sure?"

"Because I want to be. Look, don't worry about Simeon getting
away scot-free. Win a few, lose a few. Call it the luck of the game."

And the game had a good way to run yet. . . .

Those two famous Battle Creek generals, A and B, were up
there pulling strings like the men in the gloom above a puppet show.

For fundamentals, they had had the precise terms of the with-
drawal from Okinawa. For a bonus, their sources had supplied the
"walking-dead" back-up plan of the Japanese.

"That's fiendishly clever," conceded B. "How do we answer it?"

"We don't answer, we anticipate."

"In other words, we let out the secret before they do."

"Precisely. Their idea is to shock us with the horror we have
made. You tell somebody there's a demon at the top of the stairs and
he isn't frightened when the funny face turns up. The principle is the
same."

"I can see why you're A," said B, "and I'm always B."

"Nonsense." A had an endearing modesty. "Holmes was nothing without Watson. Just think of Simon without Schuster, or is it Garfunkel, Rowan without Martin, Niven without Pohl—they don't amount to much, do they?"

"If I knew who they were, I would tell," said B.

"I can see why you're B," said A, "and I'm always A."

Two greying men, they were, despite the banter, sitting on the step of a rotting bunker in the partitioned-off section of the old fort, whittling wood, squirting tobacco at flies.

The think-tank idea was gone, demolished brick by brick like the Hudson Institute after Herman Kahn had beaten Marshall McLuhan to the punch-line in a thirty-six-hour television talk-show, only to collapse from exposure and drag himself off to a shady cactus in New Mexico. Not a wise move when McLuhan was on dining terms with gila monsters.

Anyway, the think-tank idea was gone. Long since, raw energy had been throwing up some pretty raw ideas. The method now was P.F.—Poet's Friend. Which mean that you found a spot, settled down and when inspiration hit you, baby, you had to shout.

A and B happened to be risking their butts to splinters on these bunkhouse steps. Oh, and the Muse was cheaper, too—a distant legacy of those Nixon cuts on defence spending.

"Something wicker," ventured A. "You know, I still have a great deal of affection for that line of mine."

"Even if it is being overtaken by events." B downed a Michigan hopper with a full ten c.c.'s of Virginia sputum. At least I'm the better shot.

"It may be," admitted A. "But I'm glad to say we are not. The objective is to let our subjects know in advance what the Japanese have planned. You know, I never expected a freak show to travel with the Cooger and Dark carnival. It's almost too good to be true. Ideas about telling—let's fence around a little."

B worked his boot among the pile of wood shavings. "It can't be in any official form."

"Why not?"

"First of all, we're not supposed to know. Secondly, we're working with people who wouldn't help us if they thought we were the government."

"Good. Go on."

"Ergo, we have to use the forces of dissent."

"Is that a situation we can control?"

"It will balance itself—entropy."

"Such as whom?"

"Student groups."

"There are so many."

"Then we choose carefully, avoiding the edge of the spectrum, electing preferably those whose dissent is vocal rather than active."

"Who else?"

"Well, who do we have, A?"

"The John Birch Society."

"We don't want to make this too much of a political thing."

"The unions."

"One strike to you, A. What about civil rights?"

"Are they valid?"

"I don't mean the racial egalitarians, I mean the vigilantes. Ku Klux Klan—if there are any left."

A was overjoyed. "It's nice to get back in the game, Big B. I thought you were going to do this all on your own. As a matter of fact, I have a dossier from my uncle who was in the FBI—a number of names. It's a start. Who knows? These Baptists from the Bible belt may even look on it as a revival."

"I don't know that it's right to bring religion into this, either, A."

"Who said anything about religion? This is evangelism."

B was still none too sure. "Do we tell the law?"

"When the time comes—and when the time comes, there may be no need because our early movers will have done it for us."

A folded the blade into his whittling knife. "I think I'll get on back to the ranch," he drawled.

B lingered. "Questions unanswered. Uneasy feeling."

A stood up with decision. "O ye of little faith. If we make our choices right, they'll save us most of our work and they won't even know they're doing it. I think perhaps, in a little while, when we've given the Grand Wizard time for his own machinations, we'll let the Green Town authorities know the KKK are coming, even if we don't mention the mutants. Cheer up, B. It's going to be good."

B was not converted. "Supposing," he said. "Just supposing . . . the Japanese have the same idea."

"That's ridiculous," said A pleasantly. "They've already had their idea." That's why I'm always A, he thought.

Tokyo rose and shimmered. Shigajiro Malecki went back to his office. With apologies to Gilbert and Sullivan, he had a little list.

The names thereon were not alphabetical—had been added as data or inspiration came to hand. Nor were they destined for execution except in the business sense. Malecki had business for them and if they did not respond, the removal would be in name only. He could do that because the vital occupants of the list would not even know they had been approached. Better if they didn't. Controlling people was valid only as long as they were unconscious of the control. Malecki was a good enough judge of humanity to be able to extract that service painlessly.

Other intelligence agencies used persuasion, blackmail, baroque ideology, encouragement of weaknesses, good old-fashioned money, all with the special emphasis on the agent. To Malecki, the methods left too broad a margin of error. Far better, he felt, to create the situation. Then, knowing your people, you could be confident of the way they would act. But never rely on people. A cold in the nose can let you down, or a traffic jam or a sudden yellow streak.

Situations are as they stand. Make them strong to begin with and the people must act in the projected manner. If one has a cold, what matter? One face missing from a crowd. The situation persists.

Malecki had had his scenario ready for years. The affair at Station Deva had allowed him to slot it into the matrix of the future, that was all. He had long since worked out how the Americans could pay best for past ignominies.

Phase Two had been on the shelf of his puppet-shop long enough to gather dust. Phase One—Deva and reaction—was providing the launch and booster stage . . . and he was pleased to note that the fine *maestro di fantoccini* brain had not suffered in the interim of waiting.

Phase One was straightforward, in the open, clear to all—except for one small touch which Malecki, in his modest way, considered ingenious. It was so good, it belonged to Phase Two—and would get there at Green Town.

Ingenuity notwithstanding, Malecki still needed to write out a cast list for his pandemonium theatre company production.

Hence his little list. The names were not for calling but for watching. That was how the minions of his agency worked—not directly but subjunctively, checking that Malecki's scenario was building up as he had visualized.

The agency did not have that much chance to operate, so that faces were unrecognisable, unphotographed, unknown. The most that could be said of one of Malecki's men in America was that he was Japanese, that he drove a Japanese car, that he never tried to be anything else but Japanese. That made him transparent rather than requiring suspicion.

It was the best cover because it was the truth. How long it would work after Green Town, Malecki did not know and did not particularly care. There was plenty more guile where that came from.

Several of the factions on the list had been duplicated on the bunkhouse steps at Battle Creek. Several had not. Battle Creek had names filed that Malecki had missed. But very few and none of any importance.

He knew about the duplications, too, and *valued* them as essential to his brainchild.

Keio's call for prompter action had added a final spice now to the pot-pourri. Malecki scanned his cast of characters once more and set about arranging their strings.

Gingerbread Gothic

The seller of lightning rods came with a new deal. Nowhere behind, vast lightnings stomping the earth or a beast storm with terrible teeth defying denial.

No late and cloudy October but the satin-blue of June going on July on the sky. And his huge leather kit did not jangle or clang but just lay there in the back of the Buick like a mail sack.

Past a lawn which was cut all wrong.

No, not the grass. But the hair, the clothes of the myriad walkers on the parkland of Little Fort State College.

Via the lawn and down to the lake to watch the night fall so he could make his delivery.

William Filo, leaving the offices of the *Campus Calliope,* was just in time to see the Buick pulling away from the poster shop next door with its mission completed. But he knew nothing of any mission or any lightning-rod salesman and he was too ready for a steak to stop and examine the parcel in the shop doorway.

The discovery was left to Jim Ruffner the following morning. Jim, majoring in visual impact techniques, operated the shop during his free periods doing good business on a campus of around twelve thousand soulful souls. It was good for his course and even better for his finances, enabling him at times to live more or less within his means.

He tried to use a little discrimination in his wares. The poster business had seen it all by now and was in something of a throwback stage. Folk hero to atrocity, statuesque nude to oedipal obscenity, all had come and gone as web-offset printing took over from lavatory graffiti. Jim, as stated, had maintained selectivity. As long as posters were cheaper than repro art, he was solvent.

And supplies came from all directions at all times. So there was nothing very special about finding a parcel in the doorway.

What was unusual was not finding the motif of the manufacturer on the back or in some inconspicuous corner of the production. No identification. Just the stark doomwatch mushroom in blacks, whites and greys and the legend "The Survivors Are Coming."

Sonic group? Possibly, but they usually had more of a message than that: a plug for their latest psymphony or the new cassette.

After five minutes, Jim Ruffner stopped looking for an explanation because he couldn't take his eyes off the mushroom. Looking at it flat was uneventful, but he had twisted it this way and that trying to find some clue to the donor and he somehow felt an additional point had been made, even subliminally.

It was nothing to do with timing. It had to be something to do with light. He took one of the posters to the window, tilted it towards the morning sun and then away.

OKINAWA BASKETS.

Now where had that come from? The picture was unchanged by angles. He pressed it illustration outwards against the window.

A watermark, clear now. OKINAWA BASKETS.

And what was that supposed to mean?

Then a shadow blotted it out. A body-shaped shadow. William Filo looking the other way, with Allison Miller at his shoulder, peering quizzically down through the glass at Jim.

He beckoned them inside.

"Great picture of an A-bomb," proffered Filo, who doubled up on journalism studies at Little Fort. "A little old-fashioned for you, though, Jim, isn't it?"

Ruffner returned the poster to the pile. Hell, there must be a good few quire there. "Bit of a mystery," he said. "They were here this morning. No mark on them. I don't know who to pay."

"Say nothing," said Allison. "You may not sell them, anyway."

Filo was thoughtful. "I saw a car leaving here last night. Late."

"A car and not a van."

"Yes. Is that uncommon?"

"Proves it isn't my usual source."

"He could have had a breakdown and come in another vehicle."

"Breakdown and he would have used another van. With eye-catchers all along either side. That's what it's all about."

"And there's no indication in the wrapper?"

"None at all. But look—this is what I was staring at." Ruffner took another poster from the middle of the pile, flattened it against the window. Same watermark. OKINAWA BASKETS. "That doesn't mean a thing to me."

There was some kind of dawn breaking behind William Filo's brow. "But then you're not a newspaperman."

"All right, what sense does it make to you, Scoop?"

Allison was stirring restlessly. "I have a class in a half-hour and I can't face it without a doughnut. Couldn't we continue the detection in Orville's?"

Earnest William broke up with a smile. "I have to feed her to keep her."

"A small price to pay," said Jim gallantly. He rolled up the poster, tucked it under his arm and led them to Orville's, where he fed both of them. To keep them. "Now . . ."

Filo was freshening his mouth with a breakfast grapefruit juice. "One of the more celebrated Pentagon leaks has been regaling the wire services lately with a tale about how we're having to pull our last research installation out of Okinawa. Of course, there's been the usual round denial with the Pentagon not enthusing over their innocence and the public not believing them anyway. Could be it's something to do with that. But what the 'BASKETS' bit is, I don't know. . . ."

"Maybe somebody's swearing," said Allison. "I suppose there are still people who use the alchemical form."

"Not on posters," said Jim. "They can use the actual and they do."

"Then it means exactly what it says," rendered William. "And what was the rest of it?"

"'THE SURVIVORS ARE COMING.' And a mushroom cloud."

"The survivors of what? The A-bomb? Or the Okinawa pull-out?"

"The Bomb, I would say. The words and the picture are on the same medium. The watermark is another matter."

"Then why tie up the two?"

"Both Japanese," put in Allison.

"And there's another thing," Ruffner followed up quickly. "These topical spreads usually take an age to print, certainly longer than this. Lately, you said—like the last couple of days? I think we're on the wrong track altogether. A printer couldn't do it in the time. Well, physically, he could, I suppose. But this is a now event. He'd surely wait awhile to see what the reaction was and then he would design to cater for the response."

"And if he knew what the reaction was going to be?" asked Filo.

"Then he would be a most unusually astute fellow—"

"Or somebody with prior knowledge and not a printer at all."

Jim Ruffner drained his coffee. "Then I don't know what point there is in it for me."

"No, Jim." William Filo, the student journalist, was reaching for the poster. "I think the message is for me."

Moments later, Orville's diner had the first window mushroom in Green Town. While Filo took Allison to her class, Jim Ruffner made sure his place and the *Campus Calliope* had the second and third.

Charlie Frei put the word around. That is to say, he was the resident striker of banners and author of overnight murals. He reduced anarchy to hardboard squares a yard by a yard. And not just anarchy. The issues of the world were all in Charlie's repertoire.

He and Jim Ruffner were hardly complementary. By the time messages got to the mass production stage, Charlie was through with them. His genesis was paintpot, not photoset.

Charlie was underground and Jim was on top. Charlie undoubtedly broke the law with some of his polyvinyl vandalism. Jim was Charlie's idea of the commercial type who was cheapening the protest racket by getting it down to a popular level.

But they didn't throw bricks at each other, chiefly because Charlie was two busy finding other people, other issues to act as targets and Jim Ruffner had never heard of Charlie Frei.

Charlie was returning this mid-morning from a fruitless reconnaissance of one of his favourite bull's-eyes, the Monk Chemicals plant.

For the record, it was he who had circulated the authentic fact that Monk Chemicals were making liquid crystals used in the manufacture of temperature detectors so sensitive that they could pick up body heat some distance away.

The idea wasn't original, exactly, but it had worked well enough as a platform at Kent State maybe ten years before when the suggestion was that such crystals had helped to track down Che Guevara and bring him an unkempt death in the Bolivian jungle.

Lately, Lefrimo and Cabralane, heroes in the style of Guevara who had been major figures in the revolutionary struggle to liberate Portuguese African colonies, had gone the same way as Lisbon increased her pressure in line with the quincentennial celebrations of the Inquisition and Charlie figured the point had been dormant long enough to be new to a subsequent generation of college kids.

The magic had lasted six months, largely due to the persistence of the World Historians Opposed to Racism and Exploitation (WHORE—which appealed to Charlie's underground humour) but he had gone to the plant perimeter today to study how his CRYSTALS FOR PISTOLS evocations were surviving the weather and had found the walls scrubbed clean.

When he had hunted out the prime movers taking coffee and cacophony in J.B.'s, they had been unsurprised by the news.

"Autumn's come for that particular leaf," said the girl who had always looked as though she liked him. "We need something different. It's up to you, Charlie. You're the oracle. Talk or die."

And Charlie, suddenly, had been stuck for words. He even bought a newspaper to scan over his breakfast but found no new outrages. Some mumbo-jumbo about a fresh Okinawa pull-out, with reports still being denied, but couched in such guarded terms that he could not hope to get a slogan out of it.

Charlie had to admit there was a real danger of apathy setting in unless he could find something. The Muse wasn't working. He fumbled through ideas but each one came up jaded. He didn't finish his coffee and left the paper on the seat.

Then he walked south down Water Street.

And stopped. At Orville's. At the *Campus Calliope*. At Jim Ruffner's shop. Three mushrooms looking out at him and the remembrance of that Okinawa item exercising his senses for no apparent reason.

THE SURVIVORS ARE COMING.

So what?

A mushroom meant Hiroshima or Nagasaki or Mururoa or Amchitka or just a mushroom. Might as well be a record sleeve for all it conveyed. But Okinawa . . .

Jim Ruffner was at the window beckoning him in like an old friend. He went.

When Ruffner pointed, he could make out the watermark. OKINAWA BASKETS. Strange.

"I—I'm in the media business myself," he said, by way of an opening.

Ruffner looked interested. "Then what do you make of that? You know, I came to work this morning and there they were—a whole

116

stack. No knowing where they came from. Nobody to pay. Must mean something."

Charlie was jealous. Things like that never happened to him. His posterity just got scrubbed off or painted over. He was conscious presently that Jim Ruffner was waiting for a practical remark.

"It's a long time since Hiroshima," he said.

"People are still dying," said Ruffner. "What's a long time for a memory like that? People are still—surviving, I guess you could say."

"This . . . er . . . this . . ." Charlie fumbled, wishing he had taken more notice of what he had read. "This Okinawa business. It's strange, like, to have the word used twice."

"It's not so much the 'OKINAWA' as the 'BASKETS,' " said Ruffner. "That I don't understand."

"Title of a new sonic album?"

"It may well boil down to that. It occurs to me you might have some knowledge, being in the business—"

"In a small way," Charlie hastened to explain. "Nothing like this, even."

"I'm sorry." The pity was even more hurtful than the assumption.

"My choice," said Charlie. "My materials are rawer, my designs more basic. Stuff of life, you know? Never mind Beardsley birds and Toulouse-Lautrec theatre bills and Tolkienesque phantasmagoria. The medium is the . . ."

"Message," finished Ruffner. "Well, if you think of anything . . ."

"Sure. I'll come back."

"Take one," said Ruffner, and when Charlie hesitated, "No. Go on. Nothing to me so nothing to you."

"Thanks." Charlie rolled up the poster and tapped it against the denim shine at his thigh. "I'll think about it and come back with the answer. For sure."

Then he went back to his apartment, a one-room affair up steps beside a provision store on Utica Street. He passed the mailman on the steps.

"You Charles Frei?"

"I am."

"Left a parcel on your doorstep. People in the shop said you were never away for long."

A parcel? Charlie wasn't even that well in with the Red Cross.

He picked it up, closed the apartment door and set about breaking the seal.

A box containing two items.

One was the twin of the poster he had brought from Ruffner. The other was a paint pen with a red fill which wrote even when he tried it on the ceiling. On wood. On brick. On hardboard.

The unstated direction, he supposed, was that he should repeat the message of the poster. Anywhere and everywhere.

The gift made him happy because it meant he belonged on the same mailing list as Jim Ruffner.

Better yet, his parcel had something Jim Ruffner's lode had lacked.

A Michigan postmark.

Judge Charles Woodman had a house in West Bonnie Brook Lane, overlooking the golf-course. He didn't play the game, gleaning far more entertainment from scrutiny of the sportsmen toiling up and down the roughs and fairways. He kept up his membership for use of the clubhouse. The golf didn't hold him but the business exchanged over the duck and green peas was a valuable root to the city grapevine.

He was watching the ants on the play-pile when one insect loomed larger than the rest and when he refocussed he found it was Simeon hurrying up his drive.

He was almost excited, though why his sympathy should flow so consistently to a miscreant was a matter most disturbing. The door was open by the time Simeon arrived on the porch.

"Saw you from the window," said the judge gruffly. "Have you come to lodge an appeal?"

Simeon was thrown momentarily. "Appeal against what?"

"Conviction . . . Forgive me, you obviously have something very important on your mind."

He led the younger man into the drawing-room, deliberately setting Simeon away from the window so that he had to turn his back on the toilers. "Drink?"

"No—yes. I'm sorry, judge. . . . I need your help and since I'm not a talking man—not any more—I may need a little loosener for my tongue."

"Sad when a man needs a bottle for a confidante."

"Not confidante, just lubrication. Judge—what kind of authority does this town exercise over its rail terminal?"

Woodman went on pouring sherry. "There's no short answer to that. The terminal itself is a municipal installation but its users are governed by all sorts of legislation-in-absence."

"Imagine you had a dangerous cargo—"

"Then one must assume we do."

"No, no assumptions, Judge. Just supposing that in your rail-yard was a freight that was lethal. How much of the onus would be on the carrier and how much on your town as the local author-ity?"

"I'm the judge, Simeon, not the city prosecutor."

"I want information, not municipal action. Not yet, anyway."

"You said this thing was imaginary."

"I said, 'Imagine you had a dangerous cargo . . .'"

"And this freight is a threat to the welfare and safety of the com-munity?"

"It could be."

"Then there is a strong responsibility on the local authority to act and control that threat. Without specifics and being unable to cite precedents, I cannot put it any stronger than that. Our town coun-cil has over-riding powers to act in protection of the community when the need arises."

Simeon stood up and walked to the window. The golfers came and went on the fanciful terrain. "I could be wrong," he said, "in which case I am wasting your time yet again."

"If you were right, how bad would this be?"

"Can I tell you from the beginning? Last night, I was at the freight depot looking around."

"For what purpose?"

"No purpose, just whim."

"What whim?"

"Bradbury again, I'm afraid. It would take the gas chamber to shake him off. *Something Wicked This Way Comes.* I go on looking . . . maybe not for that actual funeral train, all black-plumed cars and liquorice-coloured cages but for something like a . . . same pur-pose. Like a current counterpart, you know? Cooger and Dark kept coming back with their carnival every forty, fifty, sixty years. . . . Maybe this time it could take a more contemporary guise."

Woodman drained his glass and wondered why mellow sherry should sting his eyes and why his finest hour—his most famous hour—had been half a century away and in another man's lyrical

memory. "I will understand," he said. "I will force myself to understand. . . . And you found something?"

"Two men in a black suit and a grey suit who could have been
the phantoms of Cooger and Dark and a scent of—"

"Sarsaparilla?" The judge was riding with Simeon, desperate to
comprehend.

"Rabbits."

"*Rabbits?*"

"Right. The men persuaded me away and all the time there was
this helicopter hanging above me like the Monster Montgolfier with
its Dust Witch pilot. It trailed me across the yard and buzzed
me. It was—uncanny."

"Why uncanny? Mysterious, maybe, in the absence of explanation, but not uncanny, surely."

"My feeling was fear, not curiosity."

"You were thinking in parallels."

"Perhaps so."

"You said you were there on a whim."

"And you warned me about whimsy properly used. It started off
as a whim. What I'm trying to explain is that the whole thing—my
feeling included—seemed to take on some new kind of reality. And
then I went home and learned something else."

The judge took Simeon's low-drunk glass and replenished it.

"A friend from some years ago had come to tell me about a discovery of his own. He works for the Port Health Authority in San
Francisco. A few days ago, he examined a consignment of rabbits there. They had been extensively injected. When he tried to
discover something about them, his attention was discouraged by
two seamen who looked rather more like security men.

"They told him—or rather, his chief at the PHA told him—that
the animals had been vaccinated. He feels there were too many
needles for that. He suggested laboratory animals. His chief
wouldn't hear it, but he was convinced—so convinced that he came
to me. The rabbits were put on a train heading eastward.

"Last night, my two guards told me the train was carrying bullion. But it smelled of rabbits. Now why the denials, why the security measures and why the mystery?"

"Perhaps the car was used for livestock before it took on gold."
But even Judge Woodman was not convinced by that. He was
merely testing the strength of Simeon's suit.

120

"Bullion trains have security men and they don't mind being seen. That's part of the deterrent concept. These people just stepped out of the background when they were needed."

"But why uncanny?"

"I don't know, Judge. The . . . Cooger and Dark, the Montgolflier, the menagerie . . ."

"Surely you read it as you want to read it."

"Everybody does that with life, Judge. All I am saying is that it is—uncanny—how simple the task is becoming for me."

Woodman huffed into his glass. The boy could be right over the moon and his own enthusiasm could be a concoction of sentimentallty. All the same, ho didn't like unexplained phenomena in his rail terminal and if he couldn't be convinced by his visitor then he must make some inquiries of his own. "What do you want me to do?" he asked.

Simeon could not be that decisive. "Whatever you can. Put an injunction on the train's movement, I guess, until we can get to the bottom of this thing. That's what I want. I don't know how realistic that is."

"If the situation is as you outline it, detaining that freight would be entirely proper. As an authority, Green Town can do that—depending on what kind of explanations are forthcoming."

"And will you ask for explanations? You understand why I can't take inquiries very far."

"If I don't, I don't know who does." The judge stood up, crossed the room to a glass case and unlocked it. When he turned, there was an ugly-looking rifle in his hand. He advanced on Simeon and gave it to him butt-first. When Simeon took hold of the weapon awkwardly, Woodman went back for the shells.

"I . . ." Simeon's mouth was dry. "I . . . don't."

"You don't know how to use it? You don't want to use it?"

"Both."

"Then don't shoot anybody."

"But how do I explain it?"

"Officially, you are restraining them until the law arrives in whatever form that may take. Unofficially, there are things you and I need to know and your inquiries may carry some weight with that in your hands."

"But . . ." Simeon was still at a loss.

"I trust you. That was bound to happen sooner or later, so don't fight it."

Woodman watched Simeon dwindle down the drive. The next consideration was strategy. He could make his own visit to the terminal or he could ask around. If there was lethal or sinister cargo aboard the train, local forces had to know within the terms of transit law. If nobody had any information to offer locally, it left two alternatives—a bad mistake of judgment by an impulsive young man or a violation by an authority which definitely knew better.

He picked up the handpiece of his phone. Before he could finish dialling, there was another figure moving on his drive. Going away from the house. In a brown suit, neatly cut, he didn't look like Cooger or Dark.

He looked oriental.

The Haunted House was set back from Ash Street, perched high, with the ground falling away behind to the ravine. Once upon a time, it had inspired another writer with the initials R.B. to produce a grisly and classic tale which had motivated a pasteboard replica in Hollywood, a celluloid image throughout the Northern Hemisphere, an Aurora plastic assembly kit and a highly coloured postcard from Warner Bros.

The landlord had done well enough out of its progress to ignore tenants' pleas and had thereby dispatched said tenants. After summer came autumn in his wallet, however, and when he looked around again, every would-be occupier seemed to be a student.

He took delivery of coin from their parents, set a limit of six on the inhabitants and let them express themselves with what he hoped would be sufficient freedom to keep the freshmen coming.

Very seldom were there six within the clapboard, though. A commune had come and gone, tidy in habit but strangled by its own "smash-monogamy" girdle. An intellectual circus had performed verbal acrobatics under the big maple tree that dominated the back lawn but now the tree was sick in its syrup and the garden conversations were less dialectic exercises, more functions and strategies.

And there were more likely thirty than six on occasions. It was a way station for the political itinerants who hiked from university town to university town with a toothbrush and a change of anarchy in their shoulder-bags. Regional travellers they had been called and they were a familiar if not accepted consideration in the eyeball-to-eyeball bit as the raw student received his introduction to the anti-administration.

Students for a Democratic Society had begun the breed but when SDS failed to hold members at its extremes, thereby suffering a split down the middle, the Revolutionary Youth Movements had followed on. RYM-2 went somewhere and ran out of steam. RYM-1 became the Weathermen—and still had plenty of steam.

Frank Lorensen was a Weatherman and so was his companion, and scarred Lucia, but largely because Frank was one.

Today, they were the only occupants of the Haunted House. Tomorrow Julie was a visitor but only short-term.

Lucia had led her into a large and sunlit room which overlooked the straggling glory of the garden. The carpet on the floor was expensive but ill-used. The chairs were a motley group, supposedly gathered to provide the most comfort for the most people. Good reproductions of Chagall, Matisse and Picasso hung in harvest plenty on the walls, some awry as though they had not been looked at recently. Books lay where they had been thrown—Fanon, Debray, Chomsky but no Marx.

Julie's stomach turned over and she knew in part why Lucia was sad. Good taste had fashioned this room. Lack of consideration had as surely killed it and sparked a small malignancy in the girl who had given up against overwhelming odds.

Too many feet, beer-bottles, doctrines had buried the constitution of beauty. Julie tried to convey some of this awareness to the pretty, poignant vessel who hovered now at Frank Lorensen's shoulder.

If Lucia understood this, she made no response. If she did not respond, it did not mean she did not understand. There *was* no response, none that would not have been an indictment of the man at her finger-tips or an admission of her own failure.

Lorensen stirred, uncrossed his legs. Julie had been expecting a beard or a combat jacket or jeans as narrative as a Bayeux tapestry. Instead, the man was elegant in light-grey suit over white polo-neck sweater. The black boots he swung now, catching the light, had been cut for fashion and not for trend.

At first glance, he was an anachronism, as though the tenses of living and being had become jumbled with the background past and the foreground present or vice versa. At second glance, that was an unnecessary complexity. The man was selfish. He saw to himself and to his impact and to nothing else.

Another twinge for Lucia. Another chord vibrating, way back in time, for a similarly stricken Julie.

"You came," said Lorensen, "for a reason. Are you interested in our purpose here?"

"No." If Julie were to get anywhere at all, she must be direct. "I don't see wholesale destruction as the new covenant. Hatred will never replace love."

"So you're a Romantic."

"That puts me a long way round the spectrum from you. No. I'm not a Romantic."

"What then? Conservative?"

"Liberal."

"Everybody's a Liberal. A Liberal is an apology."

"Or just too far right for your taste. I'm not here to discuss the political pendulum."

"Then what?"

"I need information."

"And you think we give it without commitment?"

"I can make an exchange."

"Money?"

Julie didn't like him, was puzzled what Lucia saw in him. He was less personable than a Svengali and less charming, even, than Simeon. Chemistry. For Lucia. For Julie. The incomprehensible formula. "You don't need money," she said. "I wasn't going to offer it. An exchange of data."

"How do I know the value of your data?"

"If I know you don't want money, I also know what you do want. I'm no charlatan and don't take me for a fool, either."

"Then what information do you require? I'm tired of fencing."

"I want a statement of your loyalties—"

"What are you, some kind of fuzz?"

"Loyalties."

"Red China, North Korea. We are against the American harlot who has maimed our young men—" It was Lucia speaking, suddenly and woodenly. Lorensen caught her wrist, dug in his nails. "Stop that!"

Lucia did not flinch or flicker but the recital dried up.

"I'm sorry," Lorensen said—surprisingly until Julie realised he was talking to her and not to Lucia. "I always say once you start reeling them off like that, you might as well stop doing it. If we cannot expound with enthusiasm, we can never impress. Lucia is —a little tired sometimes. Then it is best that she leaves the talking to me. Nevertheless, what she says is right."

He had changed his grip on the girl's wrist now and was soothing the cruel red imprints of his nail with kiss and caress. Julie was repelled, more by the recompense than by the original act.

"We favour North Korea now more than ever. We pull out of North Vietnam, fabricate a new North Korean offensive and here we are, still in South-East Asia, a stalemate held as only the richest nation in the world can hold it.

"We also believe in a lot of what China has done. We blew cold for a while when she went to the U.N. on American say-so but she has made it clear since that membership means very little to her and that is heartening—"

"And Japan?"

Lorensen lifted an eyebrow. "Nothing about Japan. Why Japan? I guess if we had been around at the time of Hiroshima or Nagasaki, we might have cultivated some dogma, but we weren't. We have enough trouble staffing today's injustices. . . ."

"People are still dying in Hiroshima. Babies are still being born mutated."

"And that makes it my concern?"

"More so than North Korea, maybe. First things first—"

"What point are you taking so long to make?"

"In the sidings here at Green Town is a product of America's dalliance with Japan. Japan has found cause to kick the U.S. out. That, I think, would be an attitude to appeal to you."

Lorensen showed even white teeth with a glint of gold away in the corner. "We're always happy about chickens coming home to roost. But it is a mistake to believe we give blanket approval to every device aimed against the establishment—"

"I'm sorry," said Julie. "I was led to understand that the virtue of your organisation is exactly that. Clear cut and unmistakable. So you're not interested. . . ."

"That's not what I said. We reserve the right to pick and choose. Our achievements wouldn't be worth anything if we weren't selective. But I cannot guarantee to do business of any kind on the basis of the information you have volunteered so far."

"You're not . . . intrigued . . . by what I've told you? Perhaps you knew already." Julie gave him an opening. He could lie if he chose to.

Lorensen would have lied, if he had wanted to, but his decision was being undermined by a doubt he could not finger, a caution he could not identify. He knew nothing already, for sure. But something told him he should.

"And if I said these were not chickens, but rabbits?" prompted Julie. Still the nagging; still the elusive reason for it.

"If I had known already," he said defensively, "I would have stopped you talking. We're discussing a deal, remember. Telling me what I know isn't going to profit you greatly. . . . What really intrigues me is where you fit into all this."

Lucia detached herself from his hands, he offering little resistance, and went to a remote lounger. She picked up a book and made a pantomime of studying the glossary and turning to pages. Lorensen paid her no attention, but to Julie the girl's animation meant only one thing. She was jealous that Julie had captured a portion of Lorensen's attention.

"My husband," Julie said quickly and carefully. "He is deeply involved in the situation. A freight-car in the yards here is carrying two hundred rabbits from Japan. They appear to be laboratory animals but that needn't be the whole story . . . in fact, our experience favours the belief that this is just one piece of a much bigger mosaic. And now Simeon knows what is in that freight-car, he has decided it is too dangerous to move. He doesn't have much support."

"Simeon . . ." Lorensen's thoughts were distant, his voice mechanical, feeding the name to his ear again and again until it registered. "Yes." His attention came back with a snap. "I was a folk hero once. . . . Did you ever hear of . . . no, I guess you didn't . . . the Anderson House . . . West Eleventh Street, New York City, February 1970. We were carrying out some—experiments—
—in tactical explosives when the lot went up in our faces. At least . . ." He seemed to bite his lip, slung a quick, embarrassed glance at Lucia, whose eyes were not on her book. "I walked out. No hair, no eyebrows, just shreds of clothing—"

"Jacob died," Lucia interrupted and she was looking anywhere but at the conversation, moving her head, filling her eyes with sunlight, dark corners, motes of floating dust, casting them back finally on the crumpled pages before her. "Carrie and Joanna, too. I still see you, Carrie."

One hand had found its way to her face, tracing the line of the jagged scar down her right cheek, eyebrow to chin.

"Jacob Honeyman," said Lorensen, slightly above a whisper as though explaining an inmate's idiocy. "He was good. Joanna Lawton, Carrie Bendix. They were our friends."

Lucia was weeping quietly. Lorensen stood up and went to her.

"And . . . Lucia?" asked Julie.

Lorensen had his arm around the girl, cradling her head, kissing the cruel cleavage in her cheek.

He said, "I found her in the rubble and pulled her out before the police came. I mean, we'd—been friendly before—well, on the run we kind of grew together. I wanted to get her to a doctor but we looked such a state he'd have known and that would have been it. I did what I could with pads. I guess there'd have been a mark anyway. . . ."

"Broken glass." Lucia loosened herself in his embrace. "My mirror did it to me. I don't trust mirrors. Frank is my reflection now. . . ."

"I'm sorry," Julie said before she remembered how hard she had tried in Orville's not to use the phrase. It was the wrong one then and even more so now.

"Don't be," said Lucia. "I wouldn't have got him otherwise."

"Lucia. Baby. You know that's not . . ."

Julie waited for Lorensen to finish the sentence, but it hung in the air as heavy as shame. "I'm sure that's not right," she said eventually.

Lorensen retreated to his chair. "I—I suppose you know just how Lucia feels. You know, you girls should talk the same language, you being Tomorrow Julie. . . ."

Julie was slow to take the point. "Why me particularly?"

"Being married to Simeon. Maybe there are times when you don't feel too sure of yourself. That's how it is with Lucia. I tell her, you know? I tell her I love her and then perhaps I'll do something or say something or more often *not* say something and I see the old gnawing start. We—Simeon and I—we love when we can, the only way we can. When our thoughts are elsewhere, we are not being unfaithful or indifferent. We are just back locked in the cells of our beings."

He laughed, just to make a new sound in the room. "I guess it's all to do with hormones."

Julie could have made a rather more damning appraisal but it wasn't what Lorensen was silently begging her to say or, she sensed, what Lucia wanted to hear.

"You have to be right," she offered. "And if Lucia has been putting up with a genius since 1970, she's a marvel. Simeon and I met four years ago. Playa 9 was the following summer, and by that time we needed it. Listen, Lucia, maybe you can give *me* a few hints."

She perched on Lucia's chair, took away her wet tissue and replaced it with a dry one. Lorensen nodded his thanks almost imperceptibly. "We were talking about rabbits," he said. "What kind of trouble is Simeon expecting?"

"The usual kind," said Julie. "He doesn't know who his friends are but he can bank on the forces of order being on the other side."

"Then we must see what we can do with the forces of disorder. If Simeon will settle for bodies, I can arrange it."

"I don't know." Julie, though she felt the three of them had come through a crisis together, learning of each other as they came, was still wary of Lorensen. The experience had revealed him as an enigma, making him more and not less of a hazard. "At the same time, I do know it wouldn't help him to have somebody capitalising on the situation. You weren't planning—"

"No riot," said the Weatherman. "My guarantee. If there is any chaos it will not be of my creation. I'll see him soon and talk strategy."

"Sooner than soon, please. We don't know how much time we have." But that wasn't the reason. Julie wanted Simeon to see what he was getting.

Lucia walked her across the lawn and past the maple tree before she would let her through the gate. "I love your home," Julie said. "I love to see pictures."

"Thank you." Lucia seemed to have regained control. "For meaning well. I know I used to love it myself. I know how I used to have it and how I wanted to keep it. But times change. Camelot wasn't right for today. I guess I should have married Walt Disney while I had the chance."

It was a brave attempt to reconcile opposing dreams. Descend-

ing Kent Street, Tomorrow Julie shed her own tears for the sadness
that bedevilled the Haunted House.

Thus she didn't see the young man in dark glasses who had
trailed her all day suddenly change his route to take in the gate, the
maple tree and the Lorensen home.

Kanichi Kuroda had been a witty man beyond fifty, habitually in
sun-glasses because his eyes saw little. He had played the guru for
the Kakumaru Zengakuren (the revolutionary Marxist faction of
the student self-governors)—played and lost. In an escalating spiral
of student violence, his "narrow, overtheoretical" views had been
described as milksop by activists who left the Kakumaru to join the
more volatile Sampa group.

In the late 1970s, his wit had not been able to save him. His
impotence was known in Tokyo and Texas, Sasebo and Illinois. His
appeal turned out to be traditional. Making comedy out of con-
formity does not work forever.

"I am Kyoso Kuroda," the young man in the shades told Frank
Lorensen. "Son of Kanichi."

"Is that so?" Lorensen plumbed the filing-cabinet of his Weatherman brain.

"I do not share my father's bland political visions. Not entirely."

Lorensen was back in his chair. Lucia had busied herself elsewhere around the vast house. "What am I to make of that? Is it a
recommendation or an apology?"

"My own experience of campus thought is more representative
of today, more like your own."

"You are an activist."

"When the need arises."

"Did you carry a stave against the U.S.S. *Enterprise* at Sasebo?"

"That was . . ." Kyoso was apologetic. "That was before my
time as a student. But I saw the tear-gas and the hoses and it
planted the seed. To my credit are the sanctuary sit-ins at Kobe and
Yokohama and much of the Okinawa turbulence between 1974 and
now. At Haneda Airport last year I also engineered the hi-jack of
a Japanese S.S.T. carrying Hirohito's well-paid widow and forced a
ransom for our funds and safe conduct here."

Lorensen relaxed. He felt more at home with his kind than with
women who talked a language of their own and displayed a hunger

to each other which he couldn't even understand. The thing with Lucia and Tomorrow Julie had disturbed him more than he liked and he welcomed the chance to get back to an arena he knew.

"Sit down. Drink?"

"Hot from Princeton. Now tell me—what do you want?"

"I have been following Tomorrow Julie."

"She's a good-looking woman."

"I . . ." Kyoso did not quite catch the nuance. "Forgive me, what has that to do with it?"

"Nothing. My joke."

"I . . . I see what you mean. I am sorry. I have been following her because that is my commission."

"From whom?"

"From Sampa."

"But why . . . ?" Unless . . . Lorenson remembered Julie and two hundred rabbits. "I take it you're anti-government."

"In the normal course of events."

"And not employed by them?"

"Not knowingly."

"Does that mean you leave the possibility open?"

"It means my instructions came as they always come from Sampa Zengakuren. Anything outside of that is not my concern."

"Then you wouldn't know anything about two hundred infected rabbits from Japan." The "infected" had been a shot in the dark, a thought he had not confided to Julie in the hope that she might confide it to him.

In any event, it went home with better effect than he had hoped.

"Not Japan, no," said Kyoso Kuroda. "Okinawa."

And the curtain lifted, the door opened, the little bulb above Frank Lorensen's head came on. The thing he should have known, he kept telling himself during his interview with Julie, was revealed. "That's nothing short of magnificent," he said.

"I don't follow you."

"Then it's all tied in with this pull-out rumour."

"No rumour. This is the *reason* for the pull-out."

"Rabbits?"

"One of them escaped from an Okinawa research establishment and killed a native. It had been implanted with Yeze fever—a disease from the rickettsial strain but much more fast-working. The government was so annoyed that they ordered the U.S. to move their installation off the island."

"And these rabbits are the tainted creatures from that installation?"

"Right."

"And they've been brought across the United States in an ordinary piggyback freight train?"

"It's safe enough. They're in strong baskets."

Zap! OKINAWA BASKETS.

The poster had come that morning and Lorensen had paid it no more attention than the demo sheets he got free of charge from Red They Were and Hollow-Eyed in New York. It was in his wastebasket now.

He stood up, sifted and found the item, smoothed it out on his desk.

OKINAWA BASKETS was nowhere to be seen, but he had it there somehow. He turned the paper to the light. THE SURVIVORS ARE COMING. A mushroom cloud. And OKINAWA BASKETS.

"Did your people print this?"

Kyoso whistled. "No. I haven't seen that before. Hey, but it's rather good."

Then who? "Does it make any sense at all to you?" asked Lorensen.

"I guess the mushroom cloud means what it always means," said Kyoso. "A kind of American trademark."

"And the baskets—they're the ones carrying the rabbits."

"I would think so."

"The survivors. The rabbits are the survivors."

"No," said Kuroda. "I know what the survivors are."

"What?"

"Phase Two."

"What's Phase Two? For crying out loud, Kuroda—"

"Two hundred maimed and mutated but rehabilitated children of the Hiroshima holocaust."

Lorensen's heart spasmed. "Coming here?"

"Wherever the rabbits stop."

"But why here?"

"This is where Simeon is."

"What's Simeon got to do with it?"

"Your government believes he can generate a good situation—he and Tomorrow Julie. We had a dead-sea problem with a desalination plant at Tsuruoka but, of course, no Simeon."

"But you're going to offset the impact of that with these—survivors?"

Kyoso Kuroda suddenly had a lot more self-assurance, obviously sensing Lorensen's ill-ease. "The survivors would have come anyway. The official feeling of the Tokyo government is that this is a goodwill gesture meant to indicate that our present admonition is not permanent."

"A strange way of doing it," confessed Lorensen.

"Only if you happen to be Occidental," said Kyoso.

Frank Lorensen was having visions—gaudy, terrible productions which made him shiver and conversely triggered his perspiration. "I'll tell you how an Occidental will read it," he said.

"No need." Kuroda was positively beaming. "He will be given a profound shock and a spat of nausea. But we cannot be blamed for that. And he cannot show it—lest he offend us."

If Sam Peckinpah II had seen Dustbowl, Utah, he would have signed it to a long-term contract and filmed it upside down, back to front and s-l-o-w-l-y to keep providing the best-selling duels between fat-bellied veteran Robert Redford and the new wow, Pat Wayne, Jr.

As it was, there were Chevies at the hitching rail and bargains at the Last Chance hypermarket and nobody had openly packed a gun since the Nixon legislation on the matter came out of hiding in late 1972.

Most of the natives had a Saturday Night Special put away, oiled, somewhere around their premises but only Slade Dexter, local branch of the county sheriff's office, could bounce a firearm around on his hip. Which he did. With alacrity.

Slade liked his image as he liked his name, with its sound that came out tight as a palomino's saddle-girth and coiled in gentle like a whiplash. For the Dexter, he could thank his father. The Slade was an addition of his own since it did no harm and possibly a great deal of good. Nobody would tangle light-heartedly with a lawman whose name was Slade Dexter.

Dustbowl didn't have a Dalton gang or even a Calamity Jane,

though some of the public wives were fairly accident-prone on the nights the mineral men came in to spend their pay.

No, Dustbowl had the contemporary version of the O.K. Corral—a ghetto.

Slade Dexter was a blond Anglo-Saxon Protestant middle-of-the-roader who studded his utterances with references to pioneer stock but didn't quite understand why he should not refer kindly to Jefferson.

Not that he often had much to say about Thomas Jefferson. His objectives were clearly defined, his activities strong on discipline. He knew where he was going and in America today that was a fine quality. He would not debate because he suspected the treachery of words. He was a lawman with a job to do and a vision of doing it.

Tonight, as he guided the office cruiser randomly across the Dustbowl street network, edging always towards the centre, the commercial section where there would be trouble if there was going to be, he was content as only a small-minded man can be content.

A local ordinance stated that all stores should keep their lights on, providing illumination for the sidewalks (and saving on street-lights) and also making it well nigh impossible for any mayhem not to be noted.

Dexter's nuisance wasn't looting since the store-owners had little more than their customers and it wasn't race violence for the same reason. The white population's living standards were not an offence to the blacks and the black instinct for community living offset any white qualms about property values, even if their homes —gingerbread Gothic the best the town could offer—had real value beyond fulfilling a function.

Dustbowl was a poor town and just as well. Everybody on a par meant few causes for discontent. Nobody would ever write a social history but that was simple summation and analysis.

Nevertheless, Slade Dexter could never quite get to grips with the ghetto. Probably because he did not understand that the word needed a context to mean anything at all. Otis Street, his "ghetto," was merely a street of homes to its inhabitants.

They were out on their doorsteps now, enjoying the cool of the evening and making their own verbal excitement. They watched his gradual progress up the street without curiosity and without guilt. Dexter was a habit, as much a part of their day as a meal-time.

They saw him come, watched him go, knew his day was over.

And it was. He turned right off Otis Street, up Seminole Street and out onto the Farmington road. A mile along, he turned right again following a tree-lined drive to his own particular piece of gingerbread.

Louella would be waiting with dinner and tonight it was southern fried chicken with black-eyed peas and trimmings.

He would enjoy it if he could just shake off this vague frustration. Nothing happened, nothing to keep a sheriff in business. But it went deeper than that. There had been a time when he was happy. Not here but farther south.

Happy with his bloodstock. A strange way of putting it but the phrase, thrust suddenly upon his awareness, bore some clue to the malaise.

Louella said, "They're calling back."

He said, "Who?"

She said, "They didn't give details but it sounded important. No inkling for the likes of me. Must be business."

And as she took the food from the oven, the telephone shrilled again, so she thrust the platters back into the warmth.

"Mr. Dexter?" said a man's voice. "Mr. Huey Dexter?"

Now there weren't too many people who knew the Donald Duck nephew name Dexter had dropped to become a frontiersman. "I am Huey Dexter."

"I am a U. S. Defence Ministry official calling from an installation in Michigan to inquire whether you would be prepared to help us in a little exercise."

"If I knew what it was—"

"I was wondering whether you might have retained your Ku Klux Klan motivations."

Dexter was seized with sudden and gripping stomach pains. "I . . ."

The man must have been expecting some such reaction. "No anxiety, Mr. Dexter. We have need of you in the role of dragon, so to speak."

"What? Against . . . ?"

"Blacks? No, Mr. Dexter. Too many of them. This particular scenario involves Japanese."

"Well, there are a heck of a lot of those."

"Just two hundred in this instance and you wouldn't be alone."

If there was any suggestion that Dexter would have been scared on his own, he missed it.

"I would have to . . ." Indeed, with the adrenaline of unscheduled discovery receding, the deputy was discovering an appetite. "I would have to have more details."

"No time right now, I'm afraid. We require you to assemble at Milwaukee tomorrow—"

"Tomorrow! But—"

"Time is of the essence, Huey . . ."

"Then, yes."

In Battle Creek, General A put down the receiver and made another tick on his list.

Meanwhile Slade Dexter, man with a badge, went blithely to his dinner. He didn't know when his next good meal would be.

Mayor Roger Mortis was usually so slow on the ball that his political foes had the habit of taking his R initial as "Rigor" . . . Rigor Mortis, huh? But tonight he had come down Highway 50 so fast that even his chauffeur, seconded from the Green Town Police Department, was sweating.

At the junction of Water and Main, bodies flickered and weaved before the headlights. Beyond them, more flickering, emanating from burning rubbish in the middle of the street.

The crowd was what he had expected. Long hair held back with Geronimo headbands, painted arms, glinting teeth, loud noise. They weren't from the reservation but from the campus.

When the faculty descended shortly to regain their charges, there would be nice banalities about degrees of activism but the point was lost on Mortis. Right now, every surging body was in violation and whether they had been inebriated by mental firewater from the out-of-town radicals and topped up with local beer made no difference.

Coming down Main, he had been in a small dilemma; whether to wind down the window to listen for breaking glass or whether to keep it up in case of a sudden Molotov cocktail in the back seat.

Now at the crossroads he knew he had done right in staying secure. With a mob like this, it went as understood that there were broken windows and an emotional assessment of around $100,000 in damage that would come down in the light of day to $15,000 or less.

Mortis was a tubby little man and the breakneck journey down Highway 59 had bounced him about like a billiard ball among cushions. So he was on his dignity before he began.

He laid a hand on the driver's shoulder and ordered a halt, unnecessarily as it happened. The patrolman touched a switch in the dashboard, handed him a mouthpiece and a copy of the statute book turned to the appropriate page.

"2923.51," it said. "Dispersing of riotous group. When five or more persons are engaged in violent or tumultuous conduct which creates a clear and present danger to the safety of persons or property, a law enforcement officer or commissioned officer of the organised militia or armed forces of the United States called to duty to protect against domestic violence shall, forthwith, upon view or as soon as may be on information, and unless prevented by such persons, order such persons to desist and disperse to their several homes or lawful employments. Such order shall be given by such means and as often as necessary to reasonably insure that it is heard, unless the giving or hearing of such order is prevented by such persons. Whoever refuses or knowingly fails to obey such order shall be fined not more than fifty dollars."

And if they all kept still and listened to that, he thought, it would be a miracle. More likely they'd take hold of the car, turn it over and set it ablaze while he was still quoting precedent.

The spirit of the Riot Act was served if the assembly was declared illegal and its members ordered to disperse. Urgency of action required some attempt at immediacy.

He cleared his throat and blew on the mouthpiece. The rumble it made outside had him wondering about dynamite. The assembly was focussing its attention on him now, pressing hard around the car.

"You are breaking the law," he said. "Get out of here at once."

The students laughed. Perhaps they saw his struggle. Perhaps they knew the problem of the cumbersome invocation and were amused by his hasty paraphrase. For himself, he was pleased enough.

"This gathering is illegal," he said. "Go to your homes."

Homes? On campus? Your dormitories, your halls of residence.

More laughter and a little good-natured pushing at the car. The driver unsheathed his Police Special.

"You are in violation of the Riot Act," tried Mortis. "I am telling you to disperse. I am giving you notice of the consequences—jail or a fifty dollar fine."

A youth with an Afro hairstyle pushed himself through the crowd. If it was possible to make any sense out of the observation "there was something odd about him" when there was so much odd about so many people, then the comment might be made about this one. He wore the inevitable dark glasses against the glare of the police lights but his face was smooth. No sideburns, no chin sprouts. Just a lot of hair on the head.

He tapped at the window. "We want to talk."

The patrolman looked at the mayor. Mortis nodded. "Three inches and cover it."

The glass went down a precise three inches. The policeman's gun hand did not waver.

"We are not here to riot," said the youth. Strange. A slight twang to his American. Maybe he came from Hawaii or the Philippines. Would explain the smooth skin, thought Mortis.

"Then why are you behaving in this way?"

"We are keeping warm."

"At the taxpayer's expense. How much damage have you done?"

"None, I swear. We brought our own combustibles. Maybe a little blackening in the centre of the road. No more."

"And your objective?"

"Information, Mr. Mayor. We would like to know about a certain lethal consignment here in Green Town or on its way—a consignment that is contrary to our pacifist persuasions."

"I don't know anything about such a consignment," said Mortis. And he didn't. He looked at the policeman, who also shook his head.

The youth was turning away from the car. "The mayor denies it," he shouted.

"Now wait a minute," said Mortis to the window. On reflection, he repeated it into the mouthpiece. "Now wait a minute. This is not a denial."

He was wary of these conversations via intermediary. He knew the damage that could be done on translation, the incendiary nature of those intermediaries. Such manoeuvres employed at Kent,

Ohio, in May 1970, at Berkeley, California, oft times since, at Stanford, at Maryland, at St. Paul, Wisconsin, had trailed into bloodshed because situations had been misrepresented by those who stood to gain politically from chaos and grievances had been created as exercises in mayhem.

"This is not a denial," he repeated emphatically. "I do not deny this suggestion of a lethal consignment—"

"Then he admits it," shouted the blinkered youth. Sporadically, at points throughout the crush, voices were beginning to strike up in echo. "Pig admits it. Pig admits it."

"Silence!" Mortis was shouting and it came out of the loudspeaker like thunder. "If you will have the grace to hear me out, you will find out exactly what I am admitting and what I am denying. I am admitting that I know nothing of this consignment. I am denying that I know anything. . . . And before I am accused of double-talk by my young friend here, let me tell you I am using his terminology. All I mean is that I don't know anything about it. That is a temporary condition. I am prepared to take whatever steps are necessary to gain information and am giving you an assurance to this effect. As soon as I have details, they will be conveyed to you."

"And what action then?" shouted somebody far back in the crowd. The youth had filtered away, moving quickly between bodies. Calling as he went.

"Required action," said Mortis. "Action to control any hazard."

"Suppose the hazard is not here and now. Suppose the danger is to coming generations."

Mortis was trying to trace the voice, but it was impossible. He was sitting, the crowd was standing. The questions just kept floating in at him with that quaint intonation.

"That's an ideological question," he said, "and outside my province as mayor. I trust you realise that unless the matter falls within the compass of my first-citizen duties, my hands are tied."

"So much for your assurance."

Mortis was close to swearing but knew he would lose them entirely if any oath took the air. "It is the best I can offer. I can only warn you and your friends that making trouble for the sake of it is easily recognisable. If you ask me to make promises which I cannot hope to keep and then issue threats at my refusal to make those promises, you show yourself up as someone who is more interested in the argument than in the solution. I can only help you if you are prepared to be helped.

"At this time, I shall waive pursuance of the Riot Act legislation on the grounds that you may have a genuine cause for complaint. But unless you give me a chance to examine that complaint, I must read your insistence as coming within the terms of violation and act accordingly."

"Fancy speech, Mr. Mayor. But we'll give you time to find out. And we'll be back here each night until you do. Right?"

"Right," responded the assembly, more enthusiastic now that it had been ruled legal. "Right on."

"Acceptable," said Mortis, "as long as you do no damage. Any vandalising or looting will be taken as signalling the end of your sincerity and credibility."

He motioned to the driver, who rolled up the window. "Now get us out of here. I'm pooped." Still with the mouthpiece in his hands.

At least, they left the crowd laughing. Rather, the crowd minus one. When participants came to consider it, none of them knew the youth who had stood them drinks in J.B.'s with the compliments of the Havana Cabal.

He, meanwhile, was making his own leisurely way up Highway 59 with the Afro wig gone to show smooth, sleeked, parted black hair and the shades off sloe-shaped Nipponese eyes.

Little Fort State College could wait for the answer. He knew it already.

Ed Rinehart could have been a wino without too much trouble. He had come close to throwing in his lot with the grape when the circus life had packed up and left town. Only the fortunate advent of the NSA had saved him from the bottom of the glass.

But there were times even now when he believed a bottle of California red could point the way to most solutions or, if there were no particular problem, could provide the current mediocrity with the complexion of a rose.

He drank now, fast and purposefully, working hard to lower the level in the bottle, and it did not go unnoticed.

"Why?" said Gaskell, away at a desk on the other side of the railroad car, writing something, drawing something.

"Why not?" The stock question retort was as close as Rinehart himself could get to a proper answer.

Gaskell laid down his stylo. "Is it Jerry?"

Rinehart had hardly known the helicopter pilot, had seen him only as an impersonal occupant of the sky. Joe Gaskell, on radio, had done all the talking to Jerry. Their very location had prohibited them from any closer contact.

"No. I don't like losing people, but if I want to be honest, I have to say the experience doesn't . . . diminish . . . me any more. That worries me, but—"

"Is that it? Maybe you feel you ought to mourn more. . . ."

"But not right now."

"Then you win. You're totally inscrutable." Gaskell reached for his stylo.

Rinehart found a catch in his throat that might have come from California. "Don't give me up, Joe. There was to be some simple explanation for these . . . blues."

"Old rocking chair's got you."

"Joe, I need . . . taking seriously."

The phenomenon, the manifestation of grief without being able to pinpoint the cause, was as surely out of the bottle as the dwindling contents of his glass and Rinehart knew that. Even so, there had to be some beginning in reality. What, for instance, had sent him to the bottle?

He walked—none too steadily, he noticed, but the imbalance could be emotional—to the lip of the car and stood where the night wind could get to his face. In the ravine north of the railroad, cicadas rattled towards destruction.

The town stretched away and the night was taut beneath it like a set of snares. One blow upon the face of Green Town now would bounce and echo. In the day, the snares came off. Maybe.

Maybe, too, the tension, the drum state of thinking was his own paranoiac paradiddle. . . .

"It's all . . ." He had a quick glimpse of the answer through wine-haze and then lost it on night-breeze. "All . . . too *easy*."

Stylo going down on desk. Subtle shift of shadows as Gaskell bulked before desk-lamp, twisted away from it. "Too *easy*? Is that an anxiety for us, Ed?"

"For me, yes."

"Do you suspect easy things?"

"No. I just like a challenge, a little difficulty. We arrive here in Green Town to try and find this Simeon and no sooner do we come to a halt than he's there, finding us. Where's the fun in that?"

"Look, Ed, the way things have speeded up, it's just as well. Besides, that's only the first step."

"One of my few, Joe, remember? I have a two-act break now and I only come back for the finale to shift scenery. I was looking forward to some kind of hunt."

"It's just one assignment, Ed. There'll be others. Don't knock it for going smoothly. I mean, it hasn't even gone smoothly. What about Jerry?"

"One of the casualties of achieving nothing."

"That's too obscure for me. A man was with us on this mission and he was killed."

"Not for the mission."

"How do we know that? He saw something, he shot at it. We heard that."

"A shadow. A rabbit."

"A rab—"

"No, not one of ours. One of the locals."

"We can't be sure."

"We can't be anything else."

"He reported he saw a running figure, dodging. Purposely dodging."

"And did we see?"

"No . . . He had the better view."

"We didn't see, he can't confirm. Whoever . . . whatever . . . it was is in the clear."

"Ed, the running guy could have led him straight into that high-voltage wire—"

"And perhaps he should have realised . . . Simeon he would have recognised, right?"

"Right."

"And he said nothing."

"Maybe he was trying to make an identification . . ."

"Don't make excuses. Who else knows we're here?"

"That depends on Simeon."

"Very much so. If he wanted to point us out to somebody, he would have to bring them. People in authority don't come sneaking. Why should they? They have a right—"

"Enough, Ed!"

"What?"

"That's enough. You wanted to chew it around and we've chewed it around. Now I've got work to do."

Rinehart backed off from the doorway, shouldered himself into Gaskell's circle of light. "Aren't you lucky."

He looked down upon Gaskell's work. Boxes, arrows, lines, small writing. It could have been a circuitry map. "What's that, anyway?"

Gaskell's tolerance was at threshold. He nearly came back with a smart answer before he realised that Rinehart was at least showing an interest, however fleeting. A straw to grasp at, a moment to make rare with mirth. He made their whole future thing sound like a wedding or some such formality. He said, "The seating arrangements."

In the split second that followed, a shot bounced and echoed on the Green Town night, from the cabin down the way, the rabbit container, and Rinehart launched himself from the door laughing. Gaskell could not be sure the joy had come from his wit. More likely, it was because this other drumskin night report was *not* arranged. Thanks, anyway.

Judge Woodman ran down the city prosecutor at the Glen Flora Country Club and he knew already that was no good place for a comprehensive answer to his inquiry.

If he knew Theo Elmwood, there would be a steak going cold as and if they talked. And Elmwood would need to make recourse to records. The secret, then, would be to get him back to his office.

He wasted no time on greetings: "Theo? Charles Woodman. Can you tell me off the top of your head whether we have any hazardous materials in the town freight-yard at this time?"

"What the . . . ?" Elmwood began an exclamation. "They would have to be of a very special sort for me to know about them, Judge."

And that meant the attorney was thoughtful. The two had known each other long enough for Elmwood to respond with "Charles" to Woodman's "Theo."

"I've dismissed the on-the-spot transport staff. It's the kind of thing you and/or the police would know about."

"What is it?"

"According to my information, tainted livestock masquerading as bullion."

Elmwood considered that. "Are you saying bad meat? Risk of infection? That sounds like a public health matter."

"Rather more to it, I'm afraid. These could be laboratory animals."

"Vivisectionists?"

"Possibly. But worse even than that. Who conducts most of such experiments?"

"The drug houses?"

"More than them."

"The—the *government?*"

"Right. And if there was any plan to run such things through here, we should know."

"Of course we should. I'll see what I can find out in the morning."

"It's urgent, Theo."

"You mean you want it done now?"

"I have been asked to take out an injunction to hold this consignment. I want to find out quickly whether the city should support the writ or fight it."

"Who asked? No, I'm sorry, Charles, I guess that's classified information."

"Not at all. He won't mind. My informer was Simeon."

Woodman heard a muffled curse at the other end of the line. "Judge—is he trying to pull the wool over your eyes?"

"I think I resent that suggestion, Theo. I know wool when I see it."

The judge recalled Simeon disappearing down the path and the man who had come from nowhere to follow him. He was no Simeon whim and a product of Woodman's imagination if he was a product at all. Perhaps the judge had better lay on a safeguard.

"I'd like to see you back at your office, Theo. If I'm not there within ten minutes of your arrival, do me a favour. Come and collect me."

Muffled movement on the line, playing direct to Woodman's inner ear so that he could not identify it easily. Elmwood, he decided, had shifted the receiver from one hand to the other.

"Look, Judge, if you think you are in any danger—if you are in a difficult situation right now, like Simeon is holding a knife on you, just give me a 'yes' or a 'no' and I'll have a car there in seconds."

"No," supplied Charles Woodman emphatically. "Look . . . Simeon is all right. He's not the one I'm concerned about."

"Then who?"

"That's why I want to see you, Theo. Now—do I get my interview?"

"And your arrangement. If you're not in my office ten minutes after I arrive there, I'll be out to you with guns blazing."

"A siren should do the job," said Woodman. Now why had he said that? "I'm preparing to set out now."

He downed the phone and the doorbell rang. The caller had the edge on him. So intent in his talk with Elmwood had he been that the drive had been left unwatched.

Was it Simeon back? Was it the slant-eyed pursuer?

He opened the door and was rooted. The eyes could have been any shape behind the white flour-sack hood.

The procession could have made laughter, but for the burning it started in his stomach. Simeon, the Asiatic and now a clown in fancy dress. Shortly, a girl who wore balloons?

"Inside," said the visitor. The small cannon in his gloved right hand said the rest.

Woodman searched the roadsides of his mind for a milestone. Green Town had been a place of moderation. No Jew-baiting, black-hunting, McCarthyism. The only Klansman ever had been—

"Good evening, Zack Shoemaker," he said. "Who's minding the store?"

The masked man just prodded with his iron, shouldering the door wide to allow access and then closing it expertly with a backward flick of the foot. "It's no good, Judge. You don't know me."

And it was no good, because the voice was not Shoemaker's.

"My identity isn't important. Just the message I have for you. I'll deliver it and go."

"Then why the gun?"

"Part of my habit," said the man dryly. "This is a difficult message and I want to know that you've grasped it."

Woodman found himself an easy chair. He didn't bother to look at the clock because he knew the future—the next twenty minutes or so, anyway. And there he had the edge on the caller. "Is it going to take long? I have an appointment."

"Here?"

That had been close to an indiscretion. "No, downtown," the judge said hurriedly. "In fact, I have plenty of time."

"Here," adjudged the Klansman. "How long?"

"Honestly," said Woodman, "my appointment is in town." Allow room for uncertainty, he thought. That's easier to accept than a lie. "Of course, I don't know what my friend will do if I don't turn up . . ."

The Klansman took a dining chair from the table. "The point's too small to matter. I won't be here that long."

This time, Woodman did look at the clock. It wasn't a question of whether Elmwood would be here soon enough, but that he might be too late.

"The message." The hooded man drew Woodman's eyes back from the mantelpiece. "The message is from the government."

The judge laughed. "They have a new line in messengers. Whatever happened to the post-paid envelope?"

"Laugh if you like but it's a fact. I didn't say I came from the government. But it looks as though you're not going to have the information unless you get it underground, so here I am."

"Being a public-spirited citizen."

"We think so."

"How many is 'we'?"

"All of us and that's as much of a figure as you're going to get. The message is that some very peculiar specimens are coming your way. They are un-American and as such a threat to the greatness of our nation."

"Rabbits," volunteered the judge.

"What?"

"Rabbits. In freight wagons. From Japan."

"From Japan, sure. But not rabbits—people."

"People?" The Klansman could see it when the judge looked askance. If the judge surprised the body behind the hood, there was little indication possible. "Any particular kind of people?"

"Mutants," said the Klansman. "Hiroshima survivors and offspring. We don't like the idea."

No more do I, thought the judge. But not for your reason. I fear for them at your hands and at lots of hands not branded KKK.

"I'm glad you told me," he said. "It is . . . un-American. What are you intending to do?"

"Primarily, we don't think this is a good thing for our people to see. Our children will be sickened and we'll be pretty uneasy ourselves in the presence of so many . . . well . . ."

"Guilt symbols?" suggested Woodman.

"Guilt symbols, nothing," countered the Klansman quickly. "We only gave as good as we got. They started. We ended it, killed a couple of thousand to save a good few million."

"The usual defence."

"We don't need a defence."

"The usual arrogance."

"I'm just telling you, Judge, that we don't want them here."

"In Green Town?" The Judge bethought a trap. How wide was his messenger's interest?

"In America," said the Klansman.

"And I'm just telling you, Faceless, that I can't fault your intentions. Now I know what the poor people are likely to have to put up with, I don't want them here either."

The Klansman stood up. His intellect seemed to falter between brute and academic. "Good. It isn't necessary for us to have the same reasons as long as we make the same decision."

He started for the door and Woodman wanted to hold him. The questions came rushing. "Wait . . . How do you know this? Why Green Town?"

There on the night wind, traversing a scale of panic, a siren leathering towards the house on Bonnie Brook Lane. Damn Elmwood for his punctuality.

The man in the hood paused on the porch, working out some intimate equation involving distance, speed and pitch.

"Ask Simeon," he said. Then he was gone.

"Out," said Simeon. "Back off and out."

He was seated on one of the upturned baskets with the rifle balanced awkwardly but at least pointing in the right direction.

A Remington .303, Rinehart noted. A sports gun but with power enough to end the game whether you were herd or human. He stayed where he was. He would not risk advancing farther, but he could take a gamble on Simeon issuing a more emphatic ultimatum before he actually pulled the trigger.

Gaskell's fast footsteps pounding on the loose chippings. "And tell him the same," said Simeon.

"Joe!" Rinehart tried to sound as though he wasn't taking it seriously. "Simeon's here. He has a gun."

"Simeon?" Gaskell's surprise was genuine. His next comment was more calculating. "I thought he didn't hold with that kind of thing."

"You mean nonviolent?" Rinehart picked it up quickly. "That's what I heard."

Gaskell joined him in the doorway with upper chest, shoulders and head above the level of the container floor.

"Put both your hands where I can see them," Simeon said quickly. Gaskell obliged, placing them palm-down on the floor of the container.

Simeon was sitting on the far side of the rabbits' run. The animals, made nervy by the shot, had gathered in a neutral corner.

"So you know me," he said. "I thought perhaps you might."

"Know you," said Gaskell. "Don't know what you want."

"Simple." Simeon's wrists were aching with the unaccustomed weight of the firearm. He shifted his legs and found a way of supporting it with his knee. "I want to know why you told me this was a bullion train when all you have aboard is rabbits."

"We're fur smugglers," said Rinehart.

"Liar."

"Then you have different information."

"That's right. But I still want to hear it from you."

"I don't think you would use that rifle," said Gaskell. "I think I could come and take it away from you right now."

Simeon had a bad moment. "It's a chance you take," he said, like a professional. And he was wondering whether it would hurt the man too much to have a bullet in the arm, and then he was wondering whether he could be sure of hitting the arm anyway and not puncturing a lung or—

But Gaskell wasn't coming because Rinehart had hold of him. "No, Joe. It's too big a risk. That thing has a hair-trigger. You make the man jump and you could lose half your head. These novices are more of a menace than paid killers. . . . What is it you want, Simeon?"

"I've told you—why the tight security on these rabbits?"

"Why do you want to know?" It was a stupid attempt to pad out the exchange and gain time but the strategy was going wrong. Simeon was supposed to be making an uproar by telling other people and here he was playing it solo. Uncharacteristic.

"I want to make sure my information is correct before I . . ." While he kept the conversation going, his mind was working on new facts, trying to find their place in the jigsaw. The men knew him. Why? Unless it was intended that they should meet him. Or he, them. And was that the reason this lethal freight had pulled into Green Town when it could have got itself lost entirely on some rail spur until the fuss had been forgotten?

"Before you what?" said Gaskell tersely.

Simeon took a chance. "Before I tell anybody."

"Like who?" queried Gaskell.

"Like whom?" said Simeon.

"What?"

"The phrase is 'like whom.'"

"Then I stand corrected. Like whom?"

"The authorities."

"Covers a multitude. What authorities?"

"Town authorities. Local transport authorities. Agencies of law and order."

"They know."

"Is that a fact? You mean they have sanctioned it."

"Sanctioned what?"

"Carrying these rabbits."

"Anybody can carry rabbits."

The rifle barrel wavered. The men at the door moved uneasily. "You're wrong," said Simeon. "There are people in authority who have no idea these animals are here."

"Maybe they just didn't want to admit it to you," said Gaskell. "After all, you're just an . . ."

"Eccentric?" Simeon smiled. "But not too bizarre to be beyond use to you, huh? What did you want to do—give me a swing and tell me to broadcast to the world? And what was the message? That these poor creatures had put in sterling service for America? That they were heading for a well-earned rest and don't believe what people say about them being laboratory animals, tainted with bugs —was that it?"

Simeon surprised himself with the fluency of the speculation. But if the government wanted him saying something, what else? He was to smooth the way for the passage of the rabbits to their eventual destination. Why him? Goodness knows. But perhaps their choice had been spontaneous on seeing that he was still gullible enough to be chasing thunder lizards. If he could remember Playa 9, how much better could they?

Yet there had been no approach as such. Latimer? No, the train had already been in Green Town by the time he arrived. Official timing would have been rather more peremptory than that.

Then it had to be that they were so certain of the way he would react that they merely had to present him with the opportunity.

In which case, his speculation might be fluent but was way off the beam. Thus he had to try it for size.

"Anyway," he said. "They're not moving from here."

Rinehart smiled. "We could just get the engine started and take you with us."

The proper response should have been "Why?" or "How do you plan to do that?" The fact that they could smile and deflect him with parlance meant the situation was under control as far as they were concerned. Which, in turn, meant it had never been intended that the rabbits should leave Green Town . . . well, not immediately. Not until something had been done.

"No, you couldn't," he said. "That's not in your instructions. It's the old wagon train manoeuvre. Get the wall at your backs and then turn and fight—except in this case the wall is Green Town and your weapon, I suppose, is me. What happens when the fighting is over?"

Gaskell was at a loss and Rinehart was admitting to nothing.

"Why don't you just give us the gun and go?" said Gaskell eventually.

"Is that to be taken as an indication that I've hit the nail on the head?"

"It's to be taken as an indication that all this talk is futile and weighing pretty heavily on my patience."

Simeon didn't expect them to admit his summation had been accurate. At the same time, if they had expected him to come to them and receive their instructions, where did he stand now, with no word coming from either of them?

"I'm not leaving," he said, on the edge of desperation. Tired mind trying to recall. Something unscheduled. Something that hadn't been all cut and dried and laid out ready to catch him.

The gun.

And he started with the recollection. And the thing jumped in his hand, hammered his ribs and filled the deathly quiet piggyback with noise.

Gaskell and Rinehart had frozen. They were watching him with a mixture of expressions but no assurance. He looked for some evidence of a wound. They were pale, shaken but alive. The bullet, in fact, had passed between Gaskell's outstretched arm and his chest and on into the night and that was as close as he wanted to know anything about.

The challenge now was to recover faster than they could, to make use of the initiative he had created to jerk some revelation from them.

"If you think I wouldn't shoot you, you've been misinformed," he said. "And when your precious cargo gets held up here, it won't be anything attributable to me, just due process of law."

"In other words," said Rinehart, "there's some kind of judge on the way here with a restraining order. How else did you think we could be so sure of staying—and securing the spotlight for you? Now whatever you're planning to do next with that gun, these animals have to be fed and I'm about to do it."

Simeon stood up and his stability, he was pleased to observe, was marvellous. Even the limb treachery of returning circulation didn't unsteady him. It didn't matter that inside he was sagging.

"I came to find out and I found out," he said with dignity. "Furthermore, I'm telling you I know what you want me to do and I won't be doing it."

Then he went to the door of the piggyback and swung himself carefully to the ground. They made way for him.

Walking away, he heard Rinehart say, "What do you think? A climb-down? He's not so anxious to shoot after all."

Gaskell kept his counsel till Simeon was out of earshot and then would only say, "Forget about the gun because that was a prop in a strange place. The fact is, the guy still thinks he has a choice."

For Simeon, the stupid weapon which weighed him down on the right side had but one purpose now: it must be returned.

He was on his way to the house in West Bonnie Brook Lane, where he would not find Charles Woodman. He would not see the judge again until many things had been made clear to him.

The desk sergeant at City Hall was less than helpful to Mayor Roger Mortis. Attorney Theo Elmwood was out somewhere on a call with Judge Woodman, so that shut down any access to legal prerogatives.

Sure, he'd been told of the street demonstration earlier on and had made all the right noises. But it had cleared up, hadn't it? And he'd been looking at the clock. And all of a sudden he had to go and see Judge Woodman in a police cruiser he had borrowed.

Something wrong with his own car? Not that the desk sergeant knew.

Strange? Mayor Mortis couldn't waste time wondering about any other machinations. "Give me Dancey, then," he said.

Clement Dancey was the Green Town chief of police, a good and reliable public servant but having not quite the astute demeanour required by Mortis. Nevertheless . . .

"Clem," greeted the mayor.

"Good evening, Mr. Mortis."

"Just a few thoughts about this unsettling business in town earlier on."

"We had the situation under control," said Dancey quickly.

"I don't question that," Mortis assured him. "No, this isn't a censure call, Clem. As I said, just a few thoughts. Have you had a report on the incident?"

"I was there myself, sir. I reported to myself."

"Sorry, Clem. In the crowd, I didn't—"

"I heard you. I considered you handled matters with a great deal of diplomacy."

"Thank you. In fact, I didn't know the first thing about what was going on. What was this . . . lethal consignment . . . they were on about?"

"No information on that at all. I have men in liaison with the college police now in the hope they can pick up some data on campus."

Mortis lowered the handpiece and looked at it. If the man could provide no answer, was there any point in prolonging the conversation?

Another thought. "Clem, if there were any hazardous materials being shipped through Green Town, wouldn't you be notified?"

"Not necessarily. Only if an infringement seemed likely."

"The suggestion here is that one seems likely."

"With respect, Mr. Mayor, that allegation has to come from a proper source."

"And don't you consider each Green Town citizen a proper source?"

Dancey laughed at the other end of the line. Somehow that irritated Mortis more than his ordeal by students. "What the heck's to laugh at?"

Dancey pulled himself together quickly. "I'm sorry, sir, I didn't know you were serious. If I can be frank with you—"

"Please do," said the mayor icily.

"Well, according every Green Town inhabitant the position of 'proper source,' 'solid citizen,' 'upstanding fellow,' call him what you like, may be good stuff to catch the voters but in the guardianship and public order, we have to be somewhat cautious about what we accept as reliable. Any claims from the student fraternity need close investigation in themselves before we even start dealing with violations allegedly caused. You know what I mean, sir. One of those people tonight tried to fool the crowd into believing you had issued a denial and that was downright dishonest. We could use up a valuable portion of our time and allotment if we chased every lion that was supposed to be loose in the streets . . ."

Mortis drew a deep breath and resolved an early end to the exchange. Everybody wanted to talk politics. "Time and allotment . . ."

"So the short answer is that you can't help me."

"Not yet, sir. As soon as the information is to hand, I'll contact you."

"Thank you," said Mortis, "and good night."

His palms were moist and the familiar ache had started up in his right side. The local police force didn't have the information or even, it appeared, the enthusiasm. Or the time. Or the allotment.

That left him one alternative, having persuaded himself that he had eliminated all others. It is doubtful whether any subsequent authority would have considered his choice wise or even made with the correct amount of objectivity.

He called the governor of Illinois, William Forrester. At mid-

152

night—which gave it the ring of urgency and the priority of an assassination.

Forrester was immediately alert, though the bedroom swam before hastily raised head and the nausea of hypertension upturned his stomach. "Yes, Mr. Mortis."

"I'm sorry to disturb you, Governor . . ." And his mouth went dry. Was it worth ringing bells in far Springfield?

"It's all right, Roger. I know you wouldn't call without it was something important."

"Tonight," said Mortis lamely.

"Yes?"

"Student unrest."

"Say no more, Roger. You need the National Guard. I'll have a couple of companies mobilised. They're not far away from you—"

"Not immediately."

"You're coping? Excellent, Roger."

"No. Yes . . . the present disturbance has been checked. There is a possibility of more. I'd like your need to summon the guard if and when the need arises."

"As you wish. Meanwhile, I'll get an officer along to you to weigh up your needs."

"The morning," said Mortis, "will do."

"The morning will do, huh?" said Governor Forrester and replaced the phone and laid down his unquiet head. He felt sick but Mayor Mortis felt sicker.

Even so, his task for the rest of the night was clear now.

He went and got himself a tall glass of clear lemon juice, drank it and felt marginally better.

He must build up his case for calling the governor, who thought at the moment that it was bed-wetting.

By the time morning came, he wanted a complete scenario from Elmwood or Woodman or both.

In his present discomfort, he could not know, did not dare even to hope, that the scenario was going to prove so convincing.

He finished the last of the lemon juice and called back on the dozy desk sergeant.

A knock on the door and it was Lucia, veiled against the night. Mrs. Dilger prodded her through into Julie's presence with a flurry of curlers and a silence that was positively verbose in regard to girls who walked alone at this time of the night.

"Is she all right?" asked Lucia after the door had closed.

"She's fine," said Julie. "She just doesn't understand that we live different hours. I guess older people never do and one day we'll be older people wanting our sleep and we won't understand it either. So . . ."

Which meant she was waiting to hear the reason for Lucia's visit.

"Frank wants to see Simeon," said the girl. "No political side-effects. He just knows something he says will benefit us all. By the way, did you know you were being followed? At least, you're not now because the follower's—"

"Followed?" Julie was puzzled. "Why?"

"Because you're Tomorrow Julie."

"You keep saying that. It's no reason. . . ."

"That's the reason he gave. Simeon has a tail, too. They're Japanese."

"Japanese?" Julie's perplexity was being replaced by a slow chill of misgiving. There was no surprise; if they were Japanese, they had to be connected with the rabbits and she had known from stepping into Green Town that Simeon would find trouble eventually even if it was only by making sure trouble found him. "Again, why?"

"I . . . I think Frank wants to tell Simeon that himself. I don't quite grasp all the connotations."

Julie made an over-all gesture. "Simeon's not here. I don't know where he is but it's nowhere bad. He'll tell me when he gets back."

"But you don't know how long that will be, I suppose. . . . Julie, do you mind if I use the telephone?"

"It's in the hall. Watch when you pick it up or you'll startle Mrs. Dilger and you may not get the peace you want."

"I'll pay her."

"No need. Our rental takes account."

"Well, I'm only ringing Frank. I think he'd better get over here and wait with me."

Julie had a sudden Mrs. Dilger thought about Lucia walking alone along dark streets. "Wouldn't it have been easier for him to come?"

"No."

"No?" Julie was thwarted. "That's a straight answer."

"I don't talk about Frank's business. . . . And that's not an admonition, Julie. I just don't . . . absorb . . . it well enough to talk about it. He's had this Japanese man with him since late afternoon —just after you left. He stopped following you and knocked on our door—and then a crowd from the college came to tell Frank there was an activist they didn't know breathing fire in Orville's and J.B.'s about this tainted freight at the rail depot. Frank was surprised but his Japanese friend wasn't.

"Then when Frank heard they were performing in the street and the Riot Act was being read, he wanted to get out and see what it was all about.

" 'Forget it,' said this stranger. 'I'll tell you what it's all about— and I doubt whether you could find this "activist" anyway because he had orders to get in and do the job and get out fast.'

"So he told Frank the reason and that is what Frank wants to tell Simeon. . . . I'd better get him over here."

Lucia went away down the stairs and Julie could hear her dialling and Mrs. Dilger's door open and shut as note was taken.

"Hello, Frank?" said Lucia. "Simeon isn't here and Julie doesn't know when he'll be back. Best if you come over and wait, I think. Will you bring—your friend? . . . No, I guess not. . . . Well, we've got beds, Frank. . . . I don't know if he—do they? . . . You know, Frank, I mean do they sleep okay on mattresses? . . . Yes, that's it. Thank you, Frank. Show him the bedroom and tell him to do what he likes with it. . . . Ten minutes, then. . . ."

The front door opened and Simeon came into the hall, blinking against the bright light.

"Frank . . . Frank? He's here now."

Simeon found his vision, saw the girl at the telephone, noticed how her hand fled now to her hair, knew her from what Julie had told him.

"Hello," he said. It's all right to show her that you know her, he thought wearily. But not because of anything distinctive. Don't say "You must be Lucia" as though she has it emblazoned on her forehead or at least down her cheek. "Were you—waiting for me?"

And Julie called them both up the stairs and rescued Simeon and made an entirely unnecessary introduction just to keep the right feeling.

"I . . . I heard all about what you did at Playa 9," said Lucia.

"My role's been inflated," said Simeon. "The hurricane did a lot more."

Lucia let him have his modesty if he wanted it. "My husband is Frank Lorensen," she said, and Simeon was at a loss again because the name meant only what Julie had told him about the man and he wanted to be an authority on it and congratulate Lucia on her choice.

"You'll remember Frank from 1970," prompted Julie. "The Anderson house on West Eleventh Street, New York . . . Frank was working on tactical bombing devices."

Simeon grasped the straw. "An explosion," he said, trying to make it sound like a memory.

"That's right," put in Lucia.

"But I remember they said everyone was killed," ventured Simeon. He saw the shadow of pain cross Lucia's face. "I'm sorry. Obviously—"

"The only people found were dead," said Julie. "Lucia and Frank lost good friends."

"I . . ." Simeon wanted to put forward some kind of comfort but was finding himself enmeshed in a time-warp of his own. "I caused an explosion once. On the beach below Point Conception. People were . . . hurt . . . then. It's never worth the effort but you don't find out until afterwards. You have your eyes set on some distant good and all of a sudden you're injuring your close companions."

That wasn't exactly how it had been with Famous Gogan, the second-hand poet of Playa 9, but Simeon had wanted the matter mellowed for his recollection. Famous Gogan was close enough— as close as any man Simeon had wronged. He wondered where the man was now but would not know, could not know that Gogan was out of reach, in Italy, in a garden of few delights.

Lucia's voice pierced the time-warp. "It isn't all bad. There are compensations."

"Lucia . . ." Julie sounded on the edge of a warning.

A knock on the door and it was Frank. "Frank," said Lucia. "We were just talking about you."

And Julie couldn't finish her warning and Frank knew where he stood, anyhow, even if he was presently unaware of Lucia's ambiguity.

He took Simeon's hand. "You know, I thought I collected trouble, but you . . . Have you ever thought of becoming a Weatherman?"

Simeon chuckled. "Never been asked. Maybe one day—"

"How about now? When you hear what I have to say to you,

you'll think my antagonism to the establishment is a virtue." Frank released Simeon's fist.

"My own stance is pretty well known," said Simeon mysteriously. "In fact, I'd say very well known, just lately. But drinks! Julie"— Julie got ready to bustle—"supply the Lorensen needs and I'll have beer in a tall glass. I'm not without a little information of my own. But we'll let the guests speak first."

He sat Lucia in the cupola room's one easy chair, directed Frank to a straight chair and sat on the edge of the bed, leaving space beside him for Julie. When she had poured and the others had possessed their glasses, on an impulse he turned out the lights and let the Green Town night shine in.

"We often do this," he said. "It's what cupolas are for."

The gesture was noble. The action meant that Lucia could look out if she wanted and the gloom rendered her a measure of equality. He wanted to see that defensive hand come to rest in her lap.

"I . . . Do you know"—Lorensen was entering into the spirit of it —"I'm not even sure we don't have a cupola in our house. I don't often go beyond the first floor."

"We have four," said Lucia quietly. "Two at the front and two at the back."

Lorensen laughed. "Then we must use them."

"I do."

"Then I must."

"Frank." Lucia was still as far away. "When are you going to tell Simeon?"

Simeon made a great play of lowering the beer in his glass. "My fault," he said. "I changed the subject."

Lorensen moistened his own throat. "I've had a man with me for some hours today and he's a Japanese. He knows you or, rather, he knows of you. He also has several insights into the situation your wife outlined to us. But what he really has is a whole lot of data which will be completely new to you. This is an eye-opener."

Simeon and Julie perched like statues on the bed. Lucia had given her total attention to the Green Town neon geography.

"It seems," continued Lorensen, "that the Japanese are backing up this rabbit consignment with two hundred Hiroshima victims, mutated but walking and rehabilitated. They're calling it a goodwill gesture, only our government doesn't know much about it yet."

Simeon was breathless and he knew Julie must be the same way. "But . . . why?"

"To show they don't bear us a grudge."

"Is that what he said? I don't believe it."

"I didn't myself. I complained I couldn't follow his reasoning and he said that was because I was Occidental and it made good sense to his own government."

"But surely"—Julie was so tense that she was vibrating like a bow string—"nobody in America is going to see it the way the Japanese want it seen. We're too . . . set in our ways."

"Which are?" Lorensen led them on to see if their reaction followed his own.

"Keep your freaks out of sight," said Simeon. "Like your mistakes."

"And how do you read that?"

"Somebody's anxious that the whole weight of America's guilt will be brought home to her. Look, I don't have much time for a lot of things done in the name of the U.S., but this is—is thirty years too late. We're not in a war context any more."

"Wrong."

"Why wrong? We're not fighting Japan."

"We just claimed another casualty."

"I don't follow you."

"The rabbits," Lorensen reminded him.

"What about the rabbits?"

"They're not from Japan, they're from Okinawa. Our biological warfare experts have filled them up with Yeze fever and one of the rabbits got away and killed an islander."

"Sweet . . ." Momentarily, Simeon was in a blind panic. He had sat within inches of the creatures. He had carried the germ. He had infected how many?

Along the landing and into the bathroom. He scrubbed at his hands with pumice stone until the skin was going and then he was sick into the toilet. By that time, Julie was with him, pulling persistently at his arm. "You're all right."

"How do you know? How does anybody . . . ?" But the events of the night had started clicking away in his mind like a newsreel.

If anybody knew how lethal the animals were, it was the people looking after them. Gaskell and Rinehart had come without special

158

clothing or even gloves. Latimer had handled them and come to Green Town unharmed.

He returned to the room feeling vaguely foolish. Thankfully, the light was still off to cover his embarrassment.

"My information was that these were laboratory animals," he said. "Nothing about biological warfare. It seems to me if we've just killed another Japanese, they've a right to retaliate. We ought to be thankful they didn't elect MIRVs."

Lorensen was thoughtful. "So you're not annoyed."

"My public indignation is not aroused. We deserve an eye-opener."

"But why would you say they were taking so much notice of you?"

Simeon spent a few seconds rerunning the evening. It appeared now that there were two agencies cultivating a close interest in him. Did the one know about the other? And was it intention or coincidence?

"You say the American Government doesn't know much about this business of the survivors."

"That's what my informant said. But I had a correspondence this morning that made it look very much as though the Pentagon does have information and is releasing is to a controlled few."

"For what purpose?"

"They want to be sure the spontaneous reaction is well organised."

"Do you think the Japanese could have fed it to them?"

"Possible. And if they did, it's because they're hoping for the same kind of reaction."

Simeon found beer in the bottom of his glass and lingered over it. He had both versions and they were going to take a lot of sifting. Much of the development was parallel as he looked at it now. But where there was variance . . . ? What did it mean? One thing.

"One thing," he said. "The Yanks don't know I'm on the Japanese calling list as well."

"How can you be sure of that?"

"I was with the rabbits tonight. In their freight-car. With their keepers. I had an idea that they were making it very easy for me to find things out and what I discovered tonight confirmed it. Bringing these rabbits to me was a set-up—an American set-up. They thought if the truth about the rabbits leaked out—at least, the 'truth' that they were laboratory animals—I'd be there to provide a focus for attention. That's how they planned it and they acted as though they had the situation very much under control.

"I went there with the judge's rifle and a half-cocked idea that I was going to scare them into some kind of admission by telling them I had taken steps to insure the animals were not going to leave town. That was exactly what they wanted. In fact, they were ahead of me."

"And why do you think they came to you?"

"I triggered a situation once and I suppose they thought I could do it again."

"And what about the Japanese?"

"I don't know."

"The same," said Julie from the window. She had been trying to match her gaze and her detachment to Lucia's but it was impossible with the men's words drumming away at her.

Besides, there was a familiar kind of burning deep down within her. Familiar from three years back when she thought Simeon couldn't possibly emerge as any kind of victor.

Then it had been only a stretch of polluted coastline, a mute and malfunctioning desalination plant to take the rap, and a handful of not very smart civil servants. Now it was the intelligences of two great countries and a pair of potential dilemmas that could spike any powder keg with cobalt.

Lorensen and Lucia went home. Julie let Simeon put her to bed and did not insist that he join her. He sat for a long time in the chair lately occupied by Lucia, with his eyes cast in a similar direction.

He had not made the sharp comparison that had so unnerved Julie, though she slept easily enough now, with all energy drained out of her. But he knew this was the biggest and he had his own doubts about his ability to produce a solution that would appease both of his masters or at least reduce each of them to an inactive level.

Just before weariness came and filled his eyelids with sandy ballast and dropped them over his eyes, he was back to thinking of the old firm—Halloway and Nightshade, Spaulding and Bradbury.

Bloodsong with Poppy Dawn

Simeon and Tomorrow Julie had escaped to the country deeps, the grass tides which had broken on Green Town in the childhood of Simeon's hero with a force that carried great sprays of prairie over the suburban breakwaters and laid them down as natural picnic grounds, parks, golf courses, moon meadows.

In fifty years the tide had turned with the currents flowing from people into pastureland and the grass going down beneath concrete headstone and copper oxide poison.

So far, but no farther.

Simeon had grabbed Julie from bed at dawn, swathed her in gingham with a wool wrap against the chill, urged her bodily into the hired truck and driven west—west until the roadside flowers became more regular than the buildings. They stopped beside one of the streams that emptied thirty wandering miles later into Lake Geneva.

At breakfast time, he had her sitting with a black-eyed Susan threaded into her hair and her hands full of asters and blazing stars while he fed her with Woodstock cheese and new bread.

"I love you," he said.

"Fine," she said. "Now what?"

"I . . ."

"You'd like not to talk about it."

"Yes."

"But you can't leave it alone. I know you well enough for that, Sim—and don't worry about me as long as you include me in."

"Julie, you know you're invaluable to me."

High time something was said of their love. In three years it had changed—at Point Conception, they had both needed a strength and a stability and would not have thought to find it in each other. Hunger drove them together—a hunger that was as much a part of the circumstances as any malnutrition of emotions.

And when the circumstances were removed? There was a mellowness, an afterglow because they had shared something bigger than a physical issue.

Simeon was a better man for his marriage, thoughtful of his prize, clear of inhibitions. Where he had sat and stuttered and sweated upon the Playa 9 swing, convincing himself that this was the only way to make words, the three years had brought the luxury of discussion.

Julie, who had only ever asked that he confide in her, found herself entrusted with the mechanics of his life and was satisfied. He did not rely on her, burdening her with the responsibility of living for him, but gave her credit for an intellect at least as able as his own and treasured her advice although, as it happened, his own was usually more than sufficient.

It was the ideal growth, then; not one the stalk and one the stick but both complementary, like the clumps of big bluestem along this stream terrace—beard grass, wheat grass and dropseed.

By the time they had finished eating, the sun was warm on Julie's back and the butterflies were beginning to traffic among the ironweed.

Simeon was laid out upon the bank, apparently at peace.

"It's beautiful," Julie said quietly, and then, by way of a broaching, "I guess it hasn't changed much in—fifty years?"

"A thousand years."

"Fifty would do," said Julie. " 'Here was where the big summer-quiet winds lived and passed in the green depths, like ghost whales, unseen. . . . In that silence, you could hear wildflower pollen sifting down the bee-fried air.' "

"That was the forest," amended Simeon.

"Do you think I don't know? The buckets of dandelion wine I've drunk? The times my harvest has fallen to the silver locusts?"

Simeon was aware that she was admonishing him gently and fondly. "I'm sorry for all those lost times," he said. "But why . . . ?"

"For you to correct me. You know it is no good until you start talking. Admit this is why we're so far gone in country deeps, we drown in tides of sleep that escape the towns."

Simeon plucked a stem of wild rye and chewed on it.

"Still hungry?" urged Julie.

He was thoughtful. Now that the time had come to talk some

sense into his lurking fear, he was . . . "Hungry like I haven't been since Playa 9."

And when Julie looked crestfallen, he hastened to add, "Please, baby, nothing to do with us. Just—a void of inadequacy. I haven't had that feeling in three years, largely thanks to you."

"This time I can't help?"

Simeon found his feet, found her lips. "I'm sure you can," he said. "First we have to appraise the problem."

"Then start."

"Well, it began with one man—the man I came here to find. You know, I honestly think that, left to my own devices, I could have reconciled myself to the changes since the days of Halloway and Spaulding, but . . . The judge said it. Julie, he did actually put his finger on it, that guy with the name straight out of page twelve. 'Find the right whimsy and genocide is in your grasp,' he said. But he couldn't possibly have known . . . The things that have happened now seem to have a kind of logic about them, a pattern entirely in keeping with my state of mind when I arrived. . . . As though someone was trying to make the best of a situation and lit upon me was a scapegoat—and not for the first time."

"The same people as before?"

"It's possible—it's all government. In any event, I played right into their hands."

"With the business in the library? But how did they know you were coming here?"

"They didn't, not then. I think I was received here in all innocence and any comparisons were of my own making. But that business made the newspapers and jogged a few memories. The design started at that point. Play a little game with me."

Simeon had dropped back onto his knees now, regarding his wife earnestly. "From what you know of Ray Bradbury's work, try and make a link with what I'm saying."

Julie shifted the flowers from her lap and dusted her hands. "Any particular book?" By the prickling of my thumbs . . .

"Try *Something Wicked This Way Comes* . . . Train."

"Well . . . train."

"Good. Rabbits."

"Menagerie?"

"The two men who told me they were carrying bullion."

"Cooger and Dark."

"The helicopter."

"The Monster Montgolfier—and the Dust Witch?"

"Whoever sent Frank Lorensen those posters."

"*The Illustrated Man?*"

"Not quite, Julie. Try again."

This one took a little time before Julie proffered, "The lightning-rod salesman."

"Great . . . you're doing so well. . . . The student protesters."

"Are *they* the illustrated men?"

"I'm not too sure, but take it they are. Frank had an idea we Americans would be putting a few of our more spectacular factions on show. Like whom?"

"If it *is* a protest, it'll be vigilantes. The Ku Klux Klan?"

"A good possibility. Where would they fit?"

"Grand Wizard. Every show needs a wizard."

"The Cooger and Dark Show didn't."

"Then . . . I don't know."

"What do they do?" prodded Simeon. "I don't want to keep pushing you, love, but I must hear these things from somebody else. They must be visible to somebody else the same way they are to me."

"The KKK make mayhem," said Julie.

"Pandemonium . . . And if they're faceless, what are they like?"

"Ghosts? No . . . shadows. The pandemonium shadow show. That one's a little baroque, Sim."

"It's not the last. . . . The Hiroshima survivors."

Julie shivered, despite the climbing sun. "I don't like to call them . . ."

"Freaks? Then don't. They're Special Attractions, like Vesuvio, the Lava Sipper, the Skeleton of the Dwarf."

"It could mean nothing." Julie was positively shaken now.

"It could mean everything . . . and behind the whole mess, somebody controlling our every gesture, working us like . . ."

"Fantoccini," said Julie. Then she wept.

Simeon went down to the stream and moistened a cloth. He returned and cooled Julie's forehead and feverish cheeks. "Good will triumph."

"How do we know what is good any more? Perhaps this display of fine feeling from the Japanese is good and meant to make for peace and love. Perhaps these rabbits are coming home for their own good. The pull-out from Okinawa, if it renders some part of the world less war-like, must be good. . . . When you're writing a book, you can *make* your heroes and villains. In real life, it's not that simple. Maybe *we'd* be the villains if we tried to do anything at all."

"Julie . . . we're innocent people and we are being manipulated. That's not a virtuous thing."

"We could be mistaken. It could be all in the mind—on the other hand, it could be a comeback for what we did three years ago, which seemed so noble but was just vandalism blessed with eloquence. . . ."

Simeon was thunderstruck. "Is that what you really think? That fine and wondrous time that brought us within touching distance of each other—that was vandalism?"

Julie was weeping afresh—against him rather than for him. "If you hadn't been involved then, you wouldn't be involved now. Nobody would have remembered you—"

"Then you see there's a link?"

"Don't try to catch me out, Simeon. All I want is for us to be left alone and you keep—keep gathering a crowd. . . ."

She was on her feet now, plunging calf-deep along the bed of the stream. Simeon let her go, knowing she would not run far. He counted to sixty, followed slowly and found her huddled on the bank, bedraggled and cried out.

She just said, "Hold me."

By noon, their clothes had dried on them and Julie was restored to something approaching good humour. Simeon had not tried to approach the subject again, though some inner clock was telling him the time left for action was ticking away.

"We can't leave it like that," Julie said eventually and he wanted to kiss her and hold her all over again, but it would have seemed he thought not of her but of the situation. "What would your friend Ray Bradbury have done?"

"A fortunate accident or two, a fairy-tale finish and virtue is its own reward. All spiked with poetry to make it sweet."

"And where does that leave us?"

"Nowhere—because fairy-tales and accidents and poetry don't apply. What is needed is superior wisdom. Bradbury had it when I didn't. Now—well, he hasn't spoken for a long time about Green Town."

"So the saviour turned out to be a plain old historian."

Simeon's despair. "Yes. I guess they knew that when they mounted this charade. There's no black marquee to topple, no merry-go-round to smash. And this time, I can't even depend on a hurricane. When Bradbury wished, it worked. I wish . . ."

Julie ran her hand down his bare arm, linked her fingers with his. "There are only things the way they are. . . ."

They left the prairie without resolution and without haste as though something precious had been taken there and set free.

They had made rendezvous at Milwaukee, the place being fairly accessible without the problems of Chicago and now they came south down the shore of Lake Michigan, singing Southern Baptist hymns—"Guide Me, O Thou Great Redeemer."

They were only semi-robed for the journey because you can't sing well beneath a flour-sack hood with holes cut for the eyes. The coach had been hired by Greyhound to a business organisation and as far as that went they could be Freemasons or candle-stick-makers or KKK; it was business within the meaning of the Act.

So the driver kept smiling secretly, himself an irony, reading more irony into their words.

Redemption. A strange word to find on the lips of a Klansman. Then, maybe not so strange because your justification was the removal of an evil and the salvation of a good. Where people differed was in their definition of the two poles.

Sam Gregory had not asked for an explanation of their journey and had not been given one. He had made up his mind they were convening somewhere quieter than Chicago, where puny law agencies might be suitably reluctant to deal with seventy sinister vigilantes. Over and above that, his commitment was to transport them to Green Town and keep them safe from turnpike clowns. It was as far as he was prepared to go.

Slade Dexter was happy. There were familiar faces here from Alabama, including his brother-in-law, Clem Goldwater. Dexter had been careful not to mention the likelihood of a meeting to Louella, Clem's sister.

The first flush of reunion was past now and the voices back and front down both sides of the bus were losing volume. A half-hearted "Rock of Ages" finished the hymn-singing. The men studied the scenery or talked quietly to their neighbours. In the stretch between Racine and Kenosha the conversation started turning towards the job in hand.

"Did they telephone you?" Dexter asked Clem, in the adjacent seat.

"No, telegram. Telegram asking me to call them collect."

"I can't understand why they didn't do that with me."

"It's not really such a mystery, Slade. You're almost one of them. I mean, an officer of a government agency. I guess they knew they could count on you."

"And why the Department of Defence?"

"Yeah . . . well . . . that threw me for a while. But no doubt it is as they say. In the interests of national security, we are required to indicate our presence."

"I don't know, Clem."

"Look . . . they knew enough about us to be able to find us, right? They know what we are and what we stand for and that's how they want us to be. Because that's how we're of use to them. It's for the good of America, Slade. We don't have to question it."

"I'm not sure. They don't even tell us very much about it."

"How much do we need to know? Look, I don't mind telling you, Slade, I'm glad to be back rendering some kind of sacred service. I sit there in my television store and I go deeper and deeper into debt because those ghetto people in Montgomery don't bother to pay their way. The law says I can't refuse their business unless there's a known trade violation against them and I say I can't pursue my money because it costs too much. I'm giving myself another ulcer bitching over that insoluble when up comes the DOD with a new situation I can help to contain. Man, I feel positively relieved."

Dexter shifted a cramped leg. "That says a lot of how I feel. But I still don't understand how we're to neutralise these Japs. Just stand there and look at them? Show them our carbines? I don't follow the reasoning. Heck, the Imperial Wizard looks more Jap than they do."

"And maybe there's something in that."

"What? We should even beat them at looking Japanese? What kind of dumb patriotism is that?"

"Slade, sometimes I wonder how you're got the brains to be a cop. . . . The Japanese have kicked us out of Okinawa. They have made us bring our rubbish back to our own trash-can—don't you read the papers? This is the insult added to the injury or—if you accept the Nipponese version—it's a goodwill delegation to show there are no hard feelings. They don't want our armour but they do want our trade. Now, we don't need their trade and we don't need their delegation and that yen gesture of five years ago was never meant to last forever. I guess the DOD just want us to show these little guys they're not welcome."

"And how do we do that?"

"By being there. By displaying solidarity with the administration."

"Couldn't we do that militarily?" Frank Jesse, Clem's chaptermate from Montgomery was leaning across the aisle.

"The whole idea is that we don't," said Clem. "That's the way I see it. We are a sector of public opinion. This is our strength."

"We're articles in the showcase?" asked Slade.

They settled back and thought about it.

Five miles out of Green Town, Bradford Williams, the Territorial Wizard, rose from his front seat, considered the effect of a bullhorn within the confined space and elected a loud but unmagnified voice.

"You all know why we're here," he said by way of introduction.

"Because we want to be," said somebody at the back, more to show that the T.W.'s remarks were carrying than to open up a dialogue.

"And what we are doing is right in the eyes of heaven."

This time there was no response. Each of the seventy had tried to study his motivation, some with more success than others. The confused were slightly less wicked than the committed. The counterfeit suggestion of a divine benediction went a long way to helping them make up their minds.

"The pagan is come amongst us," said Williams, warming to his theme, "and we are the sword of the Lord, felling the ungodly."

"What's he mean?" Slade Dexter in a whisper. "Who's felling?"

"Render unto Caesar those things which are Caesar's. Thus we are ordered. And the word from our Caesar, our great government, is that they have vital work for us to do in allaying the pagan. We are mindful of the privilege we have been given. We are determined to fill that commission to capacity. We will not falter in the face of their might . . ."

"Are they armed?" Clem Goldwater, apprehensively.
"Does Brad know something we don't?" Frank Jesse.
"Quiet." His friend from Birmingham.
"Action?" A primitive from Georgia.
"Judgment?" A Tennessee fundamentalist.

A steelworker from Detroit, a tin miner from Arkansas, a farmer from Wisconsin, a teacher from Indiana, a paper salesman from across the lake felt slight jolts as though their reasoning was derailing.

"And we *kill* . . ."

Kill?

Kill!

I don't like it. Not a few of them yielded a doubt, each one ignorant of the other. Because they could not be sure of their fellow-travellers, they shut their mouths on their tongues and let the order stay unchallenged.

Kill! Was that the government talking? And they could do it with impunity?

Sam Gregory watched his Negro knuckles go pale on the wheel of the bus, paying little attention to turnpike clowns. No need. He had a busload of the biggest.

Zebedee Company of the Illinois National Guard had been sleeping under canvas for three days, albeit in the shelter of the Janesville Greenwood Stadium, and several of them were no longer convinced of the virtue of their calling.

Teamster trouble had dragged them from their homes and their jobs and put them on a $30-a-day stipend while they scorched out some militant truckmen and stopped them shooting holes in the tyres of dispute-breaking container lorries.

It was a gruelling mixture of frustration and futility. The teamsters had their radios tuned to the citizen wave-band and its regular traffic reports, so they knew the movements of the turnpike schooners at the same time as the troops and could anticipate them a lot better, being of the breed.

Saloons would emerge from side-streets, filter among traffic, burst a few heavy-treads and be away before the Guard could get to them.

The idea was to move the trucks in convoy, with every fifth lorry spaced out by a jeepful of part-time soldiers. In addition, marksmen were placed along overpasses between Madison and Rockford. But that, in itself, was a weakness with a lot of space to cover and too few bodies for total effectiveness.

And the guys riding shotgun were less than happy. Any sniper who could wing a tyre and flee unseen could just as easily wound a guardsman, and the insurance they carried from the state legislature was hardly enough for the immediate discomfort of a slight injury, let alone the extinction of life.

Besides, the teamsters' manoeuvres were not always in the good clean tradition of conventional warfare. The first day out, a few jackets had disappeared from their tent town, probably filched by a stadium employee with a brother in the trucking business.

Anyway, when they tried to check home that night, two of the wives weren't answering the phone and the others told tearful tales of heavy breathing and foul-mouthed suggestions.

The question the wives asked—the question the guardsmen now asked—was: "What are you protecting out there when you should be home protecting us?" It was a question to which the only answer was veiled in the obscurity of the situation.

This was a union dispute and the only justification for their involvement was that the Highway Patrol was too busy with other duties and the safety of the community was paramount to their brief.

Even so, they took some convincing. And now, it seemed, there was to be another company formation with a new set of instructions. Captain James Ronald Gordon had been pulling his men off the roads and bridges all afternoon.

Now, 153 officers and men, all with the regulation six months of basic training, plus thirty-two hours of riot drill, plus varied amounts of OJT (on-the-job training), stood easy on the grass of the stadium expecting Captain Gordon to tell them anything except "You're going home."

A couple of the company's technicians had tried to get to the public-address system but somebody had locked up the control room and gone home—probably the same SOB who had taken the jackets.

So the captain was reduced to a bull-horn. And he had a great deal to say.

"First of all, men," he yelled, "I want to congratulate you on the

way you have been handling this teamster business. I know it isn't
our usual line of country and I know some of you—and your families
—have been required to exercise a tolerance and a devotion to duty
far above and beyond any such devotion sought from a civilian.

"I trust that soon we may all be able to rejoin our loved ones and
try to pick up the threads of a normal life.

"But first we have to occupy a standby condition in circumstances
that may be rather more familiar to you than these present ones."

He paused to drink deeply from a glass of water a non-com
handed him. The men shuffled their feet and waited.

"The administrative authorities at Green Town tell us they feel
there is a riot situation building up in their city. It is not strictly accurate to state at this stage that campus activists are providing the
flash point, though one might speculate that they will try to turn
the event to their advantage—"

"Not pigging students again," said the motor mechanic corporal
alongside Guardsman Conroy Mitchell. "Give me renegade truckers
any day. Boy, the way those co-eds swear—you'd never believe it.
Put me off going out with girls for a month when we tangled with
them on the North Chi campus. Do you remember?"

"Before my time," said Mitchell. Most things the company had
done were before his time and he wasn't sure he ever wanted his
time to start.

"You'll learn fast."

"Listen to the captain," said a non-com on the other side of the
corporal.

"It's been my practice," Captain Gordon was continuing, "to
point out to you our legal standing when it comes to commissions
of this nature.

"I am going to quote to you first from a pamphlet entitled 'Disturbance Control: Guidelines for Small Unit Commanders and
Troops.' You see, I need this briefing as much as you do."

The vaguest flicker of a smile here and there.

"It reads, 'Criminal sanctions may be imposed against any guardsman who exceeds his authority in accomplishing his mission. The
rule of "necessity" is the guide used to determine whether or not a
guardsman exceeds his authority. However, if acting in good faith
and pursuant to lawful orders, the guardsman's conduct is usually
not criminal!'"

The captain turned over pages. "Under the heading 'Troop Civilian Relations,'" he said, "I quote, 'The restoration of law and order in an Illinois city is not exactly a combat situation, but rather it is a situation wherein our guideline is minimum application of force consistent with our objective.'"

Leaf upon leaf as the captain found his dog-eared place: "The summary states, 'In a civil disorder, the Illinois National Guardsman continues to serve his state and country by restoring law and order and by providing an atmosphere where the rule of law will prevail. The successful accomplishment of this mission with a minimum of force must be recognised by the guardsman as one of great honour and service to his state and country.

"'And so the keynote of all operations aimed at the curtailment of civil disorder is restraint. The guardsman acts confidently and with a firmness, but he must gauge his action to the seriousness of the disorder he seeks to deter or contain.'"

The captain closed the pamphlet and shifted the heavy bullhorn to his other hand. "In accordance with procedure, I am going to give you the three occasions when you may fire your weapon. They are: when you feel your life is endangered; when ordered to do so by an officer; to save someone else's life.

"Since we are directed to maintain only a standby, there is not likely to be a fulfilment of any of these conditions. Nevertheless, it is my responsibility as your commanding officer to insure that you are all aware of the restrictions the law places on us."

He handed the loud-speaker to his communications non-com and went back to his quarters.

"It all sounds reasonable," said Mitchell.

"Huh." The corporal grunted as though he had special and greater knowledge. The sergeant beyond him in the line felt moved to make some kind of explanation for the apparent cynicism. "What Yorky means is that we've heard it many times before and it doesn't vary by a syllable."

"But if it's necessary—"

"It isn't necessary," said Yorky. "Most of it is common sense. The captain just has a sore spot like the rest of the brass over an occasion when things got a little out of hand."

"What—here?"

"No. In Ohio. May 4, 1970. Four students killed and nine injured at Kent State and they're talking yet over whether it was justified or whether a few guardsmen just got sick of getting the finger and

172

triggered a few rounds off the record. I reckon the bums got what they deserved. Where's your law and order when nobody respects the guy in uniform—"

"That's a long time ago, York," said the sergeant, drawing himself up. "It's no good for morale, the way you talk."

The corporal spat into the grass. "So we're getting formal, are we, Gus? How can you say it's a long time ago when we get that spiel every time we go into an operation?"

The sergeant looked at Mitchell. "How much OJT do you have, son?"

"Nothing in actual riot situations. Thirty-two hours in simulation."

"And did it make any impact with you?"

"Well, yes. I know you and Corporal York can probably repeat it word for word, but I hadn't heard it before. Like, read it, you know. But never . . . in an animated form. You know what I mean?"

The sergeant kicked out at York. "Do you get my point, Yorky? There's a couple of these on every trip we take. If there was only one, it would still be worth"—he looked at his watch—"fifteen minutes of your time."

The corporal spat again, as though he had been keeping something bitter in his mouth for the whole nine hundred seconds.

The Highway Patrol was too busy looking for a bus. They had a score of vehicles hard shoulder parked from Milwaukee to Green Town and the only reason the casual motorist wasn't getting away with murder was because no sooner had he got over the sight of one waiting cruiser than he was up to the next.

They worked as deterrents because they couldn't move. Not yet. Not till they began their relay pursuit behind the Greyhound loaded with the dragon brotherhood.

Each would follow the vehicle for a section, tailing off where the next in line took over. They kept radio contact with the Lake County sheriff's office and with each other. A patrol car on a busy road like the turnpike was not untoward. But the same pair of patrolmen, mile after mile, trailing the same bus was bound to mean something—particularly to the travellers in the bus.

So the patrolmen would vary their position in the southbound traffic, keeping the Greyhound in visual range. And the last in the line would follow clear into Green Town, where the local police force of seventy-four and special supplement of twenty-five would assume supervision.

"And what happens after that?" Patrolman Frank Apex in car 7D was asking his paper-chaser, Patrolman Ernest Bloch. Up and down the line, cruiser teams were popping the same question, sometimes the driver asking his buddy who filed the bulletins and took the messages, sometimes the other way about.

They had learned not to question too deeply the reasons for massive police operations but they could tell by the amount of mechanism involved that this was something almost unparalleled.

"We keep out of the way so that no toes get trodden on," said Bloch. "This one is so big, it's ridiculous. Five law agencies involved —local police, sheriff's office, campus police, National Guard and us. Something's bound to foul up."

"And all over a busload of KKK men."

"Frank, you know as well as I do that there's more to it than that. If that was all was involved, we could run the coach off the road now or at least give it an escort to where we wanted it to go."

"True, Ernie. And we don't because somebody somewhere wants it to get where it intends to go. There's a faultless military mind working behind this."

"Faultless?"

"I'm jesting, Ernie. I don't like only getting a ration of the information. I'll tell you something—I hope it *does* go wrong. Maybe next time they'll think to equip us a little better."

The short-wave fussed and buzzed. Bloch fiddled with tuners. "They have to fix this thing. It's our only bread and butter."

"Item," said the control voice, "has just quit Kenosha making sixty m.p.h. Should be with you, 7D, in six minutes twenty-five seconds. Don't look for 6D. He has a pepped-up '72 Mustang, a '74 Toyota and a '73 Cadillac between him and the suspect vehicle. You can move in closer than that—suggest one car distance. Out."

"Fantastic," said Apex, who had the task that made a circumlunar docking manoeuvre look simple. "Traffic coming past us at sixty. And we don't just have to get in behind the bus, but we have to pick our place, too. At a mile a minute."

"Child's play," said Bloch, "for a jockey like you."

"I'd like to hear if you've got any ideas."

"First of all, turn your ignition on."

"Get—"

"Careful, Frank. You'll need a cool head."

"You'll need an ice-pack. Right. I get into the slow lane. Suspect will be in the centre lane. I let it draw level and then turn on the gas and the flashing lights—and hope the hydraulics on the crates behind will take the strain."

"That's about all I can tell you, Frank."

"Don't know how I would have managed without you, Ernie."

Apex penetrated the slow lane while Bloch watched back over his shoulder, not trusting to roof and wing mirrors. They went up to forty and held it for around three minutes. Then . . .

"Coming up," said Bloch.

"Got it."

"Six vehicles . . . five, four, three, two, one . . ."

Apex hit the siren and blinker as the bulk of the coach cut out the light. The man in the Mustang had his eyes to the front and kept them on the tail of the Greyhound. Then car 7D swung out into the fast lane, with Apex gunning the motor.

The Cadillac had overtaken the Toyota at the last acceleration bay but they were both running close.

When the Caddy braked to let the patrol cruiser in, the following car was slow to take the caution. On Japanese instinct, the driver swerved left, struck the rear of the Caddy a glancing blow and was cantilevered across the central divider.

The oncoming leviathan in the northbound fast lane was spitting out bits for miles before the traffic behind would let him halt with his life.

By which time there wasn't much left to bury of the Nipponese who had been trailing Bradford Williams for two days—even a Kamikaze man likes to know when—and Apex and Bloch in 7D had handed on the chase to the next cruiser, none the wiser.

When the National Guard patrol vacated its post on one bridge spanning the turnpike, Clyde James took it over with his Tungsten rifle leaning at the ready behind one of the box girder supports, invisible from road level but handy enough if a turncoat trucker hove into view.

He didn't know where the Guard had gone and didn't much care. His role now was to spot offenders from his vantage point and signal the outriders parked at two points on the hard shoulder in the stretch of road behind him.

Whether he would get a chance to use his shooter again was speculative—a man with a gun on a bridge ahead of you lacks the surprise element of the man in the car who comes from the rear.

But no matter. Clyde had popped his fair share of heavy-duty cross-plies during the campaign so far and his cell chief had the report down in the log-book.

Clyde, like a large number of the membership, wasn't entirely *au fait* with all the niceties of the situation. He knew he, as a teamster, was supporting the longshoremen in another of their periodic container disputes and the justification offered to him was protection of job opportunities.

The Evans Refrigeration Pact of 1974 had laid down once and for all the responsibilities of the docker and the proper expectations of the trucker so that there should have been no mystery over demarcation.

But then, when diminishing U.S. commitments had put new stress on the dollar and the result had been contraction of labour, Furness Fresh Transit had decided they could not afford a teamster and an electrician for each of their freezer leviathans and had begun advertising for men qualified in both respects.

It looked like a clear violation of the Evans Pact but in fact new circumstances were calling several of the previous year's wisdoms into question.

It was a matter for a federal commission. There was, however, little haste in convening one since any judgment handed down was likely to alienate one or another section of the interested parties.

A series of disputes that year had eventually triggered the formation of a commission. It took more unrest to spark a representative calling of witnesses.

Now the pressure was on for some sagacity from the experts, and since each party might well consider itself about to be sold down the river, each had cause to begin a dispute whenever the mood took it.

Clyde James did not know that, not fully. And what he didn't know at all was that there was yet an even deeper layer of sinistration.

The American Federation of Labour-Congress of Industrial Organisations, as of four days ago, was enjoying another dalliance with the Central Intelligence Agency, acting in this instance as liaison for the NSA. This affair, predictably, had been prompted by the business on Okinawa.

The CIA/NSA was not merely insuring that no dockside trouble would arise that might draw attention to the livestock lately delivered to Bay City Terminal, San Francisco, and examined by Herb Latimer. On advice from Battle Creek, Michigan, they were making certain that any straying local focusses should be directed to this present flare-up.

In other words, the confrontation with the National Guard was a set-up. Clyde James didn't know anything about that.

In still further words, the student turbulence which had now necessitated the transfer of Zebedee Company from the turnpike to Green Town was not in the Battle Creek briefing—that was destiny working from a different, Tokyo-distant source.

All Clyde James knew was that the National Guard had moved out, leaving an enviable vantage point unoccupied and he had moved in with the blessing of his cell officials and presumably—because at this point they didn't know any different—their peers, the AFL–CIO.

Now, he straddled the traffic like a colossus, looking for renegade refrigerators.

The parade was mundane. Automobiles from every year out of the last decade, gasoline tankers, a Greyhound coach. And somewhere beyond it, a roof with ventilators turning.

He waited to make sure. Identification was difficult. It transpired the freezer truck wasn't carrying the Furness blue and white livery but an iceburg aquamarine. He ransacked his professional knowledge. Iceberg green. Jensen Cold Comfort, a Furness subsidiary.

He was just starting to turn back across the bridge to alert the outriders when he noticed the vehicle behind the coach—a Highway Patrol cruiser.

That put hit-and-run out of the question and left him with but one alternative.

Simeon and Tomorrow Julie had tracked to Lake Geneva and come east to the turnpike just below Kenosha. In the late afternoon, they were returning to Green Town, tingling from their day in the sun but with little conversation passing between them.

Clyde James watched the Greyhound pass beneath his feet, saw the prowl car nuzzling its tail and then reached for his Tungsten.

Jensen Cold Comfort loomed closer, like an iceberg itself with little whirling chimneys for the internal igloo village.

He sighted up on its right front wheel. His finger tightened on the trigger.

A piercing ray of light from the mirror of some north-going vehicle on the lane to his right took his aim out of true by a very small fraction.

His bullet ricocheted off the front grid of the truck in the heavy-traffic lane, hammered through the radiator of the little hired van in the middle lane, came up through the dashboard and made a large hole in Simeon's left arm before piercing the van roof and spending its momentum somewhere in the upper air.

Clyde James, breaking like a deer for the undergrowth, listened for the crunch and splinter of perishing juggernaut.

Police Chief Clement Dancey was furious. Apropos a call from the Lake County sheriff's office, he had stepped out upon Green Town to see a Greyhound bus disgorging hooded men.

The Highway Patrol had kept him informed of the Greyhound's passage. His compact, well-drilled force was ready. There would be no gun-play. The men would be herded back into the coach and returned whence they came.

You couldn't arrest a man for putting on a flour sack, and the ramifications if you attempted to moralise or purge were unscaleable. Let them go home, let them keep their masks on; he didn't even want to see who they were.

And here, barring his way, was an officer of the Illinois National Guard. And there, stringing troops around the City Hall, was Captain James Ronald Gordon.

Dancey rounded the guardsman and went to get an explanation from Captain Gordon.

They were well enough acquainted from meetings of the civil defence media but there was no affection. Dancey didn't see the need for para-military agencies in local law enforcement. Gordon, naturally enough, defended such need in the only way he could. Existing authority was not sufficient or by implication not competent. That was the suggestion whether diplomacy was exercised or not. Gordon had given up diplomacy.

Dancey thought he would give Gordon a way out. "Exercise?" he inquired.

"Instruction," returned Gordon. "From the governor."

"On whose recommendation?"

"That I don't know. But if you can add anything to our knowledge of the situation, Clem, I'll be grateful."

"I've had word from the sheriff's office that we are to expect a visit from the Ku Klux Klan. I have my men deployed in such a way as to deter these Klansmen, return them to their transport and remove them. Now what in Sam Hill are you doing here?"

Gordon was puzzled. "Not looking for the Ku Klux Klan. We were told there was student unrest."

"So that's it." Dancey swore vigorously at panic-stricken city officials. "Mortis sent for you."

"If you say so."

The mayor had been on the telephone to Dancey throughout the night, had made a complete nuisance of himself. The police chief was making his own inquiries in liaison with campus law officers and if he couldn't provide answers in the early hours it was because the information was not at hand.

It might have been suggested with an element of truth that he had become blasé over student situations, so that he did not afford them the urgency shown by others not so familiar with the fickleness of the young. He had not asked the campus force to turn students out of bed to get to the seat of the previous night's disturbance. Today would have been soon enough. All night he had fenced with Mortis on the point, suggesting that the matter did not warrant such harassed concern, mystified by the mayor's apparent insistence.

True, the man had put himself into something of a cleft stick by promising an assurance to student demands by the following night, but that still left all day to arrive at a proper and unhurried appraisal.

By now, having received his reports, Dancey would have been ready to supply the mayor with the facts as presented. Merely that a fireraiser unknown on the Little Fort campus had bought a conspicuous number of drinks in the Water Street bars last night and had made certain claims concerning the contents of freight-cars now resident in the Green Town terminal.

Dancey had his own information about the cars, classified and from official sources. He had not volunteered this information to the campus force and had formed the opinion overnight that if Mayor Mortis had not been told in the line of his duty, there was no need for him to hear it from Dancey, who considered him too excitable by half.

In fact, preoccupation was not to be encouraged. It had bothered Dancey that the students had been aware of the matter at all, but he could not admit—not to them, not to Mortis, not to Captain Gordon—that their claim had firm foundation in fact.

Judge Woodman and Theo Elmwood had been buzzing around a little today, too, though offering no explanation. It was likely one or both of them had been given advance notice of the KKK visitation from the same source that supplied him, but his feeling was that if they didn't mention it he wouldn't.

He had a completely free hand on how he should handle the situation and since his line envisaged no arrests, let alone arraignments, no consultation with either was necessary.

At least, it hadn't been. Now, with the National Guard playing occupation all over the city centre, the situation seemed to have been removed from his effective control.

"We don't need you," he said coldly. "We're ready for them."

"Would that be the KKK or the students?" Gordon inquired.

"Both."

"It's unlikely they would act in any concerted manner, Clem. Are you so well blessed with policemen that you can split your strength and still come out on top?"

"The Highway Patrol is offering back-up. The sheriff's office knows the score and can provide ample deputies. Look . . . ordering you guys against students is like opening the door of the explosives shed. What kind of wisdom brought you into the game?"

"A request was made, an officer sent to examine it, a recommendation passed to Governor Forrester, who sanctioned. I don't know any more than that—except we could have done without it. We were busy enough with mobile pickets up the turnpike. I'm like you, Clem. I have to take orders."

Which was reasonable.

"I don't see any students," said Dancey. "Why don't you give your boys a rest until your particular trouble starts. I'm telling you, all these guns are enough to . . ."

He never finished it because a bus turned into North Utica Street, and when his own police sentinels moved forward, the guardsmen went with them, presenting a formidable array of armaments.

The Greyhound continued on to Clayton without slackening its pace, travelled four blocks and turned west, three blocks and then turned south, two blocks and then into Lakeview Avenue, which ended where the freight-yard began.

The windows were covered, the destination unknown to observers, but driver Sam Gregory made it without hesitation. With a pistol barrel pressed to his Negro temple since the armed men had stepped forward on North Utica Street, his choices were distinctly limited.

Dr. Ichiro Domei was landsick. For nearly two thousand miles now he had sat in his upper-storey berth when his charges were not demanding his presence and had watched the United States flow by his window.

It was green and first of all that was a novelty to a man who walked on dust, breathed in dust, thought only of coming to dust.

But when he had got used to the prairie, he had tried another game. He was no naturalist and had no names for the grasses and forbs which lined the track and shuddered with his passing.

There was a particular grass he had picked out in the escarpments as they traversed the Rocky Mountains and it was back again in force crossing Nebraska, less plentiful in Iowa, confined to the uplands as the train steadied itself for the plunge into Illinois. Reddish-brown, little bluestem by name.

Sandhills, buttes, mesas, canyons, rolling plains, rivers running so fast towards the east that they seemed to be challenging the locomotive. There was undeniable grandeur. Equally unarguable was the fact that Keio and Yamaji, apparently running a goodwill tour, had not seen fit yet to stop at any point to display goodwill.

The double-deck flier was passing through a town now. "Welcome," said the signs strung out for reading at speed, "to Cedar Rapids."

And how many Cedar Rapids was that? And what was a rapid, anyway?

Perhaps he should have been grateful. In fact, his children were bearing up very well, enthralled by the rate of travel and lack of effort. He kept them at their regular exercises so that their muscles, ever temperamental, would not atrophise. But he was still disturbed at the kind of reasoning that had suggested they should walk all the miles the train had covered. In how many years?

The coach was open plan and cut away, providing a balcony effect, and now and again he got a fleeting glimpse of a bald head, a paper-thin hand, a slow hobble to the services at the rear.

Perhaps he should indeed have been grateful. The *hibakusha* were supremely content with the journey, persuaded that way by the almost hypnotic vastness of the country through which they passed.

Deep down, he hoped they would keep going until they fell off the other side of America, and then maybe they could get on a boat and go home again, their purpose served. Whatever that purpose was.

Making a stop would mean making contact with strangers and responding to that contact. He had been doubtful enough of that at the outset. As time and distance were devoured, as the *hibakusha* got into the habit of movement and spectatorship, so Domei's misgivings grew.

What he didn't realise was that the original programme had been for a much more leisurely pace across the U.S. belly. Events unforeseen and unplannable—partly due to his own insistence on his people's needs—had necessitated the acceleration.

He was landsick from monotony. He was landsick because he wanted to see the sea and get onto it and ship away from this interminable place.

He dozed for an hour and awoke in sweat and nausea because the train was slowing down. Shortly, it stopped altogether and heads were turned and gazes directed to Dr. Ichiro Domei for an explanation.

While he was thinking, Keio threaded his way down the aisle and took an adjacent seat. "We're waiting for a signal," he said. "When we get it, we—"

"Excuse me." Domei stood up, looked down upon the ruined and unnatural faces. "We have stopped," he said carefully, "at a signal. That is a red light which means there is danger ahead. But that need not be frightening for us. It means only that another train is crossing our path. When the way is clear, the light will turn to green and we will be able to go. Green means that the danger is past."

He smiled. His children turned away and went back to their windows, looking at the red light.

"When we get the green light," said Keio, "we make a small detour to the north. There we will mingle with some friendly people."

"It is a goodwill stop," said Domei, just to get it clear in his own mind.

"That's right. A typical midwestern town with a fair cross-section of the American population. Some fine buildings, beautiful parks, a picturesque lake with beaches for bathing—"

"What do my people want with bathing? Do you think they enjoy stares?"

Keio demurred. "I was merely listing facilities. What your people do there is their own affair—or yours."

"How long will we be there?"

"As long as it takes."

"As long as what takes?"

"Meeting people. Making our gesture."

Keio stood up, having said all he had planned to say.

"You never told me," Domei caught him, "what your principals said when you took it up with them about the *hibakusha* walking—"

Keio made no move to sit down again. "An error in transmission," he said. "As I suspected. I thought we had resolved that—"

"And another thing—why have we not stopped before now? We must have come at least halfway across the continent."

"So that your party could gain their own enjoyment from the trip. They have been shown striking contrasts in scenery and terrain to enable them to build up some kind of picture of the land. That knowledge must surely benefit them now when they start dealing with the people. They—"

"All right," said Domei sharply. "You can go away now."

He was tired of pat answers that did nothing to explain or ease his doubts. Even while he prayed the train would not stop, he knew that it had to come to a destination eventually. And he knew, too, that the destination had been planned and that therefore the long journey beforehand was part of the plan.

Goodwill was not sufficient reason when the manoeuvre had been so precise. He did not accept Keio's glib explanations. He did not accept, either, that the marching idea had been a secretarial error. Somewhere along the line, it had been given serious consideration. The whole point of marching was that people could see you, and even if he had been able to force a change in the method of travel, the object of the exercise remained unaltered.

The stop ahead was for people to see them. And if the reason was not goodwill, could it be ill will? Or curiosity? Or political device?

At Cicero, the train diverted into the Elgin, Joliet and Eastern (Chicago outer belt) road. At Highland Park, it switched to a track that would bring it into the Chicago and North-Western Railroad-yard at Green Town.

At the railroad-yard, the audience was beginning to arrive.

William Filo was having a frustrating day and the *Campus Calliope* was suffering for it.

He had covered the previous night's disturbance and heard Mayor Mortis's promise of an explanation for the rumour which was circulating in the Water Street bars.

But as a good editorial yardstick, he preferred anticipation to reportage and today he had been chasing usually reliable sources for some strong line on the matter. Filo, normally making his beat along the bars, had been more involved with Allison Miller at the requisite time that the inflammatory stranger had been handing out free drinks and fireworks and had picked up the trail only when the atmosphere became so electric that he could not miss it.

Even so, much of the build-up had come to him second-hand—a condition he didn't like, which made it all the more important for him to grab the initiative now if the means were available. And so far, they weren't available.

He had positive mention of lethal freight in the Chicago and North-Western rail-yard on the town's southern periphery.

He checked with the police and got a curt "We're investigating claims" from Chief Dancey. He tried to reach Theo Elmwood in the city legal department to see whether any ordinances had been violated—or would have been if they were confirmed—but Elmwood was occupied elsewhere.

He drove down to the freight-yard, looked out over the acres of static cars and decided no useful purpose would be served by a personal search. He didn't know what to look for, anyway. Time was of the essence and hours spent walking the line here fruitlessly could be put to better use with discreet inquiries to people who could know if the report had any foundation.

Back to the office and on with the futile phoning until his left ear glowed red and his pen-hand was weary of shorthand outlines that contracted into doodles.

Only then did he try the old game of putting two and two together and that was having the same kind of success before his eyes
rediscovered the mushroom cloud in the window.

THE SURVIVORS ARE COMING still didn't make much sense, without
taking the unknown activist's reference to the freight as a pinpoint-
ing of location, like THE SURVIVORS ARE COMING *here*. And the survivors. What was lethal about survivors? If they were volatile,
they'd be dead.

OKINAWA BASKETS. Well, baskets and freight had a link. What
kind of freight came in baskets? What kind of—survivors? Not human, for sure. Then animals.

That at least gave him some kind of guide to the railroad
meadow. A bogey suitable for livestock, a sound (not necessarily),
a scent (again, not necessarily)—but two possibilities.

Size must come into the equation, also. Baskets were only so big
and therefore their contents must be of corresponding stature. Pigeons? What was lethal about pigeons? Messengers? Crop-spray
monitors? He discarded pigeons.

How about rabbits? Purpose? Fresh meat? Research? Survivors—
research. William Filo had not seen all of Malecki's variations, had
not known that a man was dead and rabbits were suspect. But the
Okinawa pull-out was unmistakable and the baskets could be part
of the pull-out. It seemed like a good lead and his newsman's nose
took him right to it.

So he was looking for rabbits. First break of the day and that at
nearly dinner-time.

The door swung to admit Allison Miller. "You still here?" She
sounded surprised. "I came on the off-chance. The excitement's at
City Hall. Police all lined up. National Guard as well."

Filo's stomach churned at the mention of troops. "For pity's sake,"
he said. "They're not going to let the military loose on the students?
Not again? Now look . . ."

Allison was trailing him to the door.

"Best keep clear, sweetheart," he told her.

"But why? I've just come past. It's all right . . ."

William Filo was thinking of another Allison from another campus and another National Guard confrontation.

Allison Krause, you were killed because you loved flowers
. . . Ah, how fragrant are the lilacs,
But you feel nothing . . .

Yevgeny Yevtushenko mourning a victim of the Kent State affair of May 1970. Sub-standard Yevtushenko, but a way of remembering. And now this Allison . . .

"It's not a good place for you to be. These part-time soldiers can get trigger-happy when they see a bunch of kids—"

"Besides," Miss Miller said firmly, "I don't know if they are there to deal with the students."

"Who else?"

"I heard somebody say the Ku Klux Klan was coming."

"What the devil does the KKK want here? Where do they stand? With the students or the administration? Or in the middle? But that clinches it, Allison—you're not going to be with me. You stay here and look after the office. Please. That's vital, too, love. . . ."

So Allison stayed. Three minutes after Filo had gone, the telephone rang.

"Jim Banks," said the caller. "I've been watching this picketing business up the turnpike for the *Calliope*. Is Filo not there?"

"No." Allison was familiar with the teamster dispute, as were most of the students. Campus kept an eye on the unions almost by tradition now, ten years after the marriage happy then not so happy of students and workers in Paris of spring 1968. "He has another bit of business at City Hall. Student unrest, National Guard, possible KKK visit. You'll have to fight for space, Jim."

Banks chuckled. "You sound pretty professional, honey. . . . So that's where the National Guard went. . . . Maybe you could get a garbled message to Bill. Tell him a man's been shot by the pickets. Not a container driver. Innocent party by the name of Simeon, plain Simeon. There's something familiar about the name and Bill can check it when he gets the chance. The guy's on his way to Victory Memorial Hospital. No report on his condition yet but I think he's in a pretty bad way. . . . Did you get all that?"

Allison repeated it to the legman's satisfaction.

Then she headed for City Hall. But the ten-minute delay had made all the difference.

William Filo was already following the rest of the action towards the freight-yard.

First came the nausea as Simeon saw blood spurting from his arm. Then came the panic as Julie threw her body across his in approved assassination-widow style.

He was too busy fighting her off and trying to steer the van one-handed, with lights flashing, across the heavy lane and onto the hard shoulder to notice pain.

And when they made it safely, he had not time to thank any providence. He blacked out.

Julie tore off the sash of her dress, wound it round his arm and tightened it into a tourniquet. Hunting frantically through her handbag, she found eyebrow pencil, checked the time against her watch and wrote it on unstained skin near Simeon's wrist.

Simeon was as grey as death but that in itself didn't bother her. She had seen him that way over a cut finger and knew it was shock registering in a sudden drop of blood pressure.

The wound was more messy than serious but it needed urgent treatment. How that was going to be arranged she didn't know immediately. She could see no telephone call-box and the traffic was continuing on its way.

The men who eventually showed up at the van door had guns and protest signs—and shamefaced looks. But why?

"We're sorry, ma'am," said one. "It was an accident. The marksman will be disciplined. Meanwhile, we're using shortwave radio to get you an ambulance. Can I . . . see?"

Julie didn't have the words to reply. She could not begin to understand the situation. Her pink gingham was red with Simeon's blood, they were miles from home—for pity's sake, what home?—and the men with the guns were saying sorry. In her mind was utter confusion.

"Did one of you . . . ?" She indicated the wound weakly.

"No, ma'am. That was one of our lookout men. He must have been aiming at the tyres of the freezer van just in front of you."

"I don't . . . understand," Julie was feeling close to sickness herself.

"No, lady, you wouldn't." Another voice. "It's an industrial dispute."

"I damn well told you something like this would happen. . . ." A third voice out in the yellowing afternoon. "Did anyone see where Clyde James went? I bet the son's still running."

Highway dust and dry grass and the salt savour of fresh bloodshed. "I . . ." Julie must have slumped. Suddenly there was a flask at her lips and liquid fire going down her throat and down her chin.

Then the first man tried to force the brandy into Simeon's mouth.

"Take it easy, Sam," said the second. "The law might think these good people have been drinking."

"With a stinking bullet-hole in his arm?" contended Sam. "Look— you want to do something useful, get the emergency services back on the shortwave."

Simeon came out of the darkness, saw the state of his shirt and was sick over the cab floor, the running board and drip, drip, drip onto the roadside. With his stomach empty he felt better. He accepted the brandy and felt better still. Now he had the pain all right.

He saw Julie's dress. He swore gently, almost lovingly. "I'll get you a new one. You need pink gingham—"

"Mister." The first man pressed quietly for attention. "If you'll allow us—well, you see, one of our membership is responsible for this. It wasn't intended. A stray bullet. If you'll give us your name and address, we'll set the matter straight. That's the least we can do."

"It's all right." Simeon was benevolent and light-headed with the loss of blood.

"Tell them," said Julie almost sharply. The anger was beginning in her now. Accident it might be, but there would be hospital bills. She was relieved to find herself so practical. "No. I'll tell them."

She supplied the name and the address in Oak Street. By the time a note had been taken, the ambulance siren was wailing close-by.

On the ride into Green Town, Simeon faltered between lucidity and shallow coma. The aide who travelled in the back with him and Julie took over the tourniquet and consulted his watch. When the blood had to be allowed to flow freely again, Simeon lapsed into unconsciousness and Julie had to use one of the polythene bags supplied for the purpose.

"Nasty," said the aide. "Bullet? Looks like a large-calibre job."

"I don't know anything about it," responded Julie. "We were just driving along. The—the men back there said it was an accident."

"Doesn't make it hurt any less. What are they? Some kind of . . . ?"

"I don't know what they are." Julie was impatient. "Aside from the fact they've made a hole in my husband's arm. If you want to gossip about it, maybe you'd better go see them. . . ."

The meat-wagon was unbearably hot and she could have done without the cross-examination. The man's attitude changed from solicitous to comforting. "Forgive me. When you're dealing with shock, we're told, get your patients to talk it out. I'm not really curious about the incident. If there's any more I can do for you—"

"Just get us there," said Julie, though the edge had gone out of her voice. "Wherever 'there' is." In a little while, she wept.

Victory Memorial Hospital was on Sheridan Avenue overlooking the railroad and the industrial precinct on the lake foreshore. The emergency room was at ground-floor level and well appointed.

Julie found herself in a bright-painted waiting room with a nurse bringing strong sweet coffee while the emergency-room staff dealt with Simeon's wound.

The nurse was polished and chatty. "Funny," she said, lining up the grisly observation that is the only way to make hospital bearable, "you don't get a gunshot case for months and all of a sudden the streets are full of them."

"Are they?" Julie was only half paying attention, making the right noises while she waited for the coffee to hit bottom and worried about Simeon.

"Well, not yet, actually. But it looks as though we're going to have a lot more customers before the night is out."

Some remnant of a duty was picking at the corner of Julie's numb mind. Looking out for Simeon was just one thing. Listening for him was another. "How is that?"

"Trouble at the railway freight-yard, Police, National Guard, students. Somebody said they even saw two men in hoods. Would they be—the Ku Klux Klan?" She tailed off in superstitious awe. "What on earth can they all be doing in Green Town?"

Waiting for my husband, Julie thought. Waiting for Simeon to spark the whole wonderful thing.

"I don't know," she said. "We were out of town today. But there was some unrest with the students last night, I heard. They were complaining about dangerous freight at the yard. Perhaps that's what it's all . . . But the KKK! Are you sure?"

The nurse was emphatic. "A person doesn't make a mistake like that. You can't be wrong about a company of the National Guard, the whole city police force and a busload of men in hoods, can you? It seems to me everybody who is anybody is at the freight-yard tonight."

Not quite everybody, thought Julie. And the show can't go on without him. Can it? She knew she must try to keep Simeon away. Knew but had no hope.

And when she saw Simeon, pale and padded and full up with questions about the snatches of conversation he had heard among the medical staff, she gave up all aspirations of fooling him.

"What's happening?" he said without much strength and she told him.

When she had finished, he took her hand. "Julie . . . it looks like we're back three years ago. But that's only how it looks. In fact, we've had a thousand days of loving and learning and whatever we do now, we do that much better. These doctors want me to stay but I can handle them. You won't get in my way, will you? Because you I couldn't handle. Show me one tear and I'm lost and the game is lost and as sure as hell somebody's going to get hurt much worse than I am. You do see that, Julie, don't you? It hinges on me. If anybody is to get out of this, I have to prescribe the means. There are so many people . . ."

And if she secretly blessed the bullet that injured him because it might invalid him out of his commitment, she could not say that now. She could not trust herself to speak at all. Instead, she just squeezed the hand that held hers and let Simeon put his weight on her as he stood up unsteadily from the treatment table.

She helped him get into his clothes. She let him pick his own pace down the echoing halls of the Victory Memorial—and the worst part was bearing the glances of the simplistic medicals who thought that, if she cared, she would have brought some influence to bear.

Part-time Nurse Fenella Buchman, fresh from the Wessex greenwoods, arriving in anticipation of trouble, passed them at the hospital entrance. Simeon didn't see her, Julie didn't know her and she was too hung up on the awkwardness of the moment to speak. Long after they were gone, she watched the doors and wondered if she would get another chance.

Julie settled Simeon in a taxi and ordered the cabby to drive them to Oak Street.

When Simeon looked askance, she said, "Just one condition."
And nearly choked on the lump in her throat.
"At least, wear a decent shirt."

The bus came to a halt at the livestock market and Territorial
Wizard Bradford Williams led forth his hooded minions. The access
to the railway-yard was unbarred, for what it was worth, and the
stopover jungle of rolling stock stood unguarded against their attention.

Once all seventy were through the gate, Williams halted them
with a raised hand.

"Does anyone know where we're going?" a sweating Slade Dexter inquired of his brother-in-law Clem Goldwater. "There's an awful lot of wagons."

The shrouded bodies, crowded one upon the other just inside the
yard, were beginning to mill like the beef in the pens they had
passed near the market.

They carried their carbines reluctantly and many had found a
way to conceal the arms in their voluminous robes. The sight of the
National Guard had been disconcerting. Handling a couple of hundred handicapped Nips was one thing; shooting it out with the
military was quite another. Williams had urged the driver on with a
Smith & Wesson at his head, abandoning the plan for a terror march
through the Green Town main streets.

So they were early.

For want of something useful to do, Williams delegated half a
dozen of them to return to the bus and unpack the torches from the
luggage hold.

They were stout of handle and thick of end, these torches, abundant in cotton waste and soaked in pitchblende to burn slowly. And
when the flames died or were doused, the shafts provided formidable
weapons.

"In fact," ordered Williams, "we'll favour these over guns. Another
six, collect the firing-pieces and lock them in the hold. We should be
able to strike as hard as need be with these staves."

The rush of volunteers betrayed their relief.

A good score of the vigilantes were back at the bus, fetching or
carrying, when the bulk of the party started moving in among the
lines of trucks.

They had not seen Joe Gaskell, miraculously clad in the tuxedo

of an impresario, approach Bradford Williams in the failing light and
say, "If you'll follow me, I'll lead you to the KKK enclosure."

Police Chief Clement Dancey and Guard Captain James Ronald
Gordon had watched the coach vanish from view in an administrative dilemma.

Gordon, clear in his own mind of the commission assigned to the
Guard, decided first advantage would go to the one who opened
the prodding.

"Didn't somebody ought to follow them?" he asked Dancey.

"My cruisers will pick them up. If they're leaving town, the
Highway Patrol are alerted."

"And if they're not—if they're heading for a destination within the
town limits?"

"I'll hear about it," said Dancey. "What's it to you, anyway? You
just wait for the kids to come and take you on."

He turned on his heel, whistled up his personal transport.

"Follow that bus," he told the driver. "And don't laugh."

Restored to privacy within his automobile or at least to a sympathetic environment, he began to lay his plans over the police
wave band.

First sighting reported the Greyhound on Sheridan and heading
south. That meant it would cross city limits and head into a north
Chicago suburb or it would turn off somewhere along the way.

His information on the visitation, relayed via the sheriff's office,
had been fragmentary, a mere detailing of fact. No reason had
been offered and he had not thought until now, as they headed
towards the C. & N.-W. yard, to tie it up with anything he already
knew.

When the bus was reported bulleting down Lakeview Avenue,
he knew the rabbits had to come into it. Though not why.

Nor did he know, when he instructed his force to zoom in on the
yard and led the local fleet of cruisers through the gates from the
market entrance and along the service roads, that Ed Rinehart
was tracking him on a small transportation-artery monitor borrowed
from the local DOT office and he was going in precisely the right
direction.

"So glad you could come," said Rinehart to the string of blobs.

Frank Lorensen and Kyoso Kuroda had spent the afternoon on
campus at Little Fort, stationed at the Liberty Bell and talking

animatedly to anyone who approached. Frank had a loud-speaker, a veteran of many such rallies at Liberty Bell and on Blanket Hill, but not everybody wanted to hear him. He was too clearly identified as a Weatherman to be accepted as merely imparting information. So he soon came round to the idea that attempted explanation was a bad waste of time. Instead, he merely issued an invitation. At the C. & N.-W. freight-yard that very night, he said, was to be a happening that would end all happenings. And where the devil was Simeon?

Jim Ruffner and Charlie Frei, unhappy allies at the best of times but drawn together by their need to offer some kind of opposition to the Weathermen, had taken the Blanket Hill pitch, and since Jim was known as something of a character with no particular leftist alignment, the more middle-of-the-road students were stopping to listen to him. Charlie had little enough to say without his paintbrush and he wasn't absolutely sure he had the total content of the message, anyway. The talking was left to Ruffner. At the C. & N.-W. freight-yard that very night, he said, not in so many words, was to be a happening to end all happenings.

The procession off-campus as dusk fell with no curfew declared was massive and unnerving. Since Little Fort lay to the south of Green Town, entry was made most effectively via Foss Park Avenue and Lakeside Avenue.

By the time details of the move reached Captain Gordon he couldn't even throw out enough lines of force to catch stragglers.

His own instruction, passed from the Battle Creek aces via the governor of Illinois to his headquarters and thence on UHF to his radio staff (and not purely on the say-so of Mayor Mortis, however strongly Clem Dancey and even Mortis himself believed it) had put the estimated number of students likely to be involved at three hundred.

The estimate was based on intelligence from previous similar commitments (of which there had been none) and on the forecast response to the orthodox release of information—in other words, that transmitted via Jim Ruffner and Charlie Frei, who were on the Battle Creek mailing list. Frank Lorensen, too, though Generals A and B knew nothing of the intervention of Kyoso Kuroda or the rest of his little workers. They were still preening themselves over having found out about the survivors. B had anticipated Japanese thinking successfully—"Just supposing the Japs have the same idea," he had said—but had been ignored because A was A and he was only B.

So Captain Gordon, even though he was late to his posting, could see there was something seriously wrong with the Battle Creek figures.

The best thing he could do with the company, now rendered ineffectual by sheer mass, was to get it somewhere near the eye of the hurricane.

When Joe Gaskell swung himself into the captain's jeep at the Foss Park Avenue intersection to guide the Guard to its allotted spot, he was smiling all over his powdered shirt-front.

"Much better than we expected, Captain," he said, allowing himself a little laxity in the presence of friends.

"If 'better' is the word," said James Ronald Gordon, who had just mentally resigned his commission.

Judge Charles Woodman and City Prosecutor Theodore Elmwood had spent last night and this day busy on their own inquiries to raise situation data—with the result that they weren't available to the people who could so inform them.

Frank Lorensen had tried to locate the judge to see how much he knew and whether Simeon had given him the latest. But Woodman had given orders not to be disturbed and that was how it was and Frank had a date at the Liberty Bell.

Clement Dancey had sought consultation with Elmwood, ostensibly to provide Mayor Mortis with an answer, but had been told the prosecutor was tied up all day with the judge.

And what had their twenty-hour session yielded? Woodman had considered the visit from the Klansman to be of more immediate significance than the fact that Simeon had an Asiatic pursuer, but Elmwood had not been surprised by the KKK's emergence. That much, he had known, was scheduled in the deeply classified memorandum forwarded to him from the office of the United States Attorney General under several seals.

He was more interested in the Japanese tail, because that wasn't on the schedule. But Woodman's information in that direction was limited and Elmwood could hardly approach the Attorney General's office with a query that might just turn out to be an old man's whim (even if he did tell the judge he believed every word of it).

"Ask Simeon," the Klan vanguard had said as he fled from the judge's home with Elmwood howling ever nearer in the borrowed prowl car.

It had left the lawmen wondering just how much Simeon did know of the affair. But when they tried the house in Oak Street, Mrs. Dilger told them Simeon and Julie had gone into the mists of morn and she didn't know when they were coming back. If ever. Strange couple. They had started off like a couple of nice kids. But such hours and such visitors. Present company excepted, of course.

"Perhaps it wasn't their fault," counselled the judge, who felt there might be a need to adjust the balance in Simeon's favour. "Events might show they were being used."

"I don't follow that," said Mrs. Dilger and Woodman and Elmwood agreed by common nod that further explanation was futile.

And here they were, as the hands of the clock moved towards another midnight, driving downtown in Elmwood's car, seeing a lot of people on the streets and all walking in one direction. Hurrying more than walking.

"The freight-yard," said Woodman, with a trace of anxiety. "It must be beginning."

Elmwood identified himself to the patrolman at the market gate, secured clearance and gunned his car down the service roads. He knew what to expect and could not risk glancing at the judge's drawn features as he edged the vehicle through pressing humanity.

"We have a place near the front," he said. "Should get a good view."

But Woodman was too deep in his own thoughts to question the existence of such an arrangement or to ask how Elmwood was suddenly privy to it. He was wondering what Simeon was about to do —and how he, Charles Woodman, could help.

Three girls and one of them marked to die. But which one? Tomorrow Julie, who had married a martyr and was ready at any time for his fate as long as she could share it? Lucia Lorensen, who already felt herself marked by the punishment she carried on her right cheek? Allison Miller, with a name like another girl, and a message for William Filo somewhere in this human pot-pourri?

Events would elect, dictate and execute that death but not yet. Meanwhile . . .

Lorensen, going about his business all day, had left Lucia one standing order: find Simeon.

He and Lucia, watching the stars from the Oak Street cupola last night, had learned from Simeon and Julie something of the feeling that existed between the Playa 9 pair.

There was a permutation, then, in Lorensen's instruction: find Tomorrow Julie and you find Simeon.

Lucia had tried all the Water Street bars, had been back to Oak Street so many times that Mrs. Dilger had given up answering the door. Now she waited on the sidewalk where the lightning-rod salesman had paused so many years before.

Touring the bars, she had felt the temperature rising and heard that the target for tonight was the freight-yard—which she knew already.

But too many people were heading that way for her to be able to pick out Simeon and Julie and she never liked seeing Frank at work anyway.

So she had taken herself to the least likely place on the remotest chance. And here was a taxi drawing up at the kerb before her.

Julie got out first, gave her a quick smile in lieu of greeting and reached back into the cab to bring forth the nightmare figure.

Simeon's face so pale atop clothing so rich in the hues of tragedy took Lucia's breath away.

"Julie," she said, as though the girl was the only one left alive to speak, "what happened?"

"An accident." Simeon confirmed his survival with speech. "Just when we didn't need an accident."

Julie gripped his good arm up the steps to the Dilger door. Lucia, feeling the need to assist, was left only the injured member to hold, which was plainly out of the question. Instead, she trailed them forlornly into the house, past Mrs. Dilger.

"People have been asking," said Mrs. Dilger, apparently unmoved by Simeon's plight. "Are you in some kind of trouble?"

"No." Simeon needed to stress his fitness to cope. "No bank robberies, no jealous husband's duel. We went for a drive in the country. As we came back, we drove straight into a trucker's dispute and one of their snipers got me by mistake. All in fun, really."

"Look, I . . ." Mrs. Dilger hovered between professionalism and sympathy. "Would you like some tea?"

"Love some," said Julie. "I just have to help the man change his shirt."

"If I were you, I'd put him straight to bed."

"No bed," said Simeon. "And don't look at Julie like that. I have to go out again and there's nothing she can do about it."

"She could hit you over the head."

"Believe me, that would solve nothing. The problem would still be there waiting for me."

"And you're not in any kind of trouble, huh?"

"Not like you mean it, Mrs. Dilger. Now, please . . . I would welcome that hot, strong tea."

Simeon in a clean shirt, with his left arm in a sling and the empty sleeve pinned out of the way, looked a much better proposition. It was only when Julie had him thus that she thought to ask Lucia why the girl had been waiting.

"Frank wanted to contact Simeon. There's been this build-up all day. Mid-afternoon, the National Guard shipped in from turnpike duty—"

"I wish they hadn't," said Simeon ruefully.

"Then came the Ku Klux Klan—"

"You were right," said Julie.

"We can read them," said Simeon. "Between us."

"Now everybody's at the freight-yard. Frank put the word about."

"Any sign of those Hiroshima people?"

"Not so far. There's been no mention of them. I swear a lot of the people don't know—"

"Well, that fits, Lucia. One can recognize the cool hand of the Pentagon behind most of these machinations, but a couple are surprises—surprises even to the Pentagon, I shouldn't wonder, or twists that came too late for them to handle properly."

Mrs. Dilger came with the tea, poured it and left as though she was making her apology with a show of respect.

Lucia was a little restless.

"Is there some kind of hurry?" asked Simeon.

"Frank," she said. "I . . . I know it needs you there to function at all but . . . well, I'm worried about him."

Simeon drained his cup. "Then we'd better get moving."

He stepped it out down Oak Street in splendid style but by the time they reached Dugdale he was ready to drop.

They spotted a taxi looking for business in the suspended town and pointed the man at the freight-yard.

"What the blazes is going on down there?" he wanted to know. "An exhibition bout?"

"You're not wrong," said Simeon.

Sweeping south along Sheridan, Lucia spotted a girl she knew just standing while the latecomers flowed around her in a tide. The taxi was crawling in the midst of people. "Allison?"

"I'm looking for Bill," called back Allison Miller. "Not much hope."

"Who's Bill?" Simeon in hushed and polite tone.

"He's a reporter. Runs the *Campus Calliope*. He's sure to be at the—"

"Allison!" called Simeon.

The girl on the sidewalk looked at him bleakly.

"If you come with us, I can guarantee Bill won't be far away."

"You're . . ." Recognition started. The files Allison had double-checked before she set off with her message. "Aren't you . . . Simeon?"

"That's right. That's how I can guarantee—"

"But you're supposed to be—"

"Look, bud," interrupted the cabby, "are you going to finish this ride or am I going to put you off here?"

"No way," said Simeon. "This is a ride to the finish. Just let the lady get in."

Over the last few blocks, as housing degenerated into slum, into warehouse, Allison weighed up the man who had been the subject of her message. "We heard you were in a pretty bad way. I was just looking for Bill to tell him."

"Now you see, there's no need," said Simeon. "The show goes on."

"Is it . . . your show?" A lot of things were suddenly becoming very clear to Allison.

"The organisers think so."

"And you?"

"I don't know. I may be down-staged."

"That'll be a pity." Allison was still only half-grasping what the charade was about.

"Not for me. For whoever has to do it."

"And yet you go on."

"No choice."

"There *must* be a choice."

"No."

"Then I'd say you're selling out to predestination." Allison smiled to show it wasn't a serious comment.

"Sooner me than anybody else." Simeon smiled because that was.

A police patrolman halted them at the market gate and ran a quick flashlight check. He went away in a hurry to a telephone in the security man's booth. He came back at a run, waving on the driver. "Use the service roads," he shouted. "Follow the crowd."

The cabby swore under the hum of the engine. More loudly, he said, "Who pays me the fare? You, the cops or the military? Or you got diplomatic immunity or somethin'."

Simeon couldn't get to his pocket, Julie had forgotten her bag somewhere—maybe back on the turnpike—Allison was short as always and Lucia brought notes from her well-stocked purse.

"I'll give it to you later," said Simeon. And reflected that he might not have the chance. "Tonight ought to be worth a few expenses."

More police now and the great uncommitted public seemingly arranged in some kind of order. Simeon could think of nothing more like it than a bullfight—with him as matador? Or bull?

On went the taxi, on past traffic and people in hoods and guardsmen with rifles at unsteady ready. Until a man in an evening suit laid a hand on the hood and gestured the occupants out.

By who knows what masterpiece of shunt and filter, a palpable clearing had been made in the middle of the iron meadow. Even a clear track southward into darkness the eye could not penetrate.

Clear in that direction but right here occupied by two piggyback containers. And these pinned by arc-light.

Simeon sniffed and knew them for the trucks he had found when he chased the silver snail such a few nights ago.

With his good hand, he drew the girls out of the cab one by one, like a leading man arriving plus harem.

"Julie," he said quietly because the freight-yard was beginning to swim. "You girls keep together and you'll be safe."

Then they were gone beyond the pit-stall ranks of Guard and Klansman and the man in the tuxedo was at his right elbow. "Simeon," he said. "Good to see you again."

And it wasn't Ray Bradbury. Simeon, struggling to produce a solution that would satisfy everybody, had been hoping for some extra-sensory empathy from the distant Master but it was foolish and impractical optimism. This was Gaskell, the Cooger of the piece, and the magic wasn't going to work this time.

The *hibakusha* had abandoned their preoccupation with windows and fleeting scenes. An hour ago, night had fallen and the world beyond the glass had become dull and industrial, the two together.

In a little while—Domei didn't know how long, so could not postpone the ordeal—the train would stop and the purpose would start and he had to say something to his children to warn them in advance.

He picked his way carefully down steps and down aisle so as not to make contact with any splayed or sorry limb, but not as carefully as he was trying to pick his words.

He turned to face the two hundred of them, the majority set back four by four on the lower level, the more active in the second level cutaway, designed so that another audience on another mission (or another two hundred of them) could enjoy a reissue movie while they travelled.

"We will be stopping at a town soon," he began. "I am told that it is a nice, friendly town where people will be pleased to see us and will make us welcome.

"These are the people we have come all this way to meet. We have been shown their country—and you know how much you have enjoyed looking at it—and now we shall be talking to the people who live their lives in such a country. It will be interesting for us."

For them, too, he thought, but did not say it to the *hibakusha* because the interpretation to the sensitive would be that the Americans were weighing them up.

"We will not stay there long and afterwards"—he saw Keio come through into the coach and was glad he had timed the next assurance so well—"we shall finish our train journey, board a ship and go home.

"So do what you need to get yourselves ready, children."

He drooped. The talk was over and nothing had been said in warning because how can you warn people without frightening them and how can you alert them when you don't know what they must see?

He could only hope now that what lay ahead would not be so bad that it would destroy their trust in him or so awful that it would reopen the wounds in them.

Keio intercepted him at the foot of the steps. "Ten minutes."

Domei scanned the carriage. His charges were busy in various ways. He could afford a few words without being overheard. "And what then?"

"We arrive."

"For what purpose?"

"Goodwill."

"You still insist—"

"There is no other way I can put it to you, Doctor."

"Then why here?"

"It is typical."

"Do we meet anybody tonight? It's getting late. Perhaps we should just pull into a siding or something. Surely they wouldn't be expecting us at this time of night—"

Keio put a hand over his on the step-rail. "They surely are expecting us."

Dr. Ichiro Domei gave himself over to the inevitable.

Midnight then and the town clocks chiming on towards one and two and then three in the deep morning and the peals of the great clocks shaking dust off old toys in high attics and shedding silver off old mirrors in yet higher attics and stirring up dreams about clocks in all the beds where children slept.

Simeon heard it.

Muffled away down the cleared south track the humming of a locomotive, the slow-following dragon-glide of a train.

The faces tilted and the inner darkness moved outward from his sickening stomach and his left arm gypped him so that he stumbled in his Shakespeare/Bradbury.

> By the pricking of my thumbs,
> Something wicked this way comes.

He had climbed, under Gaskell's assistance, to the flat-car base before the piggyback-container-turned-stage for his cabaret.

Gaskell had been talking quickly, excitedly, his teeth gleaming often to match his peerless shirt-front. "We admit to the rabbits. Tell them about the rabbits and how they've given us sterling service in Okinawa and now they're going to a gracious retirement—know what I mean?"

"If you wanted it that word-perfect," said Simeon through his nausea, "you should have given me a script last night."

And kept me off the road today, he thought. Sweet Julie, this pain . . .

Gaskell's strong secret service arm around his waist. "Easy now, baby, that's quite a knock. Move at your own pace. Could you do with a seat? I . . . Believe me, this in your arm was nothing to do with me."

"About the only thing," Simeon managed to mutter. He took a big mouthful of fresh air, let the oxygen work on his lowering blood pressure and felt fractionally better.

"One accident and the rest design. Don't take this personally, but I hate your stinking guts."

Gaskell retained his glittering professional smile. "Who's personal? I'm acting on orders just as you are. My direction is dictated by authority, yours by chemistry, what's the difference? Here we are at the same point at the same time for the same reason. My people won't bother about an academic distinction, Simeon. They'll just pay you well and leave you alone."

"Sure. Till the next time."

"We like to believe there won't be any next time."

"Believe what you like, last time there wasn't going to be a next time. You Pentagon pundits will always find a use for a fool to pull you out of the mire."

"What mire? Look, Simeon, if you hadn't decided to chase thunder lizards in a library, my principals would have forgotten all about you—"

Ed Rinehart was climbing the steps to the platform with a canvas folding chair.

Simeon dropped into it gratefully, grimacing when the jolt got to his shoulder. Rinehart worked on around him with cables, brought in a microphone stand and lowered the mouthpiece to Simeon's face level.

Gaskell squatted on his heels at the side of the chair. "It's a little late now to start arguing the merits of what we're asking you to do."

"It's a little late for you to be coming out with the request."

"Please. We need your help. I can only say 'please' and pay you. Tell all these good people there's nothing to worry about from the rabbits."

Simeon looked out over the serried ranks. The faces were blobs rendered featureless by the abundance of arc-light. The KKK at least he could make out. The rest could be young, old, strange, familiar. The girls were somewhere near the hoods and William Filo had his message and was about to get his lineage.

Out there, too, Judge Charles Woodman and Prosecutor Theo Elmwood and police and students and guardsmen and the whole works.

"Big show," he said.

"You're popular," responded Gaskell.

"No, I mean big show for two hundred white rabbits."

"A conjurer's bonanza. Bound to be a big show. You sure you're —I mean, we don't want you getting delirious. Any time you feel you can't go on . . ." Gaskell unbent and moved back from the chair.

"That's all the time," said Simeon.

Gaskell tapped the microphone with his fingers and it rattled like a snare. He blew across it and made thunder. "Ready when you are."

He moved it nearer Simeon so that bending forward was unnecessary. Then he walked towards the steps down, where Rinehart was waiting.

"Do I know all I need to know?" asked Simeon. Amplified, the words hung forebodingly over the freight-yard arena.

"What else?" said Gaskell, away from the mike and just loud enough for Simeon to hear. Rinehart was digging nails into his arm.

"Yes," shouted Rinehart. "Just explain to our good friends here what it is all about."

The crowd of thousands moved like a tree troubled with a breeze.

The students were most leaf-like, turned this way and that upon their stems, Ruffner- or Lorensen-inspired, believing either and confused by both, waiting now for the happening that would end all.

Law and order agencies stood ready but ready for what? Their superiors knew but were in a minority and not discussing it, anyway.

The KKK membership, unnerved in the apparently placid presence of so many people, cursed their hoods and linen and sweated some more.

Lucia had found Lorensen, Allison Filo and Julie heard nothing, only watched the lemon paleness of Simeon's face and wondered if they all looked such ghouls to each other.

Elmwood waited for the plan to be fulfilled. Charles Woodman,

Green Town veteran, waited to fulfil a plan of his own. If only Simeon would say the right words. . . . That had been the seat of his frustration all day, the inability to talk to the boy. He had swilled over the facts with the cool water of logic. There were two forces at work. The Americans, because they knew Simeon, had chosen Simeon. The Japanese, because they knew the Americans, had also chosen Simeon.

And if they knew that much about the Americans and the way they would react, then nothing was a mystery to them and they could utilise those reactions, even to the point of—

There was movement down the southbound track, a hunched buffalo shape.

Say it right, Simeon, prayed the old man. Keep something in reserve.

The buffalo shape was caught and held in the corner of Simeon's eye. He assessed its progress as he watched the motley crowd before him.

The humming was everywhere. He had to speak soon or be drowned out. Gaskell stood as though he was impaled upon the steps, Rinehart tugging at him.

"What about the survivors?" said Simeon. Gaskell fell the rest of the way down the steps, dirtying his tuxedo and suspecting Rinehart's hand upon the ankle that had jumped from under him. If he blows it now . . .

If he tells all now, thought Woodman, there will be nothing—and then was annoyed at the banality of his thought.

But Simeon said no more. He waited on the humming, as did all, saw buffalo become double-decker car, saw double-decker car with diesel pushing come close, closer, kiss-close to the platform on which he sat, grappling with his senses.

And stop.

He sucked in air and the humming receded.

He blew it out, spent, and a door in the car opened and a gentle ramp came down, a ramp friendly to wheels and withered limbs.

He said, "The rabbits in this car behind me have been used in germ warfare research and they still carry the germ. An Okinawan died and that is why they have been sent back and are crossing our land. . . ."

The hub-bub was starting up but the lights were fading for Simeon.

There was activity at the top of the ramp.

"And now, ladies and gentlemen," said Simeon, with all the volume he had left, "it's time to meet the stars of our show. . . ."
Then his senses fled.

Charles Woodman kept his head while all around were losing theirs and wore a small smile as he climbed to the platform, pantomimed to Julie that Simeon was still breathing and passed on to his Ray Bradbury task.

Dr. Ichiro Domei, at the head of the ramp to lead his people forth for any challenge, looked out upon the reception as a heretic might face an *auto-da-fé*.

In fact, the comparison was not a bad one, with the hooded figures and the wild, wild faces turning towards him and the sound of voices surging and frothing in the midnight air.

The horde looked set for nothing other than death, and horrible, torturous death at that. He turned back into the carriage and spread-eagled himself across the doorway, hands and feet plucking at the framework for purchase, small body trying to blot out the scene that lay beyond.

But heads popped, eyes flew, shoulders pressed. He could not hold them back without an explanation and how could he explain what he did not understand himself?

Where was Keio? The dorobo must have known what to expect.

Keio, taking in the vision from the double-glazed bubble on top of the car, was well pleased with all that he saw. Malecki and his staff had done their work admirably. Close identification was out of the question from his vantage point but general appraisal was easy enough. He and Malecki had bargained on Simeon, students, law agencies and had even stuck their necks out and said Ku Klux Klan.

Lo and behold, here they were all assembled like toys to a clockwork battlefield. Not that there would be any battle. That was the beauty of it.

The Americans would see what they had done. These simple Japanese would see what kind of people had detonated their simplicity. And the whole world would see what fools the Americans could make of themselves when they put their minds to it.

Stalemate. Each entity cancelled the other out perfectly until all that was left was the posture.

No shooting, no shouting. Just shock.

From where he stood, the ramp was invisible but there seemed to be some kind of hold-up. He ran a last satisfied eye over the glorious impasse and went to see why the *hibakusha* were taking so much time to make their appearance.

He had to push his way through them, though the contact seemed to curl his fingers and toes and vitals inwards in revulsion. He found Domei clinging to the doorway.

"In Meiji's name, what is this?" shouted Domei breathlessly. "What have you done to us? Get us out of here."

"Doctor!" Keio spoke sharply. "Pull yourself together. You knew there would be people here to meet you."

"But not these—people. They are like devils."

Keio permitted himself a harsh and impatient guffaw. "There is a large crowd so the police are here to keep them in order. We are familiar with the principle in Japan."

"But the hooded men."

"Ku Klux Klan. Men are entitled to dress how they will. There is an obscure oriental link and no doubt they thought it would be fitting—"

"I'm not stupid, Keio. Not any more. I know the Ku Klux Klan and they're not just here to be friendly. They resent our presence—"

"Believe me, Doctor"—Keio was trying to prise the man's fingers away from the door frame—"the only thing they will resent is your apparent reluctance to go out and meet them. What is it? Are you still ashamed of your charges?"

"My children can face anything—"

"Then let them." And with that, Keio took hold of the doctor's wrist, swung him clear of the door and ushered the *hibakusha* into the New World.

The silence was complete—thousands of breaths drawn in and held.

In the lemon glare, in the vacuum of time between today and tomorrow, nobody stirred or spoke or lived.

Then, two figures moving.

On the piggyback container, the venerable Judge Charles Woodman.

On the trackside at the bottom of the ramp, Lucia Lorensen took the defensive hand away from her veil of hair for a final time and stepped forward with her arms outstretched to the Hiroshima scarred.

"We welcome you," she said and Julie could have howled aloud but instead she was stepping up beside Lucia, arms similarly extended, and smiling at the first nervous *hibakusha* making their unsteady descent of the ramp.

The students knew the move for what it was first because they had seen between Lucia's fingers and her marred cheek was no secret, though they played out the game if it comforted her. For she was sad and she was beautiful and those were two good reasons to play out the game.

Here, Lucia happy. Warming to those who had more need to hide themselves and yet did not. As Simeon had burned his swing, so Lucia threw off her veil and Julie, standing shoulder to shoulder with her, felt as she had done three years before on that butterfly night when she and her man had honeymooned on the cooling beach of Playa 9 hours before the sound and the fury came back to the sea.

A good feeling. A once-in-a-lifetime feeling come twice.

And somebody would pay with a life.

Two thousand come from the campus and leaning now towards the small area of action. Two thousand finding their voices and reading out a message as clear as if Charlie Frei had painted it on the sky.

WE LOVE YOU.

WE LOVE YOU. WE-LOVE-YOU-WE-LOVE-YOU. WE . . . LOVE . . . YOU . . .

Resounding like an African chant, swaying bodies and moving feet.

Two thousand voices is a lot for a National Guardsman to take. It was as though someone had placed a bucket over Guardsman Conroy Mitchell's head and was beating it with sticks.

But he still had control.

It wasn't until Captain James Ronald Gordon turned them about so that they faced the mass with rifles at the slope for an overhead volley that Mitchell's nervous fingers knocked off the safety catch of his M-1.

Corporal Matthew York saw the involuntary action from his position next along the line.

"Get that thing down before you put the catch back on," he said.

Mitchell did nothing. "Get the thing down," York repeated, louder. Still nothing. Mitchell was in his bucket with the sticks banging away.

York left his position, laid a firm but gentle hand on the barrel and swung it down towards the earth. Mitchell wasn't even conscious he was providing digital resistance until the rifle went off.

The steel-jacketed M-1 bullet dented a piece of rail and leapt back up, smashing through bone and sinew in a Klansman's hand, entering a girl's throat and leaving her body by the back of the skull and travelling another mile across the roofs of Green Town before its impetus decayed.

Captain Gordon was screaming in panic or rage or something and when the words emerged from the loud-speaker bedlam, he was saying, "Lay down your arms. On the floor with them. Stand on them. Lie on them. Don't damn well touch them with your hands again."

He remembered Kent State.

Slade Dexter, sheriff of Dustbowl, nursed his devastated pistol-hand against his white robe and watched the blood flow with almost clinical detachment. He was wondering how the hell he was going to explain this to Louella.

William Filo had heard the bullet sing and ducked. He came up looking for Allison Miller and couldn't see her. Only when he looked down and then . . . too much. This greatest story, this closest story to him had become his personal tragedy. His Allison dead. He was at one with Barry Levine, bereaved of Allison Krause at Kent. His notebook went somewhere under milling feet and he didn't see it and didn't care because the story would never be filed. If the girls had kept together, they would have been safe. . . .

The gathering hovered on the brink of insanity and only then did Charles Woodman pronounce his judgment and his sentence.

He had entered the container, opened the enclosure, directed the white flood of fur to the steps.

Rabbits scurried, jumped, toppled or squatted with noses quivering.

The crowd, of one accord, sobered itself to a statue state as the animals shuffled their way among boots and sandals and bare toes and brogues and Minnie Mouse heels.

Simeon surfaced and was aware of the judge's bulk beside him, hunched to speak into the microphone.

He heard Woodman say, "I have loosed the plague. . . ."

The night had finished wailing and Allison Miller's life was a moist and anonymous patch that would have startled like a poppy between the tracks once the sun came up. But the police emergency squad knew little about poppies and hosed the life away as a matter of routine.

With the sun would come the questions for the authorities, by the authorities, asked of the authorities, and Clement Dancey had a word or three to say about the alarmist use of the National Guard. Others were ready to hold the whole strategy up for inspection and one day James Michener would write a book about it that would make more money than this one.

Meantime, the rabbits were gone, following their leader across rails and roads and into moon meadows and thence to the prairie to feast on bluestem. The scent of July grass had caught their pink noses, tickled their pink eyes and they had trailed it away from Green Town.

They had killed no-one.

Nor could they have done, explained Judge Woodman to his packed open-air court, with Secretary Chuta Keio standing hard by to corroborate.

For the germ-carriers were dead and incinerated in Okinawa and the toughest thing that had happened to these beasts was acupuncture.

The judge laughed. He laughed for all America, he said, because the Japanese design had been to draw a laughable response.

"If the rabbits were genuinely poisonous, there would have been no need for the back-up *hibakusha*," he said. "The oriental philosophy is merely this—you do not pay back a man who has spited you. You merely fix it so that he spites himself.

"And those of you who don't laugh with me because your faces are too red or because you do not believe we have done wrong must surely admit that a weapon so selective that it manages only to embarrass those who should be embarrassed has more to offer the world than anything in our silos.

"No bloodshed, just illumination on the truth of our ways.

"We mourn the young girl who died here tonight but we cannot deny that she died at our hands because of the steps we saw fit to take. She is not the first—if only she were just the latest in a long line. But she could be the last.

"Our visitors did not want that death and did not provide for it. It was a fault in their equation, I am told, which renders them sor-

rowful with us and gives us a common platform and a foundation
on which to build.

"We would be foolish not to work on that foundation. . . ."

The microphone lost power suddenly. Joe Gaskell and Ed Rinehart climbed onto the car and started winding up the cables.

"I hadn't finished," said the judge.

"We haven't stopped you," said soiled Gaskell.

But they had.

The National Guard was forming up and shipping south to the Lakeside Avenue access. The KKK was going north to the market, where their bus was waiting.

Clement Dancey took one look at the deflated students and called in his men and sent them back to patrolling the streets of Green Town.

Dr. Ichiro Domei had walked his children up and down the tracks until they were tired and less full of questions and had led them back up the ramp.

He did not like what Keio and his government had done and could not begin to comprehend it. But the purpose had been served and there would be little time lost now in getting them all to the sea and home.

The young, the uncommitted, the ready to learn, moved in towards the flat-car. Woodman had stooped and was talking to Simeon. Simeon tapped his arm and turned him around.

"I think they want to hear from you, Simeon," said Frank Lorensen from the ground. Simeon had only the strength to smile.

"Don't reject wisdom just because it wears whiskers," he said. "Now here comes the judge."

He rose from his canvas chair and Rinehart moved in like a wraith and took it and folded it. Julie gave her husband shoulder support going down the steps.

Frank and Lucia were waiting with a new kind of ease between them.

"I'm sorry," said Simeon. "I can't stop any longer."

"We're glad you came," said Lucia.

He regarded her quizzically. "You mean here?"

"No. Anywhere. This town . . ." In all her fumbling, her right hand had not moved from her side. Tomorrow she would comb back her hair. Julie saw that before Simeon.

"We're glad, too," she said.

Going home alone with Simeon, she said, "Well, we made somebody happy."

Simeon was thinking of a girl who had accused him of aiding predestination. He said, "And we made somebody dead."

When Simeon was taking his leave in a day or a week or a month,
he would bemoan his failure to Judge Charles Woodman.

"All I did was to fade out," he would say. "How negative can you
get?"

And Woodman would refill his glass and kiss Julie like a daughter
and say, "You were the catalyst. Again. Next time you will be the
man who frees the rabbits."

But this minute, this dawn in the cupola bedroom, Simeon and
Julie watched first light moving like a tide upon the shores of the
lake.

"Do you know . . ." Simeon was tired beyond counting and
opined beyond sleep, "so far we have not met one real person who
lives in Green Town."

"What about Mrs. Dilger?"

"Is she real?"

"If she doesn't remember the last time Cooger and Dark came,
she must be real."

"I don't know. I guess we're all figments of somebody's imagination."

"Ray Bradbury lives," offered Tomorrow Julie.

"No. Ray Bradbury endures," said Simeon with emphasis.

He gave the town a last snap of his fingers.

Doors slammed open; people stepped out.

All over Green Town, new stories began.